I0823354

The GLOWING HOURS

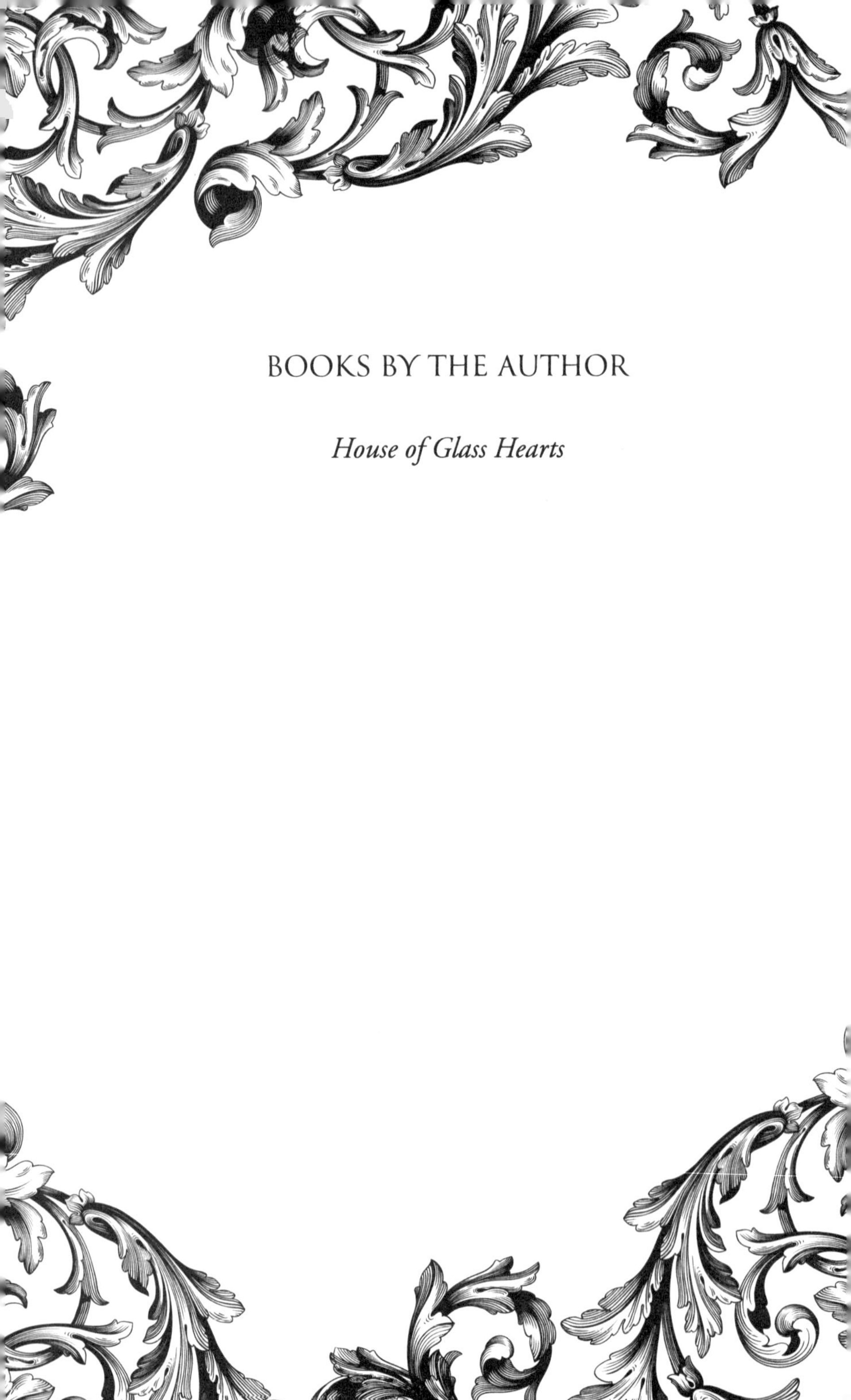

BOOKS BY THE AUTHOR

House of Glass Hearts

The Glowing Hours

LEILA SIDDIQUI

HELL'S HUNDRED

Published by Hell's Hundred
an imprint of Soho Press
227 W 17th Street
New York, NY 10011
www.sohopress.com

Library of Congress Cataloging-in-Publication Data

Names: Siddiqui, Leila author
Title: The glowing hours / Leila Siddiqui.
Description: New York, NY : Hell's Hundred, 2026.
Identifiers: LCCN 2025023543

ISBN 978-1-64129-701-1
eISBN 978-1-64129-702-8

Subjects: LCSH: Shelley, Mary Wollstonecraft, 1797-1851—Fiction | LCGFT: Gothic fiction | Biographical fiction | Fiction | Novels
Classification: LCC PS3619.I3324 G58 2026 | DDC 813/.6—dc23/eng/20250520
LC record available at https://lccn.loc.gov/2025023543

Interior design by Janine Agro

Printed in the United States of America

10 9 8 7 6 5 4 3 2 1

EU Responsible Person (for authorities only)
eucomply OÜ
Pärnu mnt 139b-14
11317 Tallinn, Estonia
hello@eucompliancepartner.com
www.eucompliancepartner.com

PROLOGUE

1858

It had taken Jane years to find her. She'd followed the river of gossip from London to Coventry, all those whisperings about an exotic and wealthy foreigner who, decades ago, had turned heads in London society for just a brief few weeks before mysteriously vanishing. A lifelong spinster, so it was told, who'd spent her life caring for her brother's children, and, when they had grown, was taken in by an adoring niece to look after her grandnieces and nephews. Jane sat in the drawing room, waiting for her to appear.

The floor creaked behind Jane, and Mehrunissa Begum Hammersmith walked in, a thick gray-streaked braid swung over a shoulder, a matronly high-necked black dress on. She was graceful and soft as she made her way across the room, sat in a chair opposite Jane, and folded her hands in her lap.

"I am delighted to make your acquaintance, Mrs. Shelley," Miss Hammersmith said.

Jane doubted it. The woman neither smiled nor

frowned; she had an unreadable expression on her face. A thick knot formed in Jane's chest. She could see, now, why her mother-in-law had been so taken by such a dignified creature. Slowly, Jane exhaled the breath she'd been keeping in and gathered the bundle of papers in her lap.

"I have begun the task of working on my mother-in-law's memorials," Jane said calmly. "Both hers and her husband's."

"Tragic, how he died," Miss Hammersmith said. "I read about it in the papers. So young, Percy. Lord Byron too. And . . ."

The woman before Jane appeared to lose her composure. But she took a moment, and a softness returned to her face. "And another man who was employed by him," she continued. "A young doctor."

Jane nodded. "You spent that summer with the most notorious man to ever have written a word in the English language. Have you ever wanted to—"

"No." Miss Hammersmith shook her head. She smoothed her black dress against the tops of her thighs. "I prefer to forget that summer, Mrs. Shelley. It was as if I were never there."

Miss Hammersmith stared hard at Jane, who realized this was not a request but a command. She would never speak of her time with the Shelleys. Jane had been gripping hard to the bundle. She let go, placed her hands on top of the pile, then cleared her throat. It was a while before the words materialized in her mind.

"As you may have heard," Jane said, "Mrs. Shelley died a number of years ago. We were very intimate. She was like a mother to me." She let out a deep sigh. She knew she hadn't fully recovered from the loss, perhaps never would. "A few years after her death, I found the journals she had written with her husband." She shifted in her seat, Miss Hammersmith watching her every movement. "And while I have tasked myself with putting together her biography, there are some things I . . ."

She found she'd been tapping her foot against the floor. She stopped, then finally stood and approached Miss Hammersmith. Jane held out the bundle of papers to her and, when she didn't reach for it, laid it delicately in her lap.

"Pages from her journals, Miss Hammersmith. From that summer. She paints a very vivid picture of you. Of what happened to all of you in that villa. I cannot, in good conscience, include any of this in her memorials. I ought to have thrown it all into the hearth, to have destroyed it before my husband could see it."

Tears sprang to her eyes, and she quickly wiped them away. "In my affection for my mother-in-law, I want you to have them. You can treasure these pages or you can burn them. They are yours to do with as you wish."

"What about her sister Claire?"

"Miss Clairmont wants nothing to do with us."

"Then what makes you think I should have them?" Miss Hammersmith asked.

"I do not know. I suppose she would not have minded that I shared with you."

Jane sat back down and watched as Miss Hammersmith undid the twine around the bundle. When she'd found the journals, she and her husband had begun to read them together. She was consumed by this window into the youth of a woman she'd worshipped. As the events of Mary Shelley's life took on a sad turn—of dashed hopes, death, depression—she hid them away from her husband, took on the sole project of consolidating it all into a biography of her beloved mother-in-law. But there were some lines, some passages, that she found herself scratching out completely. She was shocked at her own rashness and had to step away from the journals for a time. Young Mary had seemed bitter, hapless, and at times even irritating. It was not the woman she'd come to love as her own mother.

But she was still working through her grief and eventually returned to the task. As she read on, she arrived at the summer of 1816. Then it wasn't just lines or passages she found herself blotting out but entire pages. She would rip them out, hide them from her husband in various parts of the house: shoved into desk drawers and within pages of other books, some even sprinkled in the garden. It took Jane weeks, months, to decide what to do with them. And even then, there were moments from them she wished she could tell her husband about. But it would be her secret to bear.

She had a duty to her mother-in-law, who was one of

the greatest women writers of the past century. Jane would ensure her legacy stayed that way. There were times she felt possessive of her brilliant mother-in-law. Mary had lost her husband at such a young age. Jane's own husband, Percy Florence, was Mary's only surviving child. Yet Mary's delicate vulnerability had made Jane want her all to herself. To care for her, love her as a daughter might have. But the journal spoke of unbelievable things. Of obsession, prurience, madness, grotesque hallucinations . . . Jane shuddered to think about it.

Miss Hammersmith slid one page behind the other. She stopped to read, then glanced away, perhaps overcome with her own memories of that summer.

"You've read these pages?" Miss Hammersmith asked.

Jane nodded. "It was quite a summer." She leaned forward, hesitated for a moment before asking, "Is it all *true*?"

Miss Hammersmith moved the bundle to a side table. "I believe she had a brilliant mind, though often troubled. She was far too young to have gone through what she did."

Jane let out a breath. So it was true. Her mother-in-law had had a touch of madness that summer. It was no wonder, considering all she'd been through in her young life, that she had produced such a frightening tale. Perhaps the incendiary pages had just been a way to inspire her writing.

"After I heard about Mr. Shelley's death, I dreamt about her often," Miss Hammersmith said. "That she was freed of that man, the burden of his genius."

"She never married again," Jane said.

"Or perhaps could not." Miss Hammersmith stared at a point on the rug. "Her devotion to him was like a religion. She entwined her full self in that man. I will never understand it."

Jane felt the seconds tick by on the clock as she mustered the courage to ask her next question.

"Have you read *Frankenstein*?" she said at last. "You were one of very few to witness her inspiration."

Miss Hammersmith had on a faraway smile, one that reminded Jane of her mother-in-law.

"I don't have the courage to read her work," she said. "Any of it. Is it not curious, that all three of the men we spent our summer with died only a few years after? And yet we women, cursed with life instead?"

Miss Hammersmith laid her hand on top of the bundle. "Thank you for the gift."

Then she stood, moved swiftly across the room and into the hall. By the time Jane got there, Miss Hammersmith had the door held open for her.

Jane pulled a copy of *Frankenstein* from her pocketbook. It was one of a multitude she owned, multiple editions she couldn't bear to part with. But this one would do. She opened the book and, since she'd previously underlined the passages, was able to find the page quickly.

"Safie is a young Arabian woman," she said to Miss Hammersmith. "Beguiling, enchanting. She has an 'angelic beauty,' 'shining raven black hair' that was 'curiously braided.'"

Miss Hammersmith held the door wider. "Mrs. Shelley—"

"And the way she sings. 'Her voice flowed in a rich cadence, swelling or dying away, like a nightingale in the woods.'"

It brought tears to her eyes to read out this passage. She found the same was true for Miss Hammersmith.

"In her journals, she wrote about hearing you sing in the vineyard. This Safie, she makes quite an impression on the monstrous creature," Jane said softly, pushing the book into her hands.

She stepped out onto the concrete stairs and turned back to Miss Hammersmith. The older woman stared at the book in her trembling hands. She turned it over and over, touched the cover, her fingers brushing against a deformed caricature of Victor Frankenstein's creature. Then, without a word, Miss Hammersmith handed the book back to Jane and swiftly shut the door.

On with the dance! let joy be unconfin'd;
No sleep till morn, when Youth and Pleasure meet
To chase the Glowing Hours with Flying feet.
—*Lord Byron,* CHILDE HAROLD'S PILGRIMAGE

CHAPTER 1

Forty-two years earlier
1815

Mehrunissa Begum leaned over the edge of the railing as the seawater churned below her. A spray of mist landed on her cheeks. It dried and itched like old tears. The ship gave a sudden lurch as it turned, and for a wild moment, Mehr thought she'd fall overboard and be forever lost to the waves, her journey a waste, her brother and father left waiting for her for the rest of their lives.

But she'd come too far now to fail her foolish mother's dying wishes. She pushed away from the railing and stared up at the sky. The sun beamed down on her, and she shielded her eyes with her hand. There were two seagulls above, their wings moving in tandem. They veered away from each other and went their separate ways, one headed for land and one toward the sea. She followed the latter until it became a speck of dust in the air.

Then she glanced across the deck for the fifth or sixth time. She'd lost count. Waiting, waiting—it was the thing she hated to do most. But for him, she'd wait just a little longer. Finally, she spotted him leaving the lascar section of the steamship, his ayah hidden in the shadows. Mehr turned her back to the sea and acknowledged the woman with a curt nod. But the ayah kept her eyes on the child as he skittered across the deck to Mehr.

Anand threw his arms around Mehr's legs. She took a sharp breath in and shut her eyes. Her body froze. She could never find herself able to return the affection. To hold him would eventually mean letting him go. And she could not do that to herself again. She stared down at his wide brown eyes, so much like her brother's that she found she could not linger on them for long. Before she could speak, he snatched the sketchbook from her hands and plopped onto the deck.

She'd been training him to sketch his pet dog, which he'd left behind in India. He missed the creature dearly. With what little physical characteristics he could accurately describe, they began the sketch together. It was his eyes they struggled with most. Mehr resisted the urge to take the pencil from the boy's hands and draw them herself; her pupil needed to learn on his own.

Anand pushed the pencil deep into the page, his movements erratic as he filled in the fur around the dog's face.

"Take your time," she said to him in Urdu.

"It is all wrong," Anand said. "I want him to be perfect."

"He is. He always will be, because your memories of him are perfect."

He colored in the body of the animal, the tip of the

pencil creating small tears in the paper. He stopped, stared blankly at the drawing in front of him. His little fingers gripped the sketchbook as he brought it closer to his face, touching it to his forehead. Then he ripped the page out. Before she could stop him, he flung it over the side of the ship.

"Anand!" It wasn't the first time she'd had to raise her voice at him.

He slumped against the side of the ship, fighting back tears. Mehr's eyes flicked over to the lascar section. She wondered if his ayah had been watching them all along.

"I do not need the picture, when I can see him there," Anand said, pointing ahead of him.

Mehr squinted across the deck, but aside from a few passengers, she didn't see anything else, much less a shaggy dog staring back at them.

Anand laughed. "You do not see him?" he asked.

When Mehr shook her head, he sat up straighter and pointed again. "There! There!"

The sea breeze whipped around them suddenly, and Mehr held tight to her dupatta. "I see nothing there," she said.

Anand let out a frustrated sigh. "Because *I* miss him, I see him. He will always be with me until I cannot see him anymore."

"Like a ghost?" Mehr said, feeling foolish for having asked a child such a question.

The little boy had a strange smile on his face as he

continued to stare at his phantom dog. "No, something else. Something as perfect as a memory."

It had been only a few weeks since she'd met him. It was at the port in Marseille, after switching steamships, that her uncle had left Mehrunissa to travel on her own. He'd spared no expense for the journey, managing to book her with the British passengers on the upper deck. But in Marseille, as she headed up to her cabin alone, she'd been blocked by a pinched-looking pale-faced woman who managed to take up the rest of the space in the passageway with her disapproval. Not unlike the white women she'd encountered in India, carving out their comfort in a country that didn't belong to them, with inattentive husbands that sometimes didn't either.

"Are you lost?" she asked in an equally pinched voice as she glared at Mehr's clothes. She'd been dressing in simple cotton salwar kameez for the trip, her lush, silky lehengas packed away in her trunk.

Mehr drew herself up to her fullest height. "I am searching for my room, madam."

The woman stood in her way, arms crossed, severe chin pointed directly at her. Then she glanced at Mehr's ticket and snatched it right out of her hand.

"This has been forged. How do *you* have a cabin beside me?"

Mehr snatched it back from her. "Beg your pardon, madam. That is none of your concern."

The woman huffed past her, and before Mehr had even

touched the cabin door, she was apprehended by two large crewmen who hauled her back onto the deck. As she struggled out of their grip, a small voice cried out and the boy appeared out of nowhere. He threw himself at her, hugging her tightly around her waist. Mehr was taken aback, staring down at the child in as much confusion as the others.

"*Oh*," the pinched woman said, taking in Anand's small, tanned face, his almond-colored eyes, his freshly pressed and tailored clothing. The woman nodded to the burly crewmen.

"His ayah," she continued. "Poor, confused creature."

Mehr laughed out loud. Her? An ayah? She could never. But Anand had taken her hand and pulled her to follow him before she could correct the woman. She gathered her trunk and let the boy lead her away, around the deck to the lascar section, where the traveling servants and nannies of British families lodged. As the boy scampered down inside, Mehr stood on the shadowed edge, facing an older woman in a plain cotton sari.

The boy's ayah gave her a knowing smile and Mehr realized she should thank her, but her tongue was baked dry in her mouth. The indignity of the experience was still with her, boiling in the pit of her stomach. The ayah hadn't asked her where her employers had gone. She seemed to know, perhaps from Mehr's noble bearing, that she was someone else under the plain clothes.

"Traveling alone?" the ayah asked, a tragic look in her eyes.

"My cabin appears to be unready. Is there a spare here?" Mehr peered down the staircase behind her.

The ayah smiled with an infuriating amount of tenderness. She beckoned her down the stairs into a dingy passageway, across to the last remaining room. When she threw open the door, Mehr stepped back and gasped. It was little more than a closet.

"No, no," Mehr said, eyeing the room. "Something bigger."

The ayah tutted, put her dupatta against her lips, and shook her head.

"I cannot stay in there." Mehr waved at the tiny cot shoved against the wall, the complete lack of a window.

"Where else do you have?" the woman asked.

Mehr left the woman's side and wandered down the hall, trying different doors, peeking into the kitchen, the pantries. The spare rooms were occupied, and she realized there was nowhere else for her to go. She chewed on the inside of her cheek, tasted the sting of blood, then returned to the room and placed her trunk beside the cot.

The ayah had warned her not to tell anyone she was traveling alone, to pretend she was traveling with a firangi family. No one would question her. And she was right. When she'd loiter on the deck by herself, before Anand would join her for his daily lesson, they saw her clothes, her skin color, the long, thick braid she swept over one shoulder, and placed her with an imaginary family upstairs. Being a young Indian woman, if she did not belong to a father or husband, she could only belong to a firangi family, and nothing else.

Beside her now, on the deck, Anand had moved on from his phantom dog and begun another sketch. His little brown hand made carefree strokes, missteps he hardly noticed. He'd remember this voyage differently. Like Anand's father, Mehr's was a British officer, and her mother an Indian woman. After making his riches and building a large compound with his own zenana of women, Anand's father was now taking his entire family back to settle in London. Mehr felt a twinge of envy in her chest, but it wasn't the boy's fault. He was entirely blameless, unlike her mother.

The horn blasted, and they both flinched. Anand gave her a sheepish smile, then stood on his toes and stared over the side of the ship.

"There it is! London!" He pointed wildly ahead of him.

Mehr pulled herself up and squinted at the port as the ship pushed through the thick water. It had no particular distinction aside from the low, ugly gray buildings surrounding the dock. Beyond those were taller, even uglier gray buildings, crowned by needlelike spires jutting out like broken teeth. There was a formidable bridge in the distance, with dark water churning below it, spraying up ash-colored froth against its underside. The clouds lay low and heavy, the buildings cloaked in dark fog as if an idle hand had smudged its fingers across the city.

The sooty air crawled into the back of her throat and

made her cough. She braced herself against the side of the ship as it groaned and turned.

"You going home?" Anand suddenly asked in English.

She knelt in front of him and spoke in Urdu. "To my family. My father and brother."

Anand shook his head. "In English. I want to practice."

The ship made a narrow turn, and she suddenly threw her arms around him. She felt his heart beat rapidly against her chest. "Do not be afraid," she said in Urdu. She swallowed hard. These were the last words she'd said to her brother, James.

He pulled away and stared up at her, seeming unsure of what, exactly, he shouldn't fear. He reminded her of James then, the last time she'd seen him. Small yet so sure of himself. It had been a decade since, and she wondered what those years had done to him. What they'd eventually do to Anand.

Behind Anand, his ayah stepped out of the lascars section. She waved her dupatta, beckoning the boy. While Mehr moved away from the approaching view of the city, Anand returned to peering over the side, his dark eyes glaring, engrossed. As his ayah came to collect him for the last time, Mehr stood between her and the boy.

"I want you to meet him."

When the ayah gave her a questioning look, Mehr cleared her throat.

"My brother."

The ayah politely shook her head.

"But you must meet him. A pukka sahib." She gestured to Anand. "Just like he will be someday."

The ayah's smile faltered. She took hold of the boy's hand and led him away.

"Farewell!" Anand called, waving behind him.

Mehr hugged her sketchbook to her chest. She had much more to say to him, but instead she gave him a short wave back as he was led away. She was already a distant memory to him, she realized. Overshadowed by the excitement of his arrival—the clanging of ships at the dock, the bellows of the lascars called into action after they had lain dormant on the ship, the cacophonous English voices that prevailed all around them now blending into one long note, and the oppressive odor of his new countrymen.

When the boat docked, Mehr moved against the tide of passengers and retrieved her trunk. By the time she was back on the deck, the crowd had thinned and she was able to see through them to the long, claustrophobic buildings lining the dock, like grindstones waiting to pull her in and fragment her into a million little pieces. She felt her breath hitch, thinking back to the endless fields around her uncle's home that stretched as far as her eye could see. She looked for Anand one last time, but the city had already swallowed him up.

She could see nothing beyond the decay of the city. She looked up, followed the multiple craggy lines of smoke to the sky, where the sun shone through a thin layer of clouds.

Mehr followed the crowd of servants and lascars ahead

of her. A young lascar, seeing Mehr struggle with her trunk, offered to help, but she recoiled, shaking her head. She was to meet her brother, James, at the dock—her uncle had written him ahead of time, made sure of it—and she didn't want anything getting in between them.

There was an unusual chill in the air. She wrapped her dupatta around her head and tightened it against the breeze. She stood on her toes and glanced above the many heads of the departing passengers, but she couldn't see anyone who resembled her brother.

With a start she realized she blended in too well with the others, especially in her plain clothes. She moved over to a bench and stood on top of it, the better to see over the crowds. She watched as families were reunited, tears were wiped from cheeks, loaded carriages tottered down the road, heavy with their burdens.

As the crowd thinned, she took a seat on the bench, loosened the dupatta around her head and draped it over her shoulders so James could see her face while he searched for her. As she adjusted the cloth, a shadow fell over her. She brightened and looked up. But instead of James, it was a cheerful-looking woman in a high-necked dress. The apples of her cheeks were dark pink, and her gray-streaked auburn hair was severely pulled back and knotted at the nape of her neck.

"Speak English?" she asked.

Mehr nodded. She could speak and write in three other languages, but she didn't say this aloud.

"Are you Mehrunissa Begum?"

She sat up straighter. "Where is my brother?" she asked.

"My name is Miss Christy. I run the home here."

"Where is James?" Mehr asked again.

The woman chuckled nervously. "He asked me to retrieve you from the ship. He was not able to come here in time. Something about your father's health."

Mehr's heart lurched. Was their father ill?

"What do you want with me, then?" Mehr asked.

"I am to take you to a home, my dear, until he can receive you."

"A home?" Mehr stood from the bench. "I have a home."

Miss Christy moved a stray hair from her face, glanced back at the line of carriages slowly being taken by the departing families. "I know you do, dear. I have created an institution for solitary Indian women, like you. Ayahs, coming here in droves with their masters and mistresses until their services are no longer needed. It is where your father placed your own ayah—"

"He sent her away?" Mehr asked. "But she took care of James. Of both of us."

"They simply did not have use for her when James grew into a man. We looked after her and helped her find a new family."

Mehr suddenly remembered she had her father's address, and put down her trunk. She had scrawled it into her sketchbook when her uncle had given it to her in Marseille before leaving her to take the rest of the journey on her own. She pulled open her trunk and dug inside.

"What are you doing?" Miss Christy asked, glancing again at the carriages.

Mehr retrieved her sketchbook and flipped through the pages, but could not find it among old sketches and lazy scrawls. Anand. She'd watched him tear a page out and fling it off the ship just hours before. She stared back out at the sea. It was gone forever, the address crashing among the waves, floating farther and farther away from her.

The sketchbook shook in her hands. She could sit on her haunches and swear damnation on the child, but she didn't have the time to spare. The woman gave a look of pity that made Mehr feel a sickness bloom in her stomach.

"I will wait here for James," Mehr said.

Miss Christy let out a nervous laugh. "He said he will not be long. Days, perhaps, and then he will take you home."

Mehr shut her trunk and sat down on the bench. Her confusion and anger suddenly gave way to something else. An emotion she loathed to feel. Hopelessness.

"I said I will wait for him," Mehr repeated.

Miss Christy sat down beside her. "You do not want to be here after dark." She pulled the collar of her dress tight against her neck. "I know you have come a long way. Would not you like a hot bath? A warm meal? While we wait?"

Her stomach growled. Mehr wouldn't look at her, but she nodded. "Not long, you say?"

"Not long at all," Miss Christy said with a smile.

Mehr picked up her trunk and let the woman lead the way to the line of carriages. The driver helped them inside and stowed her trunk atop the coach. They rattled along in silence, Mehr putting distance between her and the woman, who stared at her through the ride and hummed under her breath. It was a while until the carriage pulled around a tight corner and then stopped outside of a nondescript building.

She had called it a home. Mehr could have laughed at the word. Though it was a tall brick building, inside it felt horrifically cramped. She thought of the long, sweeping halls of the zenana as they moved through the rooms together. Mehr was dismayed to see that the house was equally as lifeless and unfeeling as its exterior. In colors of gray and white.

"My brother and I created this home," Miss Christy said as Mehr followed her through the carpeted hall. "We took in a stranded ayah from a cousin who had brought her over from India with his family. It was fate! Our cook had just left us. And she already knew how to cook our foods."

Mehr pressed her lips together and thought of Anand's ayah, wondered if she was snug and warm in her new home as she held Anand in her arms. Wondered if his ayah understood how temporary it all was. She nearly shook her head to chase away her thoughts.

Miss Christy went on. "I thought to myself, How many other women, good, strong, hard-working women, needed a benefactor? Someone to provide them with work. A purpose. This is what I do."

"You are very charitable," Mehr said, and was surprised that she meant it.

Miss Christy flushed, a proud little smile on her face.

They stopped in a sitting room, where several brown women were seated in a circle, enjoying cups of tea and laughing over something. They immediately quieted when Mehr walked in. She averted her gaze to the windows, which were small and tight, unlike the wide curtained ones she'd left behind, the ones that had let the soft Lucknow breezes flutter into her room. As Miss Christy led her out of the room, she heard their chatter resume and wondered what they would say about her when she was out of earshot.

Miss Christy led her into a drab sitting room, motioning for her to take an armchair. It looked both lumpy and unforgiving, and she did not understand how the English could stand to be so uncomfortable in their own dwellings. The furniture was scratched at the ankles, like mice or insects had battled over the living room. The walls were tinged with yellow, the carpet dull with age. Mehr resisted the urge to shudder in front of the woman. She wrapped the dupatta tighter around her.

"Tea?"

Mehr shook her head and took her seat. The cushion sank underneath her, and she held on to an armrest to hoist herself back up. She locked her eyes straight ahead, stared around the room, anywhere but at the woman.

"We will take good care of you, my dear. Just as we did your ayah. What was her name?" Miss Christy asked.

Mehr flushed and hesitated before answering. "I do not know."

"Oh." Miss Christy's voice was small. "I am quite certain we will find her. Somewhere in our records."

Mehr looked out the window as a sudden rain began pouring. Her reflection stared back at her, muddled by rivulets of water. For a moment, she thought she saw her mother's face too. But it was only a trick of the rain.

CHAPTER 2

After several weeks, and with what little information Mehr was able to give Miss Christy, her inquiries led Mehr to the revelation that her ayah was dead. She had found work in a new home after all and, after serving the family for many years, died of a sudden fever that had swept through the house. She was the only casualty. Alone, in a stranger's home. In a foreign country.

Now Mehr was in the same position, with not a letter or a visit from James. She'd had no choice but to continue living at the home, the only one of her kind, young and of her station, in a place filled with middle-aged village women who had long ago been conscripted into service. Miss Christy knew Mehr wasn't one of them. Something about "pedigree," which she'd mutter to herself every now and then. Mehr had separate sleeping arrangements. She would eat her meals at different hours, and would lie in later and later each morning in order to avoid waking with them.

The older women spent hours in one another's company. Mehr didn't partake in their activities, because she couldn't. They had their card games, ones they'd picked up from their English families, that Mehr knew nothing about. Their sewing circles had no place for her because her hands had never needed to thread a needle. They'd trade their favorite recipes and spend hours cooking together, while Mehr had never touched a pot in her life. It mattered very little, because she would not be here for long, she told herself. James would come any day now.

But the weeks ticked by, and every time she'd visit Miss Christy in her office and ask for a word from her brother, Miss Christy would shrug her heavy shoulders and turn back to her ledger.

Mehr was confronted with the sudden fear that her brother wasn't coming for her. Perhaps he thought she would remind him too much of their sensitive and histrionic mother. After all, she did take after her in looks and complexion. Even when they were small children, their mother would cry out the loudest if one of them tripped and fell and would become hysterical if the skinned knee produced blood. But she wasn't her mother. She wished James could see it for himself.

In her quietest moments, sitting on her bed, staring at the smudged walls, a distressing thought would cross her mind: her journey had been a waste. When she'd shut her eyes to push the thought away, the face of her dead mother would linger there instead.

It was the way Mehr had found her mother, also lying in her bed, her soft face turned to the window, eyes gazing out for eternity. Mehr had stood and watched her, waited for her to blink again, but her eyes remained open. Mehr had followed her gaze to the window, then headed to the soft chiffon curtains, moved them aside, and stepped over the ledge. She'd covered her hair with a dupatta and tucked one end up to cover the lower half of her face so that only her eyes showed. The sun was low in the sky, which meant the fakir had taken his post outside. She glanced over the low wall that kept the women of the zenana hidden from public view.

The fakir stood on his toes, his hands balancing his frail frame against the wall. In his tear-stained eyes was a question. Mehr solemnly nodded.

"Ya Khuda," the fakir cried, raising his hands, palms facing their god. He began to weep, and Mehr knew she was trespassing and stepped back from the window.

Her mother was buried by the time the sun set. Hours later, as Mehr paced her room, there was a set of familiar voices whispering outside her door. She found only her uncle waiting. He was the oldest of her uncles, her grandfather's favorite heir.

He produced a frail, thin envelope from his pocket and hesitated before handing it to her. She squinted at the faded writing on the front but could not make out the words.

"With your grandfather gone, and now your mother, this is for Sikander. His inheritance."

"That is not his name," Mehr said softly, staring at the envelope in his hands. "He has a firangi name now. James."

Her uncle grimaced but quickly composed himself. "Whatever he is calling himself, this belongs to him. You must take it to him."

Mehr thought she hadn't heard him right. "Take it to where?"

"Go to London," her uncle said.

No matter that she was a woman and his niece, Mehr had an easy way with her uncle. She laughed out loud, gave him a mocking squint, something her mother would have scolded her for.

"I will do no such thing," she said. "We do not leave the zenana, unless in marriage."

Mehr had turned her back to him, but he gripped her arm hard and spun her to face him. Mehr attempted to free herself, but his fingers dug into her flesh. He trembled as he held her.

"You must deliver it to him personally." He was emphatic. "You must leave purdah, leave the zenana, and go to London."

"He should come here himself," Mehr said.

Her uncle stared hard, then realized he still had hold of her. He let go and handed the envelope to her, his hands shaking. "Take this to him. Deliver it to him personally."

She wouldn't take it from him. "Why me?"

"It was your mother's wish. You must honor it," he said. "You will not understand it now. But in time, you will."

"So I must travel far away to give Sikander everything. And what would I get?"

"God will reward you," he said, and turned to leave. "That should be enough."

She spent days arguing with him. No matter how much she protested, pleaded, he insisted she leave the comfort of the zenana, where she was surrounded by her female relatives, her uncle's wives and daughters, their petty dramas and gossip, their warm companionship, despite the shame she and her mother had brought on the family.

She had never found her uncle to be a sensitive man, but he was adamant that her mother's dying wishes be fulfilled. She refused to believe him and knew something deeper was afoot. With her mother now gone, and soon Mehr, her uncle's family would be free of the scandal caused by her mother's marriage to her father, and they could all carry on as if neither had existed. Mehr had always felt like an outsider, her feet planted in two different worlds, but her mother anchored her to the zenana. With her death, Mehr had become unmoored, untethered to the rest of her family.

He wished to be rid of her, so she resolved to leave, to find her way to James, to the only family she had left.

Mehr turned her attention to the writing table, where the letter had sat untouched now for weeks. Many times, she'd contemplated tearing it open. But she knew she'd be sickened by what was inside. Her uncle hadn't hesitated when he'd told her that a son's share was double that of a daughter's. Whatever her mother had inherited from

Mehr's grandfather that hadn't already been carved up and given to his sons was left for James. And an even smaller, negligible portion was for her.

Perhaps, Mehr thought, she could throw the inheritance letter into the fire, destroy it before James would ever see it, so he would be left with nothing, like her. Inheritance meant very little to her since it would be crucial only in her future dowry, passed from one man's hands to another's. But the respect she had for her grandfather, the nawab of Lucknow, and what he was leaving for his descendants, made her pause. If she wasn't willing to fulfill her mother's dying wish, she could at least do it for her beloved grandfather.

Mehr pulled herself out of bed and threw on the old dress Miss Christy had given her. It was tight at the throat and chest and shorter at the hem due to their height and size differences, but it would do.

The ayahs sat in a sewing circle as she crept through the sitting room and out the front door. The cobblestones shone with a fresh coat of rain. London had appeared as a maze to her the first time she'd stared at it from the carriage window. She hadn't dared venture out since. But her heart yearned to see her brother and father, to ensure her journey hadn't been a waste.

She headed down the steps of the house and onto the footpath. It was the smell that hit her first, a foul, wretched scent that was both stale and ripe. She coughed and covered her mouth, but as she drew sharp looks from passersby, eyes that lingered on her person for longer than was tolerable, she dropped her arms to her sides.

When she attempted to cross the street, a carriage careened her way, and she jumped out of the road, but not before being splashed with mud and muck from its giant wheels. Heads craned out of the carriage to look at her, and she withdrew, hurried down the footpath to find another way to cross.

Miss Christy had attempted to explain the city to Mehr, though she only ever half listened. They were somewhere called Aldgate, and the home was situated two lanes over from what Miss Christy referred to as the "high street." Mehr made her way there and found a road that was overcrowded with a population that thrilled in making as much noise as possible. She could not concentrate on where she was going over the sound of carriage wheels and horse hooves, carts clattering through the impassable street, London's denizens jostling by, stopping to leer or curl a lip in her direction, expertly weaving among one another, bolting in and out of the crowded shop fronts, in a hurry for something only they knew about.

If she felt claustrophobic in the home, she was nearly overrun outside. She longed for the silence and solitude of her uncle's zenana, even the relative quiet that inhabited the home, but she had entered a different, menacing world and it frightened her.

She kept her head down and crossed dozens of streets, maneuvered around scores of carriages, passersby, and oxcarts. The city pulled her in and she walked on, utterly directionless, expecting her father's home to materialize in front of her. The sky darkened and clouds swarmed above like a flock of fat birds, heavy and lined with rain. It was too early to light the streetlamps, and the sudden gloom made it harder for her to see.

She stared up at the sky, and as she did, the buildings stretched high over her head, unfurling like long gray fingers. Through the windows, a pale face emerged. It was her mother staring longingly at her, a cadaverous hand lying against the glass. As if her mother were reaching for her. A sudden headache pierced her temples, and Mehr felt faint. Her legs were heavy as she walked on. Thunder rent the sky above her. Mehr stopped, leaned against a wrought iron fence, and when she stumbled onward, the ground suddenly rushed up to meet her face.

SHE AWOKE IN her bed, to the sound of rain pattering against the windows, the whole ordeal a possible dream. But her dress was hanging on the back of a chair, streaked with mud. Miss Christy stood in the doorway, with that constant look of pity on her face.

"You poor creature. Something regrettable could have happened to you," she said as she entered the room and took a seat at the end of Mehr's bed. "Leaving the home unchaperoned as you did."

Mehr hugged her knees to her chest. "I needed fresh air."

"You went looking for him," Miss Christy said.

Mehr shook her head. "I went looking for a cure for boredom. That is all." She sat up a little. "Have you heard from James?"

Miss Christy tutted under her breath. "If they had not found you as soon as they did . . ." She placed her fingertips to her lips. "I should be vexed with you."

"He will not be coming for me," Mehr said. It wasn't a question; she knew the truth just from studying Miss Christy's face.

"He needs time. Your father's health—"

"You know where they live."

"At present, they are not home." Miss Christy tutted again. "You behave as if I have you imprisoned here. If I'd known, I would have taken you there myself. But a young woman cannot live unchaperoned in an empty house. You must wait."

Miss Christy reached out and patted Mehr on the leg. Mehr looked away, swallowed the terrible, bitter taste in her mouth as Miss Christy took her time leaving the room, then threw herself back onto the bed, smothered her face in her pillow, beat her fist into it. Anything to stop the tears from coming.

She'd watched as, one by one, the ayahs had found work and left the home. It was time that Mehr put away her pride and did the same, if only to save enough for passage back to Lucknow. She had already made casual inquiries of the servants—it would cost her four pounds and ten shillings to grant even the lowliest cabin back. She had no choice, even if her uncle didn't want her. Coming to England was a failure. James had failed her too, but if he wished to see her again, to make any claim on his inheritance, he'd have to look harder.

She waited a few days before lingering outside Miss Christy's office, then took as long as she could before knocking on her door and asking to be let in. She could barely bring herself to say the words, to even meet Miss Christy's eyes.

"I wish to find work. With a family."

Miss Christy immediately brightened at her request. But to Mehr's surprise and horror, the only types of work available for her were as an ayah or a housemaid.

"Me? Clean chamber pots or look after someone's brat?"

"I know it is not an ideal situation for a young woman such as yourself. But . . ." Miss Christy trailed off. "Six pounds a year and an allowance would do you perfectly well."

Mehr ran the calculations in her head. It would take her nearly a year to save up for passage. "Is there nothing else with better wages?"

Miss Christy gave her a once-over. "None as respectable." She pawed through a drawer, then handed Mehr a tattered book bound in old, withered leather, its binding loose and some pages threatening to fall completely out. Stamped across the top was *The Servant's Guide for Butlers, Footmen, and Housemaids.*

"You will have to read the guidebook. It has all the training you need."

Mehr frowned at the manual in her hands. The work was entirely beneath her. At the zenana, the women had their own bevy of servants to look after them.

"Being a housemaid is not something to be ashamed of," Miss Christy said. "You gain protection and honor by association with your master or mistress. We will find you a good home, dear."

Mehr bit her lower lip. Somehow, she'd have to make it out of England, and she needed the funds to do it. Without her brother's help, she'd have to find her own way.

She relented, and soon Miss Christy began training her. They went room by room within the home, Miss Christy pointing out instructions on what she'd have to do once employed. In the drawing room, the curtains were pulled open.

"You will have to take those down."

"When?"

"Now," Miss Christy said with an exasperated laugh. "I will show you how to wash."

Then she was taught how to brush the rugs. As she bent over the floor, the splintered wooden bristle in her hand, Miss Christy paced the room, reading aloud from the guidebook.

"'Servants are not to be seated in their master's or mistress's presence, nor offer any opinion unless asked for it, not even to say goodnight or good morning except in reply.' Do you understand?"

"So, I am never allowed to speak," Mehr said, picking

out a splinter from the palm of her hand. She stifled a sneeze from the dust billowing in the air. "For six pounds a year and an allowance."

Miss Christy gave her a pointed look, then inspected her work with a *tsk*. Once the rugs were brushed, Miss Christy led her into the basement where a fresh pile of laundry was gathered. Her next chore—ironing. While Mehr leaned over the board, running the iron forward and backward over bed linen, Miss Christy cleared her throat and continued reading.

"This section here is about any wanton suggestions from a master."

Mehr yawned, waved her hand for Miss Christy to continue.

"'Being as you are under his command, obliging to attend to his needs at any hour, you will face some difficulties in avoiding his importunities.'"

"'Importunities'?" She slowed her ironing as she listened.

"His advances, Mehrunissa. Please pay attention. 'These importunities may not be easy to surmount. But keep a steady resolution and a vigorous resistance. In time, your perseverance may oblige him to desist.'"

Mehr laughed. The English and their queer turns of phrase. "'May oblige him'? What about the mistress?"

Miss Christy clapped the book against her palm. "This is the most difficult lesson in the book without your interrupting. Please."

Mehr stared down at the ironing board and found the cloth turning a slight shade of yellow as Miss Christy went on.

"'. . . oblige him to desist. He will acknowledge *you* to have more reason than himself. After all, your duty to yourself is to endeavor it.'"

"I must not sit, speak, or oblige him. Anything else to endeavor?" Mehr asked.

"That is all for now." Miss Christy sank into a chair, then looked over at the ironing board and the miserable job Mehr was doing. "You have missed several wrinkles and now you are burning the linen. Do pay better attention to your work or they will send you back here and no one will hire you again."

Mehr scoffed. She needed only nine months, ten at best, before she'd find her own way to leave for good.

A month after she'd started training and advertisements had been placed in the newspapers, Miss Christy found Mehr a position for the family of a baronet who lived some ways outside of the city. Miss Christy hadn't wasted any time, as the first inquiry had immediately agreed to pay Mehr the six pounds of annual wages. There would be no visit or interview prior.

Mehr sat on the bed and took her time packing her belongings. If she could go back to her first morning on the steamship that had carried her across the world to London, she would have warned herself of her fate. Mehr had lain in bed all morning with a terrible ache in her stomach. Her insides were twisted into knots. She'd left the comfort of her uncle's zenana, where her every need had been addressed, every desire met, living like a veiled princess, only to become the maid for a firangi household. Her mother would have died another death had she lived long enough to see it.

The thought of seeing her little brother and father again had buoyed her and helped carry her along her journey even when she hadn't wanted to keep going. But she'd been wrong. James had forsaken her. Even her uncle ignored every letter she sent, every plea to return home. But she'd make her way back to Lucknow whether he liked it or not. James would need to come back home to get his inheritance in person. And perhaps he'd appreciate his sister more once he realized how far she'd come only to be snubbed.

Mehr twisted the dupatta in her hands and had a sudden urge to tear the fabric in half. It was the same one she'd worn on the steamship, and after so many months, the knot she'd tied in it was still there. She unraveled it and let the small silk-wrapped bundle fall into the palm of her hand. It had a faint smell of rose water. The memory of Amma that it brought her made Mehr scowl. She unwrapped the bundle and took out the taweez, a tiny silver box strung on a leather cord.

The box glinted in the palm of her hand and felt curiously warm to the touch. Mehr began to pry it open, but thought better of it. She had no business reading the contents of the taweez, though she knew it was meant to have a prayer inside to keep Amma safe. Her grandfather, the nawab, had gifted it to her mother before leaving the world behind. Now it was supposed to belong to her father. She let the taweez drop from her hands into her lap. Her father. Oh, the many times Amma had filled Mehr's ears with poison about him. Her mother had driven him away with her superstitions, her madness. And so what if, in his haste, he'd left Mehr behind? He'd fled Amma, after all, and she'd had such a stronghold on Mehr. She couldn't understand why her mother had wanted him to have it after her death, given how much she'd resented him. But there was no use reasoning with the dead.

Mehr quickly packed the rest of her trunk, except for the taweez. She would need its luck now. She pulled on an itchy woolen petticoat, over which she layered a heavy long-sleeved cotton dress, then tied a white apron around her middle. Now that she was dressed the way any plain English maid would be, she didn't know where to tie the taweez into a knot. Dupattas didn't exist here, though she'd found a similar article of clothing in the shawls that Miss Christy wore. Mehr ran her hands down her apron. Tying it at the hem wouldn't be very discreet. But at the sides of her skirt, she found pockets. She dropped it into one of those.

Satisfied, and after one last frown in the mirror, cramming a white cap on her head, Mehr headed downstairs. After the post chaise arrived and her trunk was placed into the boot, she followed Miss Christy into the carriage and prayed that by some miracle James would appear, apologize for his lack of response, and take her to her father immediately.

It was a false hope. She felt inside her pocket and squeezed the taweez as the post chaise took off. Miss Christy sat in silence beside her. Mehr assumed she was preoccupied by thoughts of her wretchedness. Her face burned. She wondered what Miss Christy truly thought of her. To be so close to her only living family yet to be abandoned by her brother. She shut her eyes and pretended to sleep, not opening them again until they'd arrived in the countryside.

The change was immediate. Mehr bit back her grief and stared out the window. London had stifled her, scared her. It was busy and dirty, and the air was rotten to breathe. But the country reminded her of Lucknow, her grandfather's verdant fields stretching as far as the eye could see. Through the window, she sniffed the sweet, pure air. The lushness of the fields, now that they were just coming out of winter, was breathtaking.

They stopped down a short lane leading up to a lovely redbrick home, tall trees shading it from the murky afternoon sunlight. Mehr took her time peeling out of the post chaise and following Miss Christy up the lane. As they made their way to the house, the front door seemed to open on its own, and a young woman appeared in the doorframe, squinting out at them. Her face was so pale it was nearly translucent. Wavy golden hair escaped the messy knot she'd tied low against the back of her neck. She wore a simple muslin dress that looked too matronly for her. Because of her tired, hooded eyes, Mehr couldn't determine her age. She could have been nineteen or ninety, or both at the same time. She peered a second too long at Mehr, which made her break away first and stare at the trees instead.

Miss Christy rubbed her hands together and nodded to Mehr, then cleared her throat. "Good afternoon, Mrs.—"

"Shelley," the young woman replied. "Mrs. Shelley."

CHAPTER 3

Mrs. Shelley stood aside as Mehr and Miss Christy entered together. As modest and beautiful as the house was on the outside, it was ugly and crowded on the inside. A scuffed staircase veered up to the right, while a threadbare rug ran the length of the hallway. They followed Mrs. Shelley down the hall but had to maneuver between piles of furniture that had yet to be placed in their respective rooms. Mehr glanced into what appeared to be a dining parlour, which was mostly empty save for a small, rickety table.

She led them into a comfortably furnished drawing room. It seemed as if it were the only room they'd had time to put together. Mehr and Miss Christy took their individual chairs across from Mrs. Shelley, who sat on a large sofa. It had once been velvet, but the cloth was scuffed from wear and its previous luster had dulled over time. Somewhat like her new mistress, Mehr thought. There was something in the way she sat, back hardly touching the sofa, that made Mehr wonder how secure she really felt in such a chaotic home. It was like she was ready to take flight at any moment, flee to somewhere greater than she might have deserved.

Mehr attempted to find a way to be comfortable in the hard chair, the cushion beneath her worn down to the wood. The room was intolerably cold. A weak fire, hardly enough to warm the room, burned in the ashen grate. Mehr was reminded that it would be her duty now to keep it clean and lit, passages from *The Servant's Guide* crawling into her mind. She stared at the grate, at the bits of coal hissing impotently, their little red eyes glaring out at her. She held her hands together to stop herself from shivering. England was a particularly cold country in the winter, but spring was only around the corner and still the country hadn't shrugged out of her winter shawls.

There was a baby's pitiful wail somewhere in the house that startled Mehr, followed by abrupt silence. She rubbed her arms, avoiding Miss Christy's stern gaze. She had warned Mehr that she shouldn't look uncomfortable in her new employers' home, that it was rude. But there was no use hiding it.

Mrs. Shelley didn't seem to notice her discomfort, her expression blank and fixated on the empty table between them. The skin on her pale face was paper-thin and unlined. A delicate blue vein trailed from one temple and dissipated into her cheek. She sat with a weariness about her that made Mehr think she'd had to grow up very fast in a very short amount of time. Mehr wondered again how old she was.

"You'll have to forgive me," Mrs. Shelley said, looking suddenly at Mehr. "I make a dreadful cup of tea."

"She," Miss Christy said, gesturing to Mehr, "makes a lovely cup."

Mehr stopped herself from grimacing at the lie.

Miss Christy continued. "You have no other help?"

"We have Agnes, our cook," Mrs. Shelley said, her words careful, deliberate. Strong voice, like a child proving herself to an elder. "Lucy takes care of Willmouse."

"The baby?" Mehr asked, trying to avoid the pointed look Miss Christy gave her for speaking before being spoken to.

If Mrs. Shelley minded, she didn't show it. "William. He's a dear, dear boy. Lucy looks after him while I look after the rest." She laughed nervously. "Mr. Shelley prefers I give up housework."

"As you should, the wife of a baronet," Miss Christy said.

The young woman flushed. "It will leave me more time to write. I am working on a novel."

Miss Christy frowned, then fell into silence. Her eyes darted back and forth, as if wishing she had something to do, like fuss with a cup of tea.

Mrs. Shelley turned her gaze once again to Mehr. "Your hair. Such a beautiful, thick braid." Her voice was full of wonder as she took her time observing Mehr.

As much as Miss Christy wanted Mehr to trim her hair and style herself in the latest fashion, she had refused. She kept her hair pulled back into a braid and slung over a shoulder, like a comforting arm, reaching down to her rib cage.

Mehr stared back at the young woman. “Thank you.”

“She seems young,” Mrs. Shelley said to Miss Christy, still surveying Mehr as she spoke.

Mehr sat up straighter. “I am older than you. Four and twenty.”

“How would you know my age?” Mrs. Shelley asked.

“Because you seem young,” Mehr said with sudden confidence.

Miss Christy shifted in her seat, the wood giving out a tired croak. Mehr didn’t need to be a mind reader to know what the woman wanted to say to her. Miss Christy kept her mouth shut and turned back to Mrs. Shelley.

“She is still learning our customs. The way one needs to speak to her mistress.”

“Her name?” Mrs. Shelley again asked Miss Christy.

“Mehrunissa Begum,” Mehr said. “I am the daughter of Sadaatunissa Begum, herself the daughter of the nawab of Lucknow, descendant of Khwaja Mu’in al-Din Chishti, himself a descendant of the Prophet—”

“You can call her Mehr,” Miss Christy said, a touch exasperated.

Mrs. Shelley smiled. “Like Mary. Like me. Your mother must be beautiful.”

"My mother?" Mehr asked.

"I said she must be beautiful," Mary said.

Mehr looked away. "She was."

Silence fell between them. "I am sorry," Mary said. "My own mother has preoccupied my thoughts since my son was born."

"Children have a way of doing that," Miss Christy said.

Mary grimaced down at her lap. "She died of infection right after I was born. Gave the gift of life, while being robbed of it at the same time."

Miss Christy sighed through her nose, adjusted her gloves, avoided looking at the young woman, but Mehr kept her gaze on Mary until Mary met hers. So, she was motherless too. She wondered if that was what fate did—bring motherless young women together in the direst of circumstances.

Then, the door flew open. A thin, long-faced man walked in, leading with his chin. He wore an expensive-looking coat, but it was frayed at the collar and cuffs. His dark blond hair was arranged wildly over his head. To Mehr, he looked like a feral lion escaped from the wilds and forced into a cramped country home to masquerade as a man.

He flung himself down beside Mary and glared at her with his red-rimmed eyes.

"Have you met our guests, Percy?" she asked.

He wouldn't look at them. "I am delighted to make your acquaintance."

"You must be the baronet," Miss Christy said with a girlish smile.

He laid his head back against the sofa and shut his eyes. "I am actually a poet. A detestable one."

Miss Christy snapped her mouth shut. Mehr enjoyed imagining Miss Christy's displeasure. Two anxious writers and not one of them acting like a baronet, whatever that meant.

"We have a new housemaid," Mary said, gesturing to Mehr.

Percy kept his eyes shut. "This house could use a bit of"—he waved his hand at the room—"anything, really."

Mary smiled with a slight tic in her jaw, then stood from the sofa. Her gaze lingered on him, on his pinched lips, his lax brow. He could have fallen into a sudden, deep sleep, the way his eyes roved under his eyelids. Mary lifted a hand to his face but didn't touch him. Instead, she put a finger to her lips and motioned Mehr and Miss Christy to follow her out of the room. She walked them into the hall and shut the door to the drawing room.

"I must take my leave," Miss Christy said. She hugged Mehr, who stood with her arms stiff at her sides. Then Miss Christy held Mehr at arm's length. "This is the best we can hope for."

Mehr glared at her but kept her thoughts to herself. Her grandfather would be horrified to know that a daughter of a noblewoman, a sayidda descended from the Prophet, was going to be cleaning up after a firangi family. Mehr's eyes prickled with salt and shame. Miss Christy furiously wiped her own tears, though she didn't look as mournful as she did relieved. Another Indian woman employed, one less burden for her.

"If anything happens—*anything*—you must tell me." She lowered her voice. "I will not let you stay somewhere if you are mistreated."

Mehr glanced back at her new mistress standing in the hall, her long, thin fingers clasped together. Miss Christy hugged her again, and Mehr couldn't bring herself to do the same.

"Good luck," Miss Christy whispered, before turning toward the door and heading out into the lane.

Mehr followed her out. "My brother," she called. "If he should write you—"

"I will tell him where you are."

She gave Mehr one last wave as she climbed into her carriage. Mehr stood in the doorway, watched the carriage turn down the lane and disappear. The sky was turning orange, and a thin, fiery line of sunlight was just over the horizon. She felt a soft touch on her shoulder. Mehr flinched and Mary quickly retrieved her hand as if she'd been scalded. She moved around her to shut the door.

"Shall I show you your room?" Mary asked.

Mehr gritted her teeth. Miss Christy was gone, and Mehr's freedom went with her. She was now headed into a life of toil and degradation. She only hoped the year passed swiftly.

"Yes, Mrs. Shelley," Mehr said.

Mary led her down the crowded hall to the cellar door. She lit two candles from one of the tables pushed against the wall, handed one to Mehr, and led her below the stairs to the cellar. Even by candlelight, it was still too dark to see, and Mehr had to squint to find her way. Inky shadows blotted the corner of her eyes, uncurling themselves like long gray limbs.

She was led to a large, frigid room with a dusty stone floor, filled with yet more decaying furniture and molded rugs, and damp bags of coal sagging against the wall. Mary led her away from these and down the other end to where a bedstead and mattress had been set up underneath a set of unbleached sheets. On one side, there was a small chest of drawers. On the other, a looking glass stood atop a washstand. A solitary chair sat in the corner.

"I hope you will be comfortable here."

Mehr gave her a small nod, unable to fully meet the young woman's eyes. She turned toward the chair and found a book sitting in the center. She couldn't make out the title, but the author's name lit up suddenly as Mary neared. It was written by someone named Lord Byron. Mary scooped it up in her hands.

"I must have left it here when I was setting up your room. You can rest tonight and start in the morning. Lucy will be here to wake you."

She headed for the shadows under the cellar. Mehr heard her soft footfalls against the cellar steps before the door opened and shut, sealing her inside. Despite the young woman's serious disposition, the cellar felt colder without another person's presence. Mehr sat on the bed and hugged herself.

A small object pressed against her knee, and Mehr remembered the taweez. She pulled it out of her pocket and held it in her hand. It glinted in the light, creating sparks against the wall. The overpowering smell of rose water grew around her. With her father's gift in her hands, she unraveled the cord and began to place it over her head. But a creaking noise in the corner stopped her.

"Mrs. Shelley?" she whispered, wondering if the woman had forgotten something else in the basement.

There was no other sound. She laid the taweez down on the bed. With the candle leading her way, she crept to the other end of the cellar and stopped, waiting for something, a noise, a movement. The bags of coal lay just as they were. She moved closer to them, then there was the noise again. It came from the pile of furniture. As she inched closer, she found that a few pieces of rotten wood had fallen off the pile.

The cellar door opened and Mehr gasped, backing away from the sudden light. It was Percy, struggling down with her trunk. Her heart racing, she moved to her corner of the cellar and sat on the bed. She heard her trunk as it was dropped to the floor. She waited and counted her breaths until he went back upstairs and she was alone again.

Mehr didn't sleep that night, though she knew it wasn't

unusual. It was her first night in a new home with its new smells and an uncomfortable bed that creaked beneath her with the slightest movements. What *was* strange, however, Mehr would realize later on, after everything that was to happen over the next few months, was that she never slept a full night after she joined the Shelleys.

CHAPTER 4

Mehr settled into her role with a resigned fury. She was grateful that she didn't need to mind the infant, whose wails sounded the alarms every morning, punctuated the silence throughout the day, then streamed in through the cellar door as she lay in bed at night. Though Mehr had been somewhat intrigued by the children in the zenana, she didn't want to care for one by herself.

With the Shelleys able to afford only a few servants, Lucy handled Willmouse along with Mary's toilette. Mehr wasn't to be seen or heard by the Shelleys while she cleaned and often had to wake early and head directly into the kitchen to help their cook, Agnes, who resembled a large misshapen potato. Her face was heavily wrinkled and tanned, and her thin lips were always set in a firm line. She was mostly a dour presence.

After Mehr would assist Agnes in lighting the large kitchen hearth and preparing breakfast, she'd wait patiently for the Shelleys to go on their daily walks. Since their cottage was situated at the corner of a large garden, they'd often disappear there as well. She'd hurry through brushing and polishing, tidying the rooms, and handling the most abhorrent of all tasks—the chamber pots. She never lingered in one room long, rushing through her tasks and cutting corners where it suited her. The work was already unbefitting of a person like her. She'd skip polishing the furniture she knew they wouldn't set foot near. Sometimes she'd sweep the dust into dark corners and take it out days later, sure they wouldn't notice.

Then, when the Shelleys would return, she'd lurk in the kitchen and watch Agnes run her knobby fingers down the pages of old cookbooks, then bark at Mehr for assistance when she needed her to help peel vegetables or set a pot of water to boil.

While they worked together, Lucy would float into the kitchen and fill the silence between them. Lucy was a rather plain-looking young woman, with no discernible figure, but she was lively in conversation, especially with her captivating and expressive set of green eyes. Gossip was a trade practiced religiously by servants, Mehr had learned, and she wasn't surprised. She'd often wondered what the zenana servants had said behind her own back, but those preoccupations felt far away to her now.

One evening, Lucy brought news that Mr. Shelley wasn't well. He was a sickly man, prone to rare illnesses and convulsions, and they had moved out to the country to allow him fresh air and plenty of space to convalesce so he could continue writing his poetry. She asked Mehr if she wanted to read Mr. Shelley's work.

Mehr slowly fed coal into the hearth, careful not to get soot on her apron. "It does not interest me," she said.

Lucy grinned at her. "Afraid you might like it?"

Agnes gave her a rare smile as she stirred a thin wooden spoon in a pot of stew over the fire, then wiped her sweaty brow with the back of a hand.

"You seem civilized enough to enjoy poetry," Agnes said with her cracked, hoary voice.

Mehr scowled. "And you seem too blind to be able to read."

Agnes and Lucy laughed together, enjoying the banter. Mehr, who often retreated into her work when she wanted to be alone in a crowded kitchen, resumed her scrubbing. She let her mind close up for the day, tucked away her thoughts so that the other two would stop pestering her for company.

After she helped Agnes serve dinner and do the washing up, she went down the rickety steps into the cellar for bed. She lay awake and counted figures in her head. She was still far from her goal—even when she scrimped every shilling of her meager pay, she still had four pounds left to go. That would bring her to the middle of autumn. She reminded herself that time was a burden only if she made it one. The rest of the year would pass by quickly, just as the ten years had since she'd last seen her father.

She was brought back to that morning, after he'd had

a terrible fight with her grandfather and uncle. There was some talk about debts and honor. Then he'd forced his way into the nursery and, as she and James sat huddled together, pried James from her and picked him up in his arms. As he hurried out, he'd turned back for a small second and glanced down at Mehr. She'd held her breath. It was that second she held on to, stretched into hours, days, years. But he'd turned back, then was gone. Day after day, she'd return to that room, sit in the very same position, stare out at the doorway, wondering when he'd return and why he chose James and not her.

She hadn't wanted to leave the zenana to find them. She'd fully expected her father and James to return to her someday, had even felt it a decade later. But now, lying in a foreign bed in a foreign country, she realized just how foolish she'd been. She rolled over and stared at the taweez glinting atop her chest of drawers. She reached out and laid her fingers on it.

Then, the air was sucked out of the room. Even her candle stopped flickering.

Suddenly she realized she wasn't alone anymore. There was a heavy presence in the cellar with her. She glared around the dark, and as her eyes adjusted to the shadows, she thought she made out a figure standing at the foot of her bed. She fumbled for the candlestick and held it up in front of her. In the sudden movement of light, she perceived her mother standing at the foot of her bed. She gasped and nearly fell out, splashing searing hot wax on her hands.

But it wasn't her mother. It was Mary. She stood with her hands at her sides. Her eyes were closed and her bottom lip was dragging the rest of her face down.

"Mrs. Shelley?" Mehr whispered.

When the woman didn't move, Mehr crept closer to her. Slowly, Mary's eyes opened and she looked to the side at Mehr. Then she looked down at her hands.

"Are you unwell?" Mehr asked.

Mary shook her head. There were tears in her eyes. Mehr hesitated, glanced around the cellar. She should have been warm under her covers, drifting off to sleep, yet she was standing in the damp cold with her agitated mistress, her bare toes growing numb.

Mehr pointed at the cellar steps. "I can bring you back upstairs."

"I will not need your help," Mary said in a desperate voice.

"There is nothing wrong with sleepwalking. My mother did it frequently." Especially in moments of stress, Mehr wanted to add, but she kept that part to herself.

"I am perfectly well," the young woman said. "Good night."

Mehr watched as Mary groped around in the half dark and found the stairs. She tripped her way up and then quickly shut the door between them. The floorboards creaked above, and Mehr imagined Mary trudging back to bed.

It wasn't curious that Mary would be afflicted with the same thing her mother had been. It was a common affliction, after all. But whenever Mehr had awoken her mother in the midst of her nighttime rambles, she'd calmly open her eyes and give Mehr a sweet smile.

"I just dreamt about you," Amma would say, though Mehr never fully believed her.

Mary, on the contrary, seemed to have been startled out of a nightmare.

Mehr returned to bed, and after she blew out the candle and the darkness took hold of the cellar, she couldn't shake the feeling that she wasn't fully alone.

MEHR AWOKE THE next morning to intense bustling upstairs. It was the first time since she'd arrived at the Shelleys' that she'd woken late. She hurriedly changed into her clothes, still fumbling with her apron strings as she headed up the stairs. When she opened the cellar door, Mary stood on the other side, holding a bundle of linen in her hands.

Mehr was so taken aback she nearly toppled back down the stairs. She held on to the wall for support and eyed the young woman. Whether Mary remembered the night before, Mehr couldn't tell.

"You should be awake and in the kitchen with Agnes by now," Mary said.

Mehr resisted the urge to roll her eyes. "Indeed, Mrs. Shelley."

"The bedsheets." Mary held them up for Mehr to see. "You must be careful when you wash them."

She unraveled the cloth and pointed out several small tears with her manically chewed fingernails. "Did you know you must sew any new tears you find before washing?"

Mehr's face burned. This was in her guidebook; she remembered reading it. But it would take much too long to sift through dirty linen just to find the smallest imperfections. It already made her skin crawl to have to touch them with her bare hands. The amount of care Mary was asking for was preposterous.

"Beg pardon, Mrs. Shelley," Mehr said. "But the quality of the cloth—"

"What?" Mary narrowed her eyes at her. "What about the linen's quality, Mehrunissa?"

What she wished to say was that the cloth was much too inferior, nothing like the silks and cottons that Mehr used to sleep in. Did Mary really expect her to treat them with such care, especially when she was meant to do the work of several people while only being paid six pounds a year? If they could not afford to hire any more souls, then she was the best they had for the particular condition of their household.

There was the infant's wailing upstairs, and it momentarily distracted Mary. She handed Mehr the bundle of linen. "Do take more care in your work."

After Mary left, Mehr sulked into the kitchen, where Agnes and Lucy were waiting. Agnes gruffly pointed at a pile of vegetables for her to peel. She dumped the linen in a tub in the corner of the room and had hardly started working when Lucy cornered her.

"Do you know whose room you have been preparing the past week?" Lucy said, a tad breathless, her hand fluttering over her chest.

Mehr shrugged as she roughly chopped a turnip.

"She arrived this very morning," Lucy said, speaking so fast she was tripping over her own words. "And she is not any ordinary guest. She is Mrs. Shelley's stepsister."

Mehr stopped and dumped the bits of turnip into a pot. She started next with a potato.

"She has a sister?" Mehr asked.

"Two of them. This one is through her father's marriage."

Perhaps, Mehr wondered, that was why Mary had been so particular about the linen. Still, her ears burned from the scolding and she wished she suddenly had the complete funds to escape the country. To think she was at the mercy of such people! She placed her anger into peeling the potato in her hand.

Lucy leaned in closer. "I must tend to Willmouse. They are in the drawing room." She gave her a suggestive smile, then backed out of the kitchen.

Mehr waited until the vegetables had all gone into the pot, then wiped her hands clean and headed out into the hall. She crept up to the drawing room, its door shut tight.

She hesitated. No, she was not an idle gossip. She had been raised with manners, not to be an eavesdropper. Their business was their business. She wouldn't be snooping around like a commoner. Like Lucy.

She tutted under her breath, incensed more at herself this time than at Lucy, and turned away from the door. But before she could make it a step down the hall, the drawing room door opened and a dark-haired woman stalked out. The woman took in her appearance with one quick glance. But Mehr took her time observing the woman. She was every bit Mary's opposite. Her hair was dark, heavily curled, and pulled back in a high bun, whereas Mary was blond and kept her fair hair messily tied back. While Mary seemed like she was still growing into her clothes with her waiflike figure, this woman's dress fitted well around her comely and plump figure. Neither was a plain woman, but their individual beauties seemed to be at war with each other.

"What are you doing lurking out here?" Mary asked from the doorway, a tad exasperated.

Before Mehr could emphatically state how well-mannered she was not to pry on private conversations, Mary turned to the other, waved her hand in Mehr's direction. "Our new housemaid. Will you say hello, Mehrunissa?"

Mehr turned to the dark-haired woman. "Hello, Mrs.—"

"Miss," the woman said, her eyes brightening. Then a soft, self-conscious chuckle. "Miss Claire Clairmont." Her voice was high-pitched and had a musical quality to it.

"Mehrunissa, this is my sister. She will be staying with

us for a while." Mary stared at *Miss* Claire Clairmont, a tic working in her jaw.

AFTER THE SECOND month of her visit, the Shelleys fell into an easy routine with their guest. She took meals with them and accompanied them on their daily walks. At times, she would seek out other society and accept the many invites she received for balls. She appeared to be more popular than Mary, who preferred to receive her guests from the comfort of her own drawing room.

It was a wonder how much Mehr learned about a person just by picking up after them. Claire's room was the messiest. She threw her dresses down on every surface. Scattered about the room were small piles of books, but they were brand-new and didn't show any signs of having been read. All their spines and bindings were intact, not one smudge of ink within them. Mehr took her time inspecting Claire's clothes, running her hands along the fabric. They felt expensive, and of a much finer material than any of Mary's dresses, though still not as fine or as delicate as what Mehr had left behind.

One morning, as Mehr tidied Claire's room, straightening piles of unread books on top of the writing table, she found an unfinished letter lying perfectly in the center. She leaned closer and made out the hurried writing, eyes scanning the page.

I steal a moment to write to you to, if possible, have again the pleasure of seeing you.

Against all reason, Mehr picked the letter up, devouring the words. You could also learn a lot about a person by the way they wrote, and this young woman wrote passionately. She could hardly keep it all in a straight line. There were ink stains scattered across the page that she'd never bothered to blot away.

Tomorrow will inform me whether I should be able to offer you that *which it has long been the passionate wish of my heart to offer you.*

Mehr flushed and nearly dropped the letter. It was personal and too intimate for her to be reading. But it also shouldn't have been so carelessly left out in the open for her to read. She scanned the lines and found to whom the letter was addressed. A man named Lord Byron. As she placed the letter back where she'd found it, she knew she'd seen that name somewhere before and tried to recall where or when.

There were voices outside the cottage. Mehr left the writing table and peeked out the window. She found Percy and Claire lingering on the path that snaked away from the cottage and into the lush greenery of Windsor Park. Claire was speaking animatedly to Percy. She gestured wide with her arms, then let out pretty giggles.

Percy had dark circles under his eyes and struggled to take in a breath. The past few weeks his coughs had rung out through the house and been interspersed with the cries of the infant. As Percy struggled to take in a breath to speak to her, she hooked her arm in his and smiled up into his face. He halted and seemed lost for words. She'd caught him mid-speech, which was a rare feat because the man loved to fill the spaces around him with his own voice. The young woman was charming, and she knew it. There was some color in his cheeks as he bent forward to speak to her. Mehr squinted and thought she saw his lips brush Claire's cheek.

Mehr drew closer to the window and searched for Mary. If she had been nearby, would they have been behaving in such an intimate way? Perhaps the letter would give her a clue. She turned back to the table, when the door creaked open behind her. It was Mary, having crept up on her as silently as a ghost.

"Oh," Mary said. "I did not know I would find you here."

Mehr remained standing where she was. Through the window, more tinkling laughter from Claire. She glanced briefly out the window and found them taking the path to the garden.

Mary let out a deep sigh. "Strange how one can find they are an interruption in another person's story."

Mehr didn't respond. She resumed picking up the books off the floor and placing them on the table. Mary sat down at the edge of Claire's bed and touched one of the dresses Mehr had folded. She undid her poor work and folded it anew.

"She is a lovely girl. Willful sometimes. But I do love her," Mary said.

She picked up another and began refolding it as well. "Percy said he needs the sun to break out of the clouds every now and then."

Mehr felt Mary's eyes on her.

"Have you any siblings?" Mary asked.

Mehr's thoughts floated over to James. She wondered where he was. If he was thinking of her at that very moment too. Had he visited the home, found her gone, realized she was better off where she was? Or was he out searching for her all over London? Perhaps his carriage was rumbling down the lane and he was so close she could nearly see him out the window. But as usual when she'd have these terrible thoughts and would glance out just in case, there was nothing there.

"A brother," Mehr said, and left it at that.

"Younger? Older?"

Mehr glanced down at the young woman. "You do not have to do that," she said.

"I am quite troublesome with my questions," Mary said with a sigh.

"I mean . . ." Mehr gestured to the third dress Mary was beginning to fold. "I will fold them better next time."

Mary dropped the dress. It slithered off the bed and fell in a heap at her feet. She seemed to be coming out of a trance. "Percy says I often ask too many questions. Asking despite having already heard an answer."

Mehr waited for her to say more, but Mary continued staring at her knees. Mehr moved across the room and knelt in front of the young woman. Their eyes met for the briefest moment, and Mehr was startled to see how endless her gaze was, just how bottomless the depths of her eyes were. Mehr looked away first and picked the dress up off the floor. She shook it hard, then roughly folded it on top of the bed. Then there were the ones Mary had worked on. Once she'd made a stack of them, she felt a touch on her hand.

Mary stared up at her with bleary, bloodshot eyes.

"I enjoy at times being the quiet one in the room. But you are silence personified."

Mehr moved her hand away. She had a sudden urge to ask what Mary wanted from her. One moment she was scolding Mehr for her poor work, now she needed a friend? A confidant? Mehr wanted to be neither. Mary was her mistress, and she was paying her meager wages to wash her inferior linens and refill her washstand every morning. The indignity still riled her.

The infant began crying in the other room. Mary moved toward the door, while Lucy had already thumped up the stairs and was in Mary's room before she'd reached it. Mehr heard their urgent whispers as the infant quieted.

Mehr returned to her work and began airing the bed. She stripped the bedding and pillowcases, then lifted the mattress to turn it. The floorboards creaked behind her. She dropped it and wondered if Mary was going to join her again, telling her whatever was left unsaid. But the footsteps receded down the hall and she was left alone.

Downstairs, the front door opened and shut. Mehr returned to the window and followed Mary's solitary figure as she left the cottage and headed down the path to the garden. Moments later, she was swallowed by the trees.

After she'd done her chores for the day, Mehr met Agnes in the kitchen and helped her set the table. As they went between the dining parlour and the kitchen, Agnes declared Mary to be an excellent mother and the infant to be a perfect little boy. Agnes's thoughts often came out at random, like she had previously had a conversation with herself and then shared the last of it out loud with Mehr.

Mehr drowned out her voice and returned to her thoughts, where she liked to live alone. She'd traveled far and wide with her thoughts. She was still ashamed of how Mary had admonished her over her work. She, a sayidda, granddaughter of the grand, highly respected, and much beloved nawab of Lucknow. It made her heart ache. But the work was necessary. Every minute that passed ensured she was closer to leaving.

There was such a thing as irony, and she had no choice but to watch it play out in front of her, like a Shakespearean comedy. Even he couldn't have dreamt up the ridiculous satire of her life. Why had Mary wanted to confide in her? Mehr had already lived two lives—and now she was entering into a third that intersected with the drama of the Shelleys, their strange marriage, the glamorous new guest in the house, and the men she was entangled with. As much as it pained her to admit it, she was intrigued by the spectacle of the Shelleys. Yet nothing told her at that moment that her fascination would soon take a dangerous turn.

CHAPTER 5

In the morning, Mehr stood at the kitchen door listening to an argument between the Shelleys. Through the crack in the door, she glimpsed Claire pacing up and down the hall, stopping here and there to glance upstairs when Percy's voice rose. His was the louder of the two. It was rough, punctuated by the odd cough. Mehr recalled Lucy had once chattered on to Mehr about Percy's sickness.

Behind her, Lucy and Agnes stopped whispering after Mehr turned and shushed them. Usually the Shelleys were artful in their arguing. This time, something was drawing out their fervor. She pushed the door open a little wider and placed her ear against the crack.

"We are not trapped here," Mary said. "This is our home. I cannot, in good conscience, drag Willmouse across to the Continent."

"For a good cause. *Our* cause," Percy said.

"And if he fell ill?" Mary's voice cracked; she seemed on the edge of tears. "I could not bear it."

Mehr heard the bed creak above her and imagined Percy had flung himself on top of it.

His voice was muffled. "We moved here for my health. You know I am ailing. My spasms. The pulmonary attack. Yet I am still willing to travel."

"We finally have peace in our lives," Mary said. "And now with her—"

"Do you remember when we eloped years ago?" Percy asked. "What an adventure it was. Do not you miss it?"

It was a while before Mary spoke. "We were in constant pursuit by my family."

Mehr bit her lip, savored that last bit of drama. Percy was the only one who did not leave his letters out so carelessly, but Mehr had briefly scanned the few Mary had begun before throwing them into the hearth unfinished. They were sad, desperate letters to her father, often with apology for having run off with Percy years before. What her father's responses were, Mary would never know.

She went on. "We stayed in dirty French auberges in the midst of a war and hardly found anywhere to bathe." She scoffed. "We traveled by one donkey among the *three* of us."

Lucy was at Mehr's elbow, tittering in her ear. Mehr nudged her away.

Percy again. "We did not have the funds. We do now. I will spare no cost for our comfort."

"But we will have *her* oppressive presence yet again," Mary said.

There was that mention again of a mysterious woman. By the way Claire was glaring upstairs, Mehr didn't need to venture far to guess who she was.

Percy's voice was softer now. "I know you hated France."

"But I loved you," Mary said.

"*Loved?*"

At the last word, Claire flinched and stepped down from the staircase. She wandered back into the hallway and leaned against the wall, still devoutly listening to the conversation upstairs. She wrung a handkerchief in her hand, then paused to dab at her forehead and neck.

Percy let out a loud, rattling sigh. "I have only just begun my new literary plans, and I need inspiration. He will inspire me. Both of us. I know your imagination is trapped here as well."

"Windsor Park is an apt setting to work on your literary plans," Mary said.

"Maie . . ."

Here Mehr imagined him clasping her arms, squeezing her to his bosom.

"This is our chance," Percy said. "We can finally meet Lord Byron."

That name again. Mehr remembered where she'd seen it. The book Mary had left in the cellar. It was the same man to whom Claire had written her lovestruck letters. Now she wished she'd had the chance to read the full letters. The disparate threads of these four were intersecting with this mysterious man. The intrigue was too much for her. But she reminded herself that these were James's people, that he was a pukka sahib now. This was how his half of society lived, not her own.

Mary's voice was muffled, her head likely buried in his chest. "The fuss you caused with *Queen Mab*. He should be pursuing *you*."

"Maie, his publisher is John Murray," Percy said.

They stopped speaking, and there was a ringing silence in the cottage. Percy stomped down the stairs, with Mary close behind him. Claire backed away, busied herself by picking up a random book on the table in the hall.

Mary moved between the two. "How well do you know Lord Byron, Claire?"

Claire flushed and looked down at her book, appeared to realize it was upside down and quickly turned it the other way. "We have been acquaintances for the past month or so."

Mehr smiled to herself. Mere acquaintances didn't write so ardently to each other.

"And you say he is expecting us?" Mary asked, gently taking the book from her.

"He is very keen on meeting you. Both of you." Claire drew closer to Mary. "To have an audience, just the three of us, with Lord Byron. You know what that means."

Mary nodded down at the book in her hands, though she didn't seem as resigned as she pretended to be. Percy wasn't the only one in pursuit of his muse. Mehr was often cleaning up scraps and balled-up pieces of manuscripts from both of their rooms. Yet Mary was writing at a much more feverish pace than Percy. Literary ambition, she realized, was a trait shared by both of them.

"When is he expecting us?" Mary asked.

Claire let out an excited laugh. She took her sister's hands and pulled her into a hug. "We must go now! Now!"

She was breathless and giddy. Percy smirked at her, amused at her girlishness. When she realized he was studying her, Claire flushed and glanced away from him. All the while, Mary stood stoically in her sister's embrace.

"I need to write," Percy declared. He reached for his coat on a rack next to the front door and stepped outside. Behind his back, Mary threw an exasperated look at her sister, then hurried after him.

THOUGH IT TRIED Claire's patience, it took them two frenzied weeks to arrange the trip. They decided on taking the full summer for their holiday and would depart at the start of May and return in September. Lucy and Mehr were consumed with helping the three pack, with a separate trunk dedicated entirely to all the books they planned to read over their holiday.

Percy took to his literary plans with a new and profound mania. Every day, he'd fly out of the house and into the woods with his pencil case and journal tucked under an arm, refusing any company from the women. Mehr found his room to be overrun with pages and pages of writing and dared not touch any of it. She let the pages lay where they were, allowing his madness to take its own shape.

Claire was in a different state of turmoil, ordering new dresses to be made, then abruptly canceling her requests. Lucy later shared that the young woman agonized over every item she packed, at times dumping out her trunk and redoing the whole process again.

Meanwhile, Mary was preoccupied over her son. Mehr heard how worryingly obsessed she was becoming, not sending for Lucy at all but minding him on her own, keeping him within reach at every hour. Even with Percy's reassurances that the trip would be quicker and more comfortable for them this time given the few luxuries they could now afford, especially after the death of Percy's grandfather and the small windfall he'd recently received, some nights Mary kept the baby clasped to her bosom well after he'd fallen asleep.

The day before their trip, Mary summoned Mehr to bring a tray of tea to the drawing room. Mary was already seated and waved her over once she'd entered. Mehr set the tray down and sat across from her, watched as Mary poured a cup of tea for each of them.

"You may have heard by now," Mary said, stirring sugar into the cup. "We relieved Agnes of her duties this morning."

Mehr had woken to crashes in the kitchen upstairs and then sudden silence. She knew something had gone rotten with Agnes, especially when the woman was no longer at her usual post at the hearth.

"We could not afford to keep her or pay her wages while we are away for the summer." Mary handed her a cup. "And Lucy is very important to me, to William."

Mehr stiffened in her seat. Her mouth was dry, but she couldn't bring herself to sip the tea. Instead, her mind went over the figures and how little she had saved for her way back home.

Mary continued. "I know it has been difficult for you. It is evident to me that you are not accustomed to this sort of work. Though you have made some improvements."

Mehr put down her cup. "You are relieving me of my duties," she said. "You may as well say it."

Mary took a slow sip and stared hard at her. "I have thought about it. But we will keep you through September. If I see improvements, we shall discuss more when we return."

Mehr finally breathed out. Again, she made quick calculations in her head. She would have enough funds by the end of October. But she also had the jewelry she'd brought over with her and could easily sell off the gold—even below its value if needed—to make up the rest of the ticket cost. Then she'd be the one to decide whether she wanted to continue working for the Shelleys. The thought of it loosened the knot in her throat.

Mary smiled at her, as if she'd granted her the sweetest of mercies. "We shall be ready to depart by morning."

Though it greatly pained her, Mehr forced her lips into a smile and took a sip of the dreadful tea Mary had poured. "Till September, Mrs. Shelley."

The young woman gave her a questioning look, then nodded for Mehr to leave the room.

Mehr waited until evening to pack. When she was a little girl, she was told she'd become a world traveler. As she'd run through the halls of the zenana, her ayah would scoop her up in her arms and tickle the bottoms of her feet. Mehr had a large freckle in the center of her right foot, and this meant she was going to travel far and wide when she was older—a joke, perhaps, because she was never really meant to.

She laughed at the cruelty of fate. Here she was, halfway across the world, sitting on a cold bed in a damp cellar, dressed in plain maid's clothes. The prophecy had found her. She covered her face with her hands and breathed through the gaps of her fingers. Her mind drifted to Amma on her deathbed, before she had ceased to speak. Over the years, her mother also lost the will to cry because her tears had lost their salt. Even if she could, it just wouldn't taste the same.

Now, months later, Mehr had lost so much time on her fruitless mission. She should have been in the warmth of her father's home. She cursed aloud at James, hoping the fury of her words found its way to him. It was dishonorable for him to have abandoned his older sister. She'd spent months making excuses for him. In her mind he was always in his carriage, always inching closer to her. But that image was replaced now. She imagined him sneering, scowling at the thought of her, laughing aloud at her plight.

She turned her ire on her uncle for forcing her to pursue someone who cared so little for her. And then her mother and her damned final wish.

Mehr located the taweez in her bedside drawer, then unraveled the cord and held it out in front of her, allowing it to swing back and forth like a pendulum. There was, perhaps, something powerful in the desires of the newly deceased. She'd yet to see it for herself from the little trinket dangling in front of her, but she knew what it meant for her father to have it. Even if only to be reminded of what he'd lost two decades before and of the woman he'd once loved.

She slipped it on over her head, then tucked it under her collar. The cool metal rested against her chest. With her fist, she ground the taweez in, pressing further and further till her skin puckered around it. She let go and felt the delayed bite of the metal, the small cuts it had made.

She fished the locket out and put it in her mouth, sucked on it like she would as an infant. There was a mineral sting to the taste of her blood, and an uncomfortable lingering of her mother's scent, what the taweez would have picked up from decades of it resting against her skin. For a moment she was a child again, cradled in her mother's arms, her natural perfume enveloping Mehr, the taweez pressed between them as if it were always going to be the three of them in that embrace. But that was before.

Then a creak from the cellar steps. Lucy called out to

her, needing her help in the kitchen now with Agnes gone.

She dropped the taweez from her mouth and tucked it back under her collar, finished folding then placing her clothes into her trunk, and, with one last look around the cellar, went upstairs to help the young woman.

CHAPTER 6

Mehr leaned against the side of the packet boat, watching the water whisk past below. It was early morning, and she was the only one of their travel party outside. She wrapped her shawl tighter around her, tucked it under her elbows to keep out the breeze. When they'd left Portsmouth, they'd been told it would take only a few hours to get to their first stop on the Continent—Le Havre in France. With the turn in the weather and the increasing fury of the waves, those hours stretched out even further.

The last time she was on a ship, she'd been beset with mild seasickness the first several weeks. But now, her body had settled. It had changed in the past few months, become hardened, tougher. Maybe, she thought, she'd continue to harden until she was nothing but a large misshapen stone.

She felt movement beside her and found Percy placing his hands on the rail.

"Lovely, is it not?" It was the first time he'd spoken directly to her since the day she first met him. "The sea."

He swept his hand out in front of him. "Have you ever seen such a sight?"

"Of course, Mr. Shelley," she said, stiffening now as the wind howled around them.

"The last time we went adventuring, it was just this time two years ago," Percy said. "And it was intolerably warm. I am not quite certain when summer will arrive, but she is dreadfully late."

Mehr shut her eyes and wished for the man to go away. Instead, she felt his gaze on her.

"What is that?" he asked, staring at her chest.

She looked down and found that the taweez had wriggled its way out from under her dress. It had settled itself on top of her shawl.

She placed a gentle hand upon it. "It belonged to my mother."

"But what *is* it?" he asked again, this time reaching for it.

When Mehr closed her fist around it, he dropped his hand.

"A taweez."

Percy looked befuddled. "A—talisman?"

"It wards off the evil eye," Mehr said. "Used for luck." She tucked it back under her loosened shawl, then wrapped it around her again.

"Good," Percy said, rubbing his pale, dry hands together against the chill air. "You can protect us all."

What Mehr wanted to tell him was that this talisman hadn't done much good for her mother or for herself.

Whatever was its intended purpose, it may have to wait a good while before it saw her father again. Mehr glared up at the sky, wondered if Amma was up beyond the clouds watching her wretched daughter now. She wanted her to get a good look at what she'd created.

Percy remained at her side, staring at the sky as well. "I have dreams, vivid ones, where I am underwater. Thrashing and thrashing, but not drowning. I can *breathe* underwater. Yet I fight against it. If we were to pitch over and fall, if this boat were to sink, would your talisman save us?"

She felt the heat of his stare on the side of her face.

"Well?" he asked.

"I suppose the real question is"—she turned to him—"would you want it to save you?"

Percy frowned at her. The boat went up a tall wave, and both of them held tighter to the rail. Around the corner, there was the distinct sound of someone vomiting over the side of the boat.

"Poor Maie," he said. "She can never handle the waves. Even on the mildest seas."

"Perhaps she needs our help," Mehr said.

Percy shrugged, beckoned Mehr to follow him down the length of the boat, then around the corner outside the cabins, where they found Mary hunched over the railing. Claire stood beside her, dutifully holding back her hair, though her sister was pushing her away.

Mehr moved into the cabin. The boat pitched, and she held on to the wall, surveying the four rows of bunk beds tightly squeezed into the small room. She reached for the nearest bed and pulled the thin blanket off. Then she dragged it outside with her, careful not to lose her step as the boat rolled again.

Mary had successfully shoved Claire off while Percy was backing away with both hands raised in surrender. Quickly, Mehr dropped the blanket over Mary's shoulders. She was startled and had halfway turned around before she'd been wrapped into the blanket. With her arms around Mary, Mehr felt Mary's breath puff softly against her chin. She leaned into Mehr, and finally looked up at her.

"Would you like to lie down?" Mehr asked, still holding on to her.

She nodded weakly and let Mehr walk her to the beds. There, she let Percy tuck his wife into a lower bunk. As she headed out of the cabin, Mary called out to her.

"Will you stay?"

Mehr glanced at Percy, who looked like his life depended on it. Before she could answer, he was already quitting the cabin.

"Perhaps your talisman can cure her," he muttered as he passed her by. He joined Claire, who was peeking in at her sister. He took her arm and led her away.

Mehr lingered in the doorway, but the waves were incessant and she finally moved to sit at the foot of Mary's bed. The young woman was fast asleep and slept the rest of the trip. Mehr realized she didn't need to be there at all, but she stayed by her side until Percy had magnanimously sent Lucy to trade places with her.

Once the boat arrived at the Le Havre port, they hired a stagecoach. The driver arrived with a shotgun in his lap, which alarmed Lucy. Claire patted her hand and explained it was only for protection, just in case there were bandits stalking the road. However, on their last journey two years prior, they hadn't been attacked at all, Claire reassured her.

"They tell those stories to keep us off the roads," she said. "When you have traveled as much as I have, you know."

Behind her sister's back, Mary rolled her eyes. While Percy helped the driver stow their luggage atop the carriage, Mary prodded Claire, who'd stalled to watch the men work, into the stagecoach. It required a few more pushes before Claire took her seat in the carriage. Mehr realized Mary wanted to sit between Claire and Percy.

When they'd first left London, Mehr had learned she was not to sit inside the carriage because it was not meant for servants. Lucy had stopped her from clambering in and, with an apologetic tone, told her she needed to sit up with the driver.

Mehr had stood aghast, watched as the others piled in. She had never felt so insulted in her short life. Now, she drew herself up, then headed to the driver and took his hand as he helped her up to the seat beside him. At least, she thought, she'd be able to see the view better from up there.

It was her first time abroad, and she had grown quite tired of England. A change of scenery would help distract her from her negligent brother, perhaps even from the appalling conditions of her current life.

As the carriage took off, though the weather was mild, the breeze chilled Mehr. She wrapped her arms around herself and resisted the shivers. The driver stared at her from the corner of his eye, then wordlessly took a blanket out from under the seat and laid it in her lap. She was comfortable, then, for the first hour, but by the second, her rear was sore and the stinging smell of horse dung made her nose run. She prayed for them to have a break to stretch her limbs.

They eventually stopped on the side of the road and Mehr stood from her seat, though she felt too indignant to join the others. She stared down at them as Mary and Percy appeared to be in an argument.

"Did you remember to visit the post office before we left?" Mary asked.

Percy was digging for something in his pockets. "I may have forgotten."

"You were to give my father word when we set off," Mary said.

"So he can badger me for money on our holiday?" Percy asked.

Mehr had seen Mary's father's letters scattered among Percy's manuscripts and pages. She'd given up on resisting, especially if they so artlessly kept their belongings in disarray, cared so little for discretion; she had no choice but to glance here and there.

Mary's father wrote in large, demanding blocks of sentences chastising him for running off with his daughter yet in the same breath asking for money to cover his debts. It was then Mehr realized that the two weren't actually married, even though Mary insisted she be referred to as Mrs. Shelley.

The more she learned about them, the more she pitied them: their dramas were so tepid, so unsophisticated. She resisted the urge to laugh, pressing her lips together and averting her gaze to the sky instead.

"I would not want him to worry," Mary said quietly.

He grimaced at her. "You know that he and his wife"—he stared pointedly at Claire, who lingered nearby—"*your* mother, care for little else."

Mary headed over to Lucy, who sat on the ground with the infant, and took him in her arms. For something to do, Mehr realized, and watched her fuss with his collar. She straightened his cuffs and gave him a soft kiss on the forehead. The infant stared between his parents, surely aware of some unease between them.

Percy sighed. "When we arrive in Versailles, I shall alert him of our whereabouts. And I need to write to Harriet."

"Why?" Claire and Mary said at the same time. Mary glared at her until she looked away.

"Ianthe and Charles have come down with a fever. If anything were to happen to my children—"

"Very well," Mary said. "For your children."

He kissed her forehead and resumed rummaging in his pockets. Mary smiled to herself and stared up at him. Her eyes were large and full of adoration.

Mehr sat back in her seat, disgust coating her throat.

AFTER TWO OVERNIGHT stops at inns of ill-repute, they reached Versailles. From there, they were detained for a week while Percy sorted out their passports for Geneva. Since the Revolution in France, the government had strict laws against travelers. They didn't have any letters of introductions to any known persons in Versailles, so they were to stay confined in their rooms until the government granted their passports.

With plenty of time and nothing to do, Mehr took to her sketching, but Lucy grew bored of their involuntary confinement and filled the silence between them with gossip. Since Lucy had spent intimate hours with the Shelleys and Claire, she was able to share more about their history with her.

"I was not raised to be a gossip. We had manners," Mehr told her emphatically, scooting her chair closer to the little window where she'd stare out to sketch.

"So, you were raised in the jungle, alone with no society at all."

Mehr narrowed her eyes at her. "Pardon?"

"Everyone *loves* gossip, even you. If you were raised with as many sisters as I was."

"I was not," Mehr said, training her focus back out the window.

"Brothers, then?"

She could no longer call James her brother, and she wished that he'd cease to exist in her heart. But at times, when the night was still and quiet and she felt she was the only one awake in the world, and even though she'd stripped him of that honorific, she thought of that little boy who would follow her around the zenana like a devoted duckling, who wouldn't sleep until Mehr had muttered a made-up prayer and softly blown air onto his brow. That child had grown into a devious, spiteful man. Perhaps she'd ceased to exist for him as well. And perhaps it was all for the best.

Mehr didn't respond to Lucy's question, though Lucy didn't seem to care. She continued with her chatter while Mehr forced herself to focus on the facade of the pub across the road, the broken cobblestones, the scratch marks in the wooden door, the crooked chimney on the roof.

Some of the gossip she'd already pieced together herself. Mary and Percy had eloped when she was sixteen years old and he was one and twenty. He was already married. That was the woman, Harriet, that he had mentioned, Mehr remembered, as she sketched the stream of smoke rising up from the chimney. They'd taken Claire with them on their honeymoon and traveled around the Continent, pursued in part by Mary's family. But when it became clear Percy and Mary were serious about their intentions, her family had given up.

They'd returned to England, and Mary was often left alone with Claire for long stretches of time while Percy moved around the country, dodging his creditors. Mehr put down her pencil and stared out the window. It was as if she'd heard this story before and couldn't remember where.

Eventually, when Mary became pregnant, Percy and Claire became closer to each other. Mary suffered greatly during the pregnancy. She was often bedridden or unable to accompany them for hours at a time. Her suffering didn't end, though; the child was delivered early and passed after just a few weeks of life.

Mehr stopped completely. "Oh, the poor little thing."

Lucy laughed. "You are not above a little gossip. I knew it."

Mehr turned to face her. "You speak of the death of an infant. And she was alone for it."

"They have William now."

Mehr turned back to the window. "Indeed, they do."

They didn't seem to be any better off to her. Claire was back in their life, and Mary was obsessed with the well-being of their child. Mehr felt only the slightest amount of sympathy for the young woman. The slightest. Especially for the way Mary was surrounded by such deceitful people—her husband, her sister, even Lucy. Perhaps she knew it too, because she seemed so stern and serious at such a young age. But it was a fleeting moment, and Mehr returned to her sketchbook.

After their papers were obtained, and Percy sent money

to both Mary's father and his wife, they hired another carriage and headed in a southerly direction through the plains. For three days, their route took them past several villages, each with its own stories of desolation and war. As they rolled through, Mehr found that few had passable inns and there was a total lack of farm animals in the fields.

"Spoils of war," Percy said to a curious Lucy, as they stopped again to stretch their limbs. "That is how to win a war. Take their livelihood one animal at a time."

Claire and Percy tsked and tutted, expressing their pity as loud as they could. Mehr didn't know much about the recent war, but Lucy's look of horror prompted Claire to happily give her a history lesson, with Percy interjecting his own facts. It was apparently due to some political or social fracas. Once the French monarchy had been felled and the monarch executed (Lucy shuddered at this last point), from the ashes rose a new hero—the militant Napoleon Bonaparte. He led the country through a series of wars with Britain until he was deposed.

Mehr's mind drifted to Lucknow, and for a moment, there was a surge of dread. Would it be the same to her when she returned? She'd been gone about a year, but it felt longer. She knew she had changed, felt it in her body, her face, even the palms of her hands. Would her beloved country have changed as well? Her uncle refused to write to her; she was bereft of news from India.

Her country had its own sets of kingdoms and monarchs. The crumbling Mughal Empire to the north and east, the tribal Rajputs to the west, and the rebellious Marathas and Kingdom of Mysore to the south. She recalled her grandfather's stories about how, for generations, the Mughal Empire had consolidated power and established feudatories across the land, such as with Rajput chiefs, through marriage and other alliances, resulting in relative peace and prosperity.

But since the firangi had begun arriving in the name of trade and commerce fifty years prior, the Rajputs, Maratha Confederacy, and Mysore Sultanate were stirring, and skirmishes between each and the increasingly dilapidated empire were constant and worrying news. There were rumors among the zenana about firangi merchants creating their own armies of local sepoys on behalf of the various kingdoms.

Could the gradual unrest give rise to a militant king like Napoleon? She shuddered to think about the possibility, about what was happening that very moment while she sat in the carriage with her brother's people. She was far away and useless. Would there be the same scenes of devastation in the villages and her grandfather's vast fields when she returned home? She shut her eyes and avoided looking over the carriage for a while.

After they'd left the plains, the terrain gave way to fragrant pine forests. The Swiss mountains were slowly encroaching on them. She felt exposed on top of the carriage, the rocky outposts sharp and forbidding as they neared. Before long they were climbing up the hills. The higher altitude brought snow down upon them, and her fear was replaced with enchantment. She had never seen snow before. She held her palm up to receive the flakes. Her skin tingled where they melted. If only she could keep one, pocket it forever, and show it to her remaining family back home. But they melted too quickly and disappeared just as she withdrew her hand to the warmth.

When the snow showers became heavier, she wrapped herself completely inside the blanket. But it was both cold and wet outside, making the blanket less of a cover and more of an accomplice. The driver was barely wrapped in a shawl. The English were well accustomed to the cold, even appeared to enjoy it. But Mehr was shivering uncontrollably, snot running down her nose and freezing when it hit the air. It was unbecoming of her to be in such a state. As the carriage made its way up the treacherous craggy hills, she held on tight to the seat below her as the carriage rocked perilously on.

She was grateful that the weather was intolerable even to her master and mistress, who were safe and warm within the carriage. They stopped prematurely to shelter at an inn. By now, Mehr had grown used to this routine. She and Lucy would be cramped in a room together, forced to share a cot. She'd lie awake at night listening to her stories, and no matter how much Mehr pretended to sleep, Lucy would prattle on and on.

Mehr spent most of the evening warming herself at the fire, fuming at the injustice of it all. She hardly spoke to

Lucy, and when it was time for bed, Mehr rolled away from her. But Lucy was persistent. She poked Mehr's shoulder.

"What do you know about Lord Byron?" Lucy asked.

Mehr groaned, threw an arm over her eyes. "I care to know nothing."

Lucy giggled in the darkness, then poked her again. "He is a magnificent poet."

"And you have read these poems," Mehr said.

"No, no. But I hear he is a literary genius. Beloved in London society. Though he is a bit of a rogue."

"A rogue?" Mehr asked.

"He has a way with women. Far too many women. Only recently separated from his wife with whom he has a beautiful infant daughter. He has been called 'mad, bad, and dangerous to know' by a former lover." Lucy yawned, then her eyes widened. "Oh! And he is lame in one foot."

"A poet and pirate in one," Mehr said with a shrug.

"And there are rumors . . . scandalous ones," Lucy said.

Mehr's ears perked up in the darkness. "None more so horrific than the ones you have already shared about people I will never meet."

Lucy yawned again. "They were spread by his estranged wife. About his close relationship with his half sister."

Mehr turned to Lucy, her curiosity getting the better of her. But she had fallen asleep and was breathing deeply, too deeply to be roused for more. Mehr moved away from her, unable to sleep. She spent the night staring at the same spot on the floor, her mind working around the man that had bedeviled the Shelleys and Claire, and what his appearance would look like. She imagined him with a wooden leg, a long, waxy coat that flapped in the wind behind him. He had sunken-in eyes that were lined with malice. And with the addition of a large, matted beard, in her mind's eye he was the poet and pirate in one.

IN THE MORNING, with the snow and winds abating, they journeyed the rest of the way over the mountain before finally descending upon Geneva. As if awaiting their arrival, the clouds cleared from the sky and the haze lifted. They were perfectly able to see Leman Lake. The mountains were gnarled and ancient as they hulked above the water, protective of its beauty. It gleamed at them like a solitary bright-blue eye. Mehr shrugged off the blanket and enjoyed the warming rays of sunshine.

By late afternoon, they arrived at the Hotel de Sécheron, having to weave between other carriages and chaises. It being the summer months, the entrance was crowded with travelers seeking the moderate, pleasant climate during their holiday. Mehr was relieved they'd finally arrived. She was extremely fatigued after weeks of journeying atop the rocky carriage and having to listen to Lucy's incessant chatter. Now that their destination had been reached, she was looking forward to the stability of staying in one place for the next several months. It also pulled her ever closer to the day she could finally leave Europe for good.

Claire bounded out of the carriage. She frantically

searched the crowd of hotel guests, as if the Lord she'd so passionately written to were waiting right outside to whisk her away.

Mary and Percy were having a hushed argument to the side. Mehr clambered off the carriage, moved closer to the couple to retrieve her trunk from the driver's hands, and overheard Mary worry about the cost of the hotel. But Percy insisted they stay there because the Lord was as well, no matter the cost.

Mehr walked away from them and stared out at the lake. With dusk on the horizon, the waters stilled like dark glass and prettily reflected the clear sky, while sailboats etched lazy lines across her surface. The sun was warmer here than in England, and there was a verdant brightness in their surroundings that surpassed the beauty of the country where the Shelleys lived. Unlike noisy London, which was in a constant dark shroud, the rain merciless and the inhabitants thorny, Geneva was unsettlingly beautiful yet quietly composed, just the way she remembered home. She'd already decided it was one of the most beautiful places she'd ever seen. She could be happy here, she thought. She would attempt it despite her circumstances.

SEVERAL WEEKS PASSED before the Lord made an appearance at the hotel. By then, both Mary and Percy had gotten caught up in the romance of their holiday. They were in a tizzy, like inseparable young lovers, constantly in each other's arms. They'd disappear for hours, taking long boat rides together across the lake. Sometimes, Claire accompanied them, watching them with stubborn defiance as they sat together in a tight embrace.

Mehr and Lucy had settled into the servants' quarters tucked behind the kitchen. Mehr's duties had relaxed; she wouldn't be needed to look after the Shelleys until Percy had found a cottage for them to lease. She spent little of the extra time in her room. It was often stuffy and hot from sharing a wall with the kitchen. She took walks in the hotel's garden to find new things to sketch.

On one such excursion, the garden was full of hotel guests, more than she'd encountered before. If she was ever seen on her own, she'd get plenty of curious looks and some furtive whispers behind hands as she'd make her way to a solitary spot to sketch. But this time, no one was looking at her. There was a particular agitation in the air, and she even found Lucy outside, bouncing the infant William in her arms and clearly distracted by something. Mehr wove her way to the low garden wall, nudged Lucy with an elbow to get her attention.

Lucy turned to her briefly, but her gaze returned to the lake, which made Mehr look out as well. Then she realized what had stirred the guests. Lord Byron, who inhabited a large part of all their imaginations, had finally arrived. He was one of two men who stood on the lakeshore watching a boat approach.

It was easy to identify which of the two men was the Lord. He was particularly distinguished, had that way of standing that commanded the air around him. He had a lofty comportment, and his jacket and shoes appeared to be brand-new and were impeccably styled. She could tell by the way the man leaned that he was bearing his weight on his good leg. And he was no pirate. He was dressed far more richly than the other man, who stood pale and sullen beside him.

Mehr found her eyes drawn to the Lord, going over every part of him as a fury erupted from the hotel guests. There was a rustle of clothing, sharp intakes of breath as the crowd became animated, and several jolted forward to get a better look.

"There! There! Look!" a flushed young woman called out, though appearing to resist pointing.

Their heads swiveled this way and that as they sought the object of their fascination.

Even from a distance, Mehr could tell the Lord was devilishly handsome, with a strong, jutting chin, eyes so large they could make you feel you were in a warm embrace without him even touching you, and roiling, windswept curls.

A man grabbed hold of a woman beside him. "My dear, take your aunt's hand, she may faint."

As the matronly woman he was referring to swooned on her feet, there were more voices, now mingling into a chorus of adulation and wonder. The air was thick and intoxicating, and Mehr felt the oppressive force of their obsession blanketing her.

"A remarkable poet. Remarkable!"

"I hear he has a new mistress."

Mehr was stuck shoulder to shoulder with the spectators, and when she attempted to free herself was shoved aside. She wove her way out of the crowd, through their breathless gasps and exclamations.

"And who are his companions?"

Mehr stopped to look. Mary, Percy, and Claire were on the approaching boat. With Byron's eyes locked on them, Claire sat up straighter. She fussed with the tresses that had come undone by the wind while Mary and Percy leaned forward, almost as if they were ready to leap out onto land to make his acquaintance.

She could see why Claire was so flustered by the man, why all the guests were, though none dared to venture closer to the scene.

Mehr gave Lucy a look, and without a word, they moved out of the garden and took a quick walk around the hotel. Then they crept up the end of a lane that led directly to the shore. Lucy beckoned to Mehr to hide behind a hedge. The baby began to fuss, and Lucy absentmindedly rocked him in her arms.

Byron and the other man were in the midst of an argument. The other man had an obvious tic, periodically pulling at the cuffs of his jacket and staring up at the sky. She couldn't hear what they were saying, as they kept their voices artfully low and out of hearing range of the boat. Byron signaled to the man to follow him down the dock and walked on ahead. He had a noticeable limp, though Mehr was now sure he hadn't a wooden leg underneath.

As Mary, Percy, and Claire climbed off the boat, the Lord surveyed each of them. He pushed the other man forward so that they could take his hand and be helped onto the dock. The man begrudgingly aided them off, then with an angry glance back at Byron, stepped into the boat and yanked the oar away from Percy.

Mary and Percy were taken by surprise, nervously laughing at the man as he rowed out onto the lake and ruefully glanced back at them. But Byron didn't notice, his demeanor lighting up when he saw the Shelleys. Then his generous lips curled into a sneer when he spotted Claire hiding behind them. Mehr could tell Claire had been holding her breath until he'd noticed her. When he gave her a curt nod, she visibly deflated.

Mehr had imagined the spirited girl would have had a more significant response to seeing the object of her obsession after so long. But she averted her gaze and appeared to tremble slightly, because of the wind, perhaps, or of the man himself.

The Lord turned his attention back to Percy.

"The damned atheist who wrote *Queen Mab*," Lord Byron said.

Percy rocked on his heels. His eagerness was distasteful, but Mehr couldn't look away and strained to hear their conversation.

"And you, Childe Harold in the flesh," Percy said with the briefest stammer, though the Lord didn't notice.

He was on to Mary next, sweeping forward and lifting her hand to his lips, while Percy watched, sullen and frowning. Perhaps he had wanted a grander introduction to the Lord. Something planned and less spontaneous than this. Mehr knew he had been agonizing to meet the man; it was all he would talk about.

But Lord Byron's attention was diverted now. Mary visibly flushed, giving him a beatific smile. It was a rare one—Mehr had only ever seen the young woman frown, or perhaps force her lips into what may have resembled a smile. But her face, now, was transformed.

Byron gestured to the pale man who had taken off with the boat, several feet away, bobbing up and down and staring at them.

"John Polidori, my personal physician. If he drowns in the lake, you will not miss him."

The young man, with some difficulty, turned the boat around, but not without a final glance back. Mehr was startled for a second because he'd looked directly at her. Had he seen her from where she hid with Lucy so far away? But he had just as quickly turned back to the lake, doggedly pulling at the oars and creating even more distance between him and Byron.

"And you," Byron said to Claire.

She shrank even further. "My lord," she said, and stumbled into a brief curtsy.

"I should thank you for introducing me to your . . . family." With his obvious grin, Mehr realized the man knew more about their history than he should have.

But Claire flourished under his look. Her color brightened, and she appeared to stifle a gasp as he offered her his arm. She took it eagerly, allowed him to pull her along up the lane.

As the group moved toward the hotel together, the guests moved out of the garden and, with excited murmurs, headed back inside to continue to watch the spectacle.

The wind whipped around Mehr. The infant began to fuss, shaking his head at the sudden change in weather. He gnashed his gums and curled a tiny fist at the sky. Mehr shooed Lucy away, and watched her head back to the hotel. Now alone, Mehr felt the call of the lake. The clouds moved across its surface, like children's plump hands. On the horizon, dark clouds roiled over the mountains, and she realized by the sudden chill in the air that it was going to rain soon.

She headed down the trail and, when she turned the corner, bumped right into Lord Byron's physician. It had been so silent on the trail, so serene, that she hadn't heard him appear. She took a few steps back, tightening her shawl around her.

He'd also been startled by her appearance. But when he recovered, he took in every inch of her. She realized he was attempting to place her in his world, that he was more curious than dismissive. From afar, his looks had been dwarfed by Lord Byron's obvious beauty, but on his own, she realized how handsome he was with his dark, piercing eyes and firmly set jaw. He was as raven-haired as the Lord. They could have been brothers. But there was a magnetic, brooding quality to his countenance.

When he realized she was studying him as closely as he was her, he raked his hair back with his fingers.

"You . . . you are not from here." He gestured around him and gave her a questioning look.

"I am not Swiss," Mehr said.

He smiled at her. "Of course not."

"I work for Mr. and Mrs. Shelley."

He took in her dress again. "Their housemaid?"

Mehr nodded, then chastised herself for her eagerness; like Percy, she was short of bouncing on her heels. The clouds that had drifted in from the mountains threw a murky light around them. He stared up at the sky a moment, then turned back to her. She gave him a small smile, an invitation. There was something so boyish and tragic about him, secrets he was carrying on his gloomy brow.

"I am Mehrunissa," she said. "Daughter of Sadaatunissa Begum. My grandfather was the esteemed nawab of Lucknow."

"John Polidori." He scratched the side of his jaw. "Er, son of Gaetano Polidori."

At her raised brow, he stammered, "My grandfather was a physician and poet, called Agostino."

"A physician like you?" Mehr asked.

He let out a nervous laugh. "Indeed, although I do on occasion take pen to paper for more than just correspondences."

"Pleased to make your acquaintance, Doctor," she said.

He stared at her a long while, hesitating before speaking again. "Beg your pardon, Miss—"

"You may call me Mehr."

He cleared his throat. "How long have you worked for the Shelleys?"

"I have been in their employ for four months," Mehr said.

"And what are they like?" he asked.

She hid her frown and turned away. "You will find out soon enough. Good day, Doctor Polidori."

As she headed down the trail, he followed after her. "I did not mean to offend you."

She turned back. "Everyone here is enamored with your lord. And you wish to know about the Shelleys?"

"I was asked by his lordship's biographer to document his travels. Of which the Shelleys are now a part."

She shrugged and continued down the path, his frenzied steps behind her.

"Their . . . living arrangements are fascinating," he said.

"They are no more fascinating than a sofa in a pretty parlour," she said. "There are far more fascinating creatures that exist aside from the Shelleys."

"Then prove it to me," he said.

She turned to face him, suddenly out of breath. A large drop of rain fell on her forehead and streamed like a tear down the bridge of her nose. She stopped and wiped it away. A sudden deluge came down upon them, thrashing the leaves and trees. Polidori shrugged out of his coat to hold it over Mehr's head, but she refused and used her own shawl for cover. She hurried back up the trail, and he followed after, slipping in the wet grass behind her.

She put distance between them as the rain came down more heavily. Then as the hotel appeared, she ran around the back.

"Wait," Polidori called out over the din of the rain shower. "I hope you do not find me rude."

His jacket was drenched, and he hadn't done a good enough job keeping himself dry. The rain streamed down the sides of his head. His hair was riddled with water droplets and attractively disarrayed.

"Good day, Doctor," Mehr said back, then hurried into the hotel.

In her room, she peeled off her wet clothes—the dress, the apron, even the petticoat had been soaked through—and arranged them on a clotheshorse to dry. She had only one other dress left, one she'd had to shell out her own wages for after subtracting what she still needed to save in order to buy her ticket home. The rain had felt unseasonably cold, and she couldn't stop herself from shivering as she changed. After undoing her braid to give her hair a better chance at drying, she slunk into the kitchen to warm herself at the stove. There, she feasted on bread and day-old cheese, then headed back to her room.

As night fell, she lay in bed and let her thoughts drift to the young doctor. The Shelleys were hardly the sort of people within whose shadow she had to exist. She was the descendant of Shaikh Mu'in al-Din Chishti, for God's sake. People from all over India made their pilgrimage to his shrine, to ask for health, good luck, and sometimes their wildest desires. Her grandfather's lineage was worshipped, immortalized in marble, mother-of-pearl, and gold. And deservedly so.

The Shelleys and Byron were mere mortals.

She pretended to sleep as Lucy eventually came in and readied herself for bed. But somehow, the hours passed like minutes. She had a dreamless sleep. Then it was morning and Lucy was shaking her.

"I have so much to tell you," she said once Mehr had sat up and rubbed the sleep out of her eyes.

"Let me fully wake," Mehr said.

"Oh, it was a sight," Lucy said. "Everyone in the dining parlour was straining to hear their conversation."

Mehr yawned herself awake. "I presume it was all about books and writing."

"Indeed. And his lordship is a wicked man. You can see it in his eyes. The way he looks at you, it is as if you—" She put a hand to her face, then made the sign of the cross. "I cannot say it."

"What about his lordship's physician?" Mehr asked, fully alert now.

"He hardly touched his dinner. He looked unwell. And

poor Miss Clairmont." She tsked. "All night, leaning over the table in want of the Lord's attention, and he would not oblige her."

Lucy took her time dressing, going on about each of the foods that were consumed over dinner, then left to look after William. Mehr stayed in bed through it, pretending to listen until she was left alone. She glanced out the window, noticed there was a break in the rain and watched as the sun peeked through the clouds. She rolled out of bed and stretched, then ambled over to the small window high up on the wall. Standing on her toes, she was just able to make out a corner of the lake, the rest obscured by the garden wall. It was unfortunate that she couldn't get as beautiful a view as she could outside. She considered dressing and stepping out with her sketchbook, until a movement on the lake distracted her.

Two figures sat in a boat and moved into her eyeline. She squinted and pressed her nose against the glass. One was a blond woman, huddled with a book open in her hands. The other was a dark-haired man, clumsily handling the oars. Once or twice, the woman looked up from her book to visibly laugh at his struggles. She found him slouching, relaxing now.

The boat glided out of view, but Mehr continued staring out just in case it reappeared. It was unmistakable who they were. Mary and the young doctor. She looked away from the window and leaned against the wall. It puzzled her that these two wildly disparate people would want to spend time together. She, a timid beam of bright light, and he, an odd, timorous man. What could they possibly want from the other?

She stopped herself. No, she had no use for him or for her, or for any of these people. They weren't hers, after all. But a cruel realization again muscled its way into her mind. They were her brother's people. Their paths had so severely diverged that the thought of it made her dizzy. He'd likely been transformed from a joyful Indian boy into a taciturn English man. Did he also holiday on the Continent with a group of like-minded friends?

Then another horrible thought emerged. Had she been taken away with James, raised an English woman, would *she* be out on that boat with Mary and the young doctor? Would she be one of them?

Hatred, pure and black, coursed through her body. Her mother. It was her fault that she'd managed to imprint herself onto Mehr. Of course whenever her father had looked at Mehr, he'd been reminded of the woman he wanted to run away from. It was why she was destined to be left behind. Why perhaps even James wanted little to do with her.

She touched the taweez under her blouse, gripped it in her palm, then glanced back out the window, where Mary and Polidori's boat floated back into view. Mary was no longer reading; she was deep in conversation with the young man.

Mehr yanked the curtains closed.

CHAPTER 7

The Shelleys found a chalet to rent in the nearby village of Cologny. It was called Chapuis. Mehr wasn't surprised to hear from Lucy that the Lord had chosen something far more extravagant to stay in, a sprawling pink villa surrounded by a lush vineyard and secluded from the rest of the village. The Villa Diodati, as it was known, was a short walk away from the Shelleys' lodging.

The Lord traveled with two manservants—Berger and Robert. Among his many belongings was a large carriage that had space for a library and a dining room. Both curiously and a bit morbidly, the carriage was modeled after one that belonged to Napoleon Bonaparte. Hardly a convenience, it took several horses to cart from one country to another, the burden far exceeding its value. Mehr wondered what a man needing to carry such strange, ostentatious trinkets around the Continent said about his ego.

Once the lease had been finalized on the Shelleys'

cottage, the party set sail across the lake in a boat Percy had jointly purchased with the Lord. As much as Mehr had become enamored of the lake, she'd yet to sail on it. Leman Lake shone brightly that day, welcoming Mehr as she carefully found a seat in the boat beside Lucy. As they glided across the water, Mehr looked over the edge. The surface reflected the mountains as clearly as a looking glass. The water lapped against the side of the boat, smooth as a whisper. The lake reached for her with its watery hands. She took a private moment to dip her fingers in; though the water was light to the touch, it was astonishingly cold. She pulled her hand back as if she'd been stung.

They docked not far from Chapuis, and she found it to be a very charming cottage. The first floor had a well-furnished drawing room and a separate dining parlour with windows that looked out over the lake. Mary's, Percy's, and Claire's bedrooms were on the second floor. Mehr was placed in the attic on the third floor, which was much brighter than the last room she'd inhabited.

From the shore, Villa Diodati was plainly visible, its pink hue washed in blood whenever the sun set against it. It sat upon a hill and looked down at the lake with a haughty glance, its windowed eyes long and dark. There were handsome columns on its facade, but to Mehr they looked like the jawbones of a feral animal. Its sheer beauty terrified her, and at times when she accidentally glanced at it through the window, it appeared to shift closer and grow more predatory in its size. She found herself hating the sight of it, because it was always in view of the cottage. No matter where she turned her eyes, and even when she wasn't at the window, she could feel it glaring at her, as if it were capable of reaching out and grasping her.

In the mornings, Percy would steal away to Diodati, leaving Mary and Claire to suffer each other's company. Mary had grown colder to her stepsister, hardly speaking to her when they were in the same room together. While Claire moped about the cottage, writing even more frenzied letters to the Lord, ones she eventually tore to shreds and tossed out her window, Mary was hard at work on a novel. She'd often sit at the lakeshore in solitude, absent-mindedly staring out at both Percy and the Lord on their boat, scratching at something on her neck.

The novel, Mehr learned, was called *Hate*. Mehr wouldn't venture further than investigating the title and what her progress looked like because, she reminded herself, she didn't care what her mistress was or wasn't doing. She did notice, however, that the stack of pages increased at a dawdling pace. There were more and more balled-up pages for Mehr to clean out of the grate, some of them with hardly any writing on them at all, and half-chewed pencils littered the room.

As Percy began to spend longer periods of time in Byron's company, completely removing himself to Diodati, his literary plans were bearing fruit. Mehr realized the Poet Lord had become his muse. As Mary worked away on *Hate*, Percy began something called a "Hymn to Intellectual Beauty."

And so Byron's presence materialized all around them. He had them enthralled. When the Shelleys weren't spending long hours with him in the evenings, they were consumed by their work, burying themselves in pages and pages that Mehr would have to tidy several times a day. Sometimes they'd forgo eating for creating, and Lucy would reprimand them to take their meals.

The Lord paying the odd visit to the cottage sent Claire into a new mania, her room again becoming unmanageable, clothing and belongings in complete disarray. She spent hours with her toilette—she couldn't decide how she wanted her hair to look each time she saw him. As the Lord was a late riser, he wouldn't saunter over until afternoon. They'd all starve themselves in wait for him.

On one of his visits, Lucy and Mehr went to work, setting the table outside in the garden with platters of bread rolls, fresh cream, marmalade, and fruit.

As Mary, Claire, Percy, and Byron sat in the garden, the afternoon sun gleamed brightly off the lake. They all shaded their eyes as they spoke to one another.

"Will the doctor be joining us?" Mary asked, delicately placing cut strawberries into a bowl.

Mehr was coming out with a pot of tea but lingered in the doorway, out of sight.

"He is making himself comfortable in society," Percy said with his mouth full.

Byron waved the thought away. "I care not a lump of sugar for society. We should be here, traversing Rousseau's ground. Men like him live in little circles and petty societies—"

"Petty?" Mary interrupted. "He has endeared himself to a Madame Einard and Monsieur Odier."

Mehr peeked out the doorway as Byron frowned at Mary. He turned his full attention to Percy. "Leigh Hunt has written a very good poem, do not you think?"

Mary touched Claire's hand. "You should go with him next time they are holding a salon."

Claire was sullen. "There is nothing in Geneva that I wish to do."

Percy lolled back in his seat, distracted by both conversations. Byron gave a dismissive glance at Mary from the corner of his eye, then continued. "A devilish good one with a substratum of originality."

"He said Madame Einard is having a ball," Mary said to Claire. "You love to dance. I am certain he is a fine dancer."

Byron slammed his fist on the table. Both Mary and Percy flinched.

"I do not give a damn about him. Or society," Byron said. "To spend your time in these circles, precious time, when you can be writing."

They sat in stunned silence, except for Claire, who seemed not to have noticed any of it. With trembling hands, she pulled apart pieces of bread. Percy reached out and put a hand on top of hers to stop her from continuing, while Mary watched it all with a deep scowl.

Mary returned to scratching at her neck. It was a nervous habit that had started on their journey and spread to her snaking her fingers into her sleeves and scratching at her wrists. Almost daily now, there were dry red welts appearing on her neck, creeping up to her pale cheeks.

Percy cleared his throat. "Yes, Leigh Hunt's poem. A devilish good one."

"Tell me, my lord," Mary said, narrowing her eyes at him. "Would you think Leigh Hunt's poem a 'devilish good one' had he not inscribed it to you?"

Byron gave her a strange smirk, and Mehr couldn't tell if he was amused or insulted. Then, he turned his eyes in Mehr's direction.

"You can stop hiding," he called to her.

The rest of them turned their attention to the doorway. Mehr felt as if she'd been plunged into the icy lake water. She trembled as she stepped out of the cottage while Byron kept his steely gaze on her. As steady as she could, she placed the teapot on the table.

"And what divinity is this?" Byron asked.

He reached out and took hold of her wrist. He ran his smooth fingers across her knuckles, and despite herself, Mehr shuddered. She wondered if he'd felt it, because his smile grew wider. Slowly, he turned her hand so that her palm was facing up.

"Pink palms," he said. "And yet such saturnine skin. 'If

I must die, I will encounter darkness as a bride, and hug it in mine arms.'"

Shakespeare, Mehr thought, just as Percy said the name aloud.

The Lord's beguiling eyes were on her face. "Now, where did they find you?"

Mehr glanced at Mary, who'd been watching the two. "She is from India," Mary said.

Byron smacked his lips. "A Hindoo beauty."

"No," Mehr said. "Born a Mohammedan."

Byron was stunned that she'd spoken. There was a challenge in his stare, and Mehr was ready to meet it, until Mary interrupted their silent exchange.

"You must forgive her. Their customs are not like our own," Mary said.

"Ah." Byron sat back, satisfied. "I spent much time in Turkey with the great Ali Pasha. I have been in all the principal mosques, a virtue rarely permitted to infidels."

Mehr realized he was speaking to her now. He still had a strong hold of her wrist.

"He told me to consider him as a father while I was in Turkey, and said he looked on me as his son," Byron said.

Percy and Mary made awestruck noises, but Claire continued to stare down at the table.

"It is singular that the Turks," Byron went on, "who have no hereditary dignities, and few great families, pay so much respect to birth. There, I found my pedigree more regarded than my title."

He gazed up at her. "How would your people regard it?" he asked her sweetly.

Claire stood from her chair. Her teacup rattled and fell onto its side. As it made its way to the edge of the table, Percy dived over and caught it before it fell. With this distraction, Mehr pulled her hand away and retreated to the cottage door.

She moved into the drawing room and caught her breath. The Lord had a way of making her feel the wickedest of sensations. Her body prickled; goose bumps arose on her arms. It was clear she, along with the others, was not immune to his charms. She laughed to herself, suddenly self-conscious.

Mehr stayed hidden in the cottage until after they'd dined. Byron and Percy returned to their boat, while Mary and Claire went for walks in opposite directions. With the house emptied, Mehr was free to do the most hated and abhorrent of her duties. To prepare, she made sure her sleeves were rolled tightly up to her elbows. Then, she wrapped a clean scrap of cotton around her face, covering her nose and mouth.

She headed out the back of the house and retrieved two buckets—one of water that had been previously brought in from the lake and boiled for purity. The other was empty. These she took with her into the first bedroom up the stairs, which was Claire's. The room was in complete disorder again. She wound around piles of clothes to the toilette, where she emptied the washstand basin and water glass into the empty bucket. Then, she rinsed them with fresh water and refilled the jug.

Now, the accursed chamber pot. She held her breath, the cotton being too thin to block the horrid smells she'd have to endure. As she drew the lid off the pot, she was surprised yet again to find vomit in the receptacle. It was the third morning in a row. Quickly, she poured its contents into the empty bucket, then rinsed it with fresh water and replaced it.

As she went about the other rooms doing the same, she kept thinking back to Claire. The young woman hadn't seemed herself lately. Her usual vivacity had transformed into a sullen withdrawal since they'd left England. She hardly had an appetite, and whatever little she was eating was ending up in her chamber pot.

It was obvious what was ailing the girl, however not *who* had been the cause of it—yet Mehr once again reminded herself she did not care about any of them. No matter how much they intrigued her, no matter how much she couldn't help reading their hastily scrawled letters, or listening in on their boring conversations. No, they were just a couple of writers, yearning to be distinguished in an already crowded world. They fascinated her only because she pitied them, just as she pitied her wretched brother.

AFTER A MONTH of settling in Geneva, Mary finished her novel. It sat on the writing desk for several days, tantalizing in its stillness. Mehr wouldn't touch it. She'd carefully clean around the stack of pages. But curiosity took hold of her, and she decided she'd take just a small peek the next morning. She hadn't read anything by Percy or Byron, had no interest. But she would make an exception for Mary.

With Mary and Claire out for a visit to Diodati, she built up a resolve to read only the first page. But when she entered Mary's room, the manuscript was gone. Its remnants were charred in the hearth. Mary had replaced it with Greek phrase books. It surprised Mehr. She'd never witnessed Mary behave in such an impulsive, unconstrained way. Her brief admiration was replaced by an even briefer disappointment.

With her afternoon duties completed, Mehr chose between going on her own rambles around the village or visiting the lake. She unearthed her sketchbook, stole some pencils from Percy's and Mary's rooms, and chose to sit out on the dock until the sun set, ignoring the eerie face of the villa watching her. When she found herself glancing back at it, something stirred in her. It wasn't the same literary spirit that had taken hold of the Shelleys. It was something else, crouching inside her chest, that would fidget whenever she glimpsed the house. It pressed upon her rib cage, and she realized what it was. A longing. But not her own. It came from Diodati.

A warmth spread across her chest, like a beating heart outside her skin. Absentmindedly, she touched the taweez and realized it had turned warm. Perhaps her body was giving off more heat than normal. But the summer nights were cool, and she found herself shivering. She took it off and dangled it in front of her face. In her mind, she had another one of her one-sided conversations with her mother. They always started with a question. Her mother never answered.

Mehr laid the taweez in her lap and, for the first time, attempted to open it. There was a tiny clasp under which she dug her thumbnail. No matter how much she pushed against the clasp, it remained locked by some mysterious mechanism. She shook the locket, held it up to her ear. Was there something rattling inside? Or was that just the water lapping against the shore?

She placed the locket against her mouth and positioned her teeth under the clasp. With her fist, she pushed in as hard as she could. Still, it wouldn't open. She sighed, then put it back on over her head, lest she break a tooth. The villa watched her all the while, its dim yellow eyes flickering, glaring. As the sun began to set, Mehr removed herself from the dock and headed back to the chalet. She stopped to look up the hill. Diodati's many eyes burned brighter. The front door shifted, and for a moment, the villa appeared to be smiling at her.

CHAPTER 8

Then the rains came. Gently at first—beginning with foggy mornings and layers of mist rolling in off the lake. Those gave way to heavy showers that steadily turned the world cold and gray. The moisture crawled into the cottage, making everything soft and wet to the touch. Condensation dribbled down the walls, and there was a general dampness in the air.

With the sudden downpours, the Shelleys and Claire retreated to the villa, taking Lucy and the infant with them. In the meantime, the chalet was drowning. There were leaks in the windows and the ceilings. Mehr was running out of buckets and pots to spread out in the rooms. For two days, she hardly left the chalet, and cleaning it became useless with no one living in it. On the third day of her being left behind, the rains slowed and tapered off.

As she was airing out the chalet, opening windows and doors to dry out the interior, a stranger approached the window. He tapped on the pane just as she was about to empty a bucket of rainwater out the window. His sudden appearance startled her, and she nearly dropped the bucket.

"I did not mean to frighten you. My name is Robert," he said.

One of Byron's manservants. His black coat had two rows of polished silver buttons running down each side, and underneath he wore a crisp white shirt and black breeches. Before she could ask any questions, he offered to take the bucket from her hands.

"I have come from Diodati."

Mehr handed the bucket over to him, and after he'd poured the water out, she returned it to the leak behind her.

"Are they well and alive?" she asked. Her voice came out a croak. It had been some time since she'd last spoken to another person.

He laughed. "They have not forgotten about you. You are needed at the villa."

The taweez warmed against her chest where it lay under her collar. "Do they intend to stay long?" she asked.

Robert glanced up at the sky. "We do not know how long this dry spell will last. It has been an unusual summer. If I had known it would be raining this heavily, I would have stayed in London."

Mehr stared out the window. There were large, fat clouds just over the mountain. She knew the downpour was imminent.

"Perhaps I ought to wait for them here," Mehr said.

Robert glanced into the drawing room, unimpressed. "We have room enough for one more person."

Even in the constant deluge, she was fond of having the empty chalet to herself. She craned her neck out the window to stare at Diodati. The haze made its usual pink facade look like it was made of bone. She found its irresistible pull repulsive and looked away.

"You received a summons, not a request," he said. "I shall wait outside while you gather your things."

He walked down the lane and out of sight. She left the remaining buckets where they were and went from room to room shutting the windows. There was no telling how long she would need to stay there with her master and mistress, so she packed all her belongings just in case. When she stepped out of the chalet, her boots squelched in mud. The pretty garden at the front of the chalet was nothing but sodden roots and muck.

She quickly tightened her laces so that she wouldn't lose her boots to the mud, then headed down the lane to the Lord's manservant. As she followed him along the lakeshore, the wind picked up and knocked her from side to side. She held tight to her shawl with one hand and her trunk with the other. The mud made the walk slippery and treacherous, so she lagged behind. But she wasn't ever going to get lost. Diodati, stately upon its hill, was hard to lose.

They headed toward the bottom of the hill, which was surrounded by lush green vineyards. It was melodic the way the vines moved in the air, like they were rebab strings and the wind their bow. Mehr stopped to listen, putting even more distance between herself and Robert. A wave of mist rolled in, and as the manservant faded into it, she realized what she was hearing.

It was singing, coming from dense, deep voices, though there was something feminine in their pitch. It was a strange song, in a language she hadn't yet heard. But it was the humming that accompanied the song that made the hair on the back of her neck stand on end. It was heavy and persistent, longing and resentful at the same time. She stepped closer and thought she could make out bodies moving between the vines.

A hand reached out and grabbed her. She whirled around and pulled away.

But it was Robert, an impatient look on his face. "Come along," he said.

"Who are they?" she asked.

He continued onward, shouting over his shoulder, "Vinedressers. Leave them to their work."

The path led to an incline lined by stone steps. They were damp from the heavy mist, and Mehr made her way up carefully until they had reached the top. As the fog swirled around them, Mehr stared at Diodati's face. It grimaced back at her.

Reluctantly, she followed Robert through the front door. After he shut it behind her, she was instantly plunged into near darkness. The dark's cold fingers caressed the back of her neck, and she shivered. As she breathed in, the shadows sighed around her. Her eyes slowly adjusted to the gloom.

She was standing in a large hall and there was a sensation of movement, like she was thigh-deep in rushing water. An invisible wave nearly lifted her off the floor. But it just as soon dissipated. She instinctively touched the taweez, then followed the manservant as he led her through the hall and past a drawing room. She peeked in, noticed the lush fabric on the silk sofas. Normally she'd have enjoyed viewing the opulence of a house like this. But it wasn't for her to enjoy.

Robert lit a candle, and she followed him down the hall, where a brightly polished oak staircase led up half a flight, then diverged in two directions. Robert led her past the stairs to a tight corridor that branched off to the right. At the end was the cellar door. Down the cold stone steps was yet another corridor, which gave way to a large, open kitchen.

Lucy was speaking animatedly to the other manservant, who was sweating over a lump of dough, kneading it roughly in his hands. She tended to a pot over the stove.

"I said you are not to be in here when I am cooking," he snapped.

Lucy sniffed. "Not the politest way to ask for help."

"I work for Lord Byron, not you," he said, throwing the dough between his hands. He angled his body away from her.

Lucy finally noticed Mehr. She wiped her hands roughly on her apron. "Is the chalet still in one piece?"

"As much as I could manage," Mehr said.

She shivered, even in the warm kitchen. Her clothes

clung to her skin, having soaked in the air's moisture during the walk over to the villa.

Lucy motioned to Robert to get his attention. "Make sure Berger does not burn down the kitchen."

Berger replied in terse Swiss, a string of words that Mehr felt certain was not meant for timid ears.

Lucy walked Mehr around the kitchen. "Have you seen the size of this villa?"

"Very large and very cold," Mehr said with a frown. "Where are our rooms?" She'd dragged her trunk down with her and needed a place to put it.

"You have not seen it?" Lucy gave Robert a stern look, then led her out of the kitchen and cellar. Mehr wondered if she'd be able to retrace her steps later; the house was cavernous. At the main staircase, Lucy brought her up the landing, then took the stairs on the right. Mehr followed her into a long gallery. One wall was adorned with elaborate paintings, dim lamps dotted between the frames, while the other side contained four bedroom doors.

"Mrs. Shelley's and Miss Clairmont's rooms are there," she said, pointing at the farthest two doors. "I have a cot in Mrs. Shelley's room."

"And mine?" Mehr asked.

"Down the other way. Come along."

They headed down the landing and up the opposite set of stairs. This gallery had the same layout as the first—paintings on one wall and four bedrooms on the other. But at the end of the gallery was a solitary door.

"This is where the men are staying. I was vexed at first," Lucy said. "This house is too large for the two of us to look after. But we have his lordship's manservants. We shall only look after our own."

Mehr scoffed. "There is still too much to be looking after."

Lucy hid her smile and, without another word, pushed open the door. She handed Mehr a ring of keys and turned back to the gallery. Mehr peeked inside to the set of stairs that spiraled up to an open landing. When she ascended the steps, she found two doors side by side. One belonged to Byron's manservants, she realized. But the other was ajar. She pushed it open and peeked in.

For the first time, she felt trepidation about her new surroundings. The villa was sprawling, and she'd have half the large attic to herself. A place filled with dark corners and shadows. While she usually thrived on being alone, here she felt lost, like the house had swallowed her whole and landed her in a labyrinth.

The room was sizable. There were two large windows opposite each other, with thin curtains blocking out very little light. Mehr counted the beds lined against the wall—three of them. Against the opposite wall, there was disused furniture gathering dust—a few sets of dressers and a chipped washstand.

Mehr headed to the farthest window and found a discreet corner where she could sleep. She pulled over one of the beds, struggling as it snagged against the old rug on the floor. The smallest, closest set of drawers she half dragged, half lifted to her side of the room. Finally, the dusty washstand. She'd have to find a basin and pitcher for herself, but in a house this large, she'd be able to have some of her own luxuries.

The rain lashed against the pane, hollow thunks like knocks from an angry fist. There was a noise underneath the squall. She cocked her head to the side to pick it up better. It was a low pulsing sound, not unlike the one she'd heard from the ship's engine when she'd made her way to London. She pulled the curtain aside. From where she stood, she was able to view the lake. The mountains' jagged lines were softened by the downpour. Below, as she traced the shoreline and then the trail that led to the chalet, she could just make out the blurry shape of the house she'd just left.

Then she spotted the vineyard. The mist had made it impossible to see, but now she had a vantage point from which she could make out the rows and rows of vines. If she squinted hard enough, she could see plump clusters of grapes dangling heavily within. But there were no longer any vinedressers among the stalks. They may have run and taken cover from the rain.

She unpacked her belongings and opened the drawers of the dresser she'd managed to pull over. In the top drawer, she found a few travel guides written in English and some scraps of ink-stained newspapers, though they were written in a language she couldn't read. She felt around in the second drawer, produced a box of matches and well-used candles that still had visible wicks. She stowed them away in her apron for future use.

The third drawer contained a solitary leather-bound journal. She lifted it and held it up to the dim light. Slowly, she undid the leather cord and flipped through the first few pages. They were written in an unfamiliar language, a hurried scrawl that she recognized from somewhere else. She sighed and shoved the journal with the rest of her clothing into the drawers.

She stood and stretched her arms over her head. A sudden weariness had taken hold of her, the pitter-patter of rain nearly lulling her to sleep. But she was needed downstairs. By the chimes of the large clock somewhere in the bowels of the villa and from the waning sunlight, she knew it was time to prepare for dinner.

She found a spare lamp and lit a candle inside it, then crept down the staircase and into the gallery. There was a palpable hush surrounding her amidst the occasional gusts of wind shoving against the sides of the house. She headed for the staircase and took it down to the landing. With a sudden panic, she froze and realized she'd forgotten how to get to the kitchen. Her ears strained to pick up sound, anything to help lead her there, but the villa was solemn and quiet, a cloak of silence all around her.

She held her lamp up in front of her and descended the rest of the stairs. The villa absorbed all sounds, even those of her footsteps. She followed the remaining light as the sun was swiftly setting and the dim, yellow glow of the gas lamps adorning the walls. She found herself in a billiards room. It had a tinge of stale smoke in the air. Three cues lay haphazardly on top of the table.

She moved on to the next room and was in a short hallway. A heavy door lay on the other side. She tested the knob. It gave gently, and she pushed it open. It was an abandoned sitting room. Not one lamp was lit, and the windows were shut tight by heavy velvet drapes. There were sheets on the furniture; they looked like a mass of huddled old women. She shuddered and turned her lamp to the other side of the room.

A small face stared out at her. She gasped and backed into a table, nearly toppling over it. She shined her lamp at the figure; she was staring into a mirror. She inched closer to it. The ornate gold frame glinted in the lamplight. She saw her own stricken face, the stray brittle hairs that had escaped her braid, the dark circles under her eyes.

Her mother would be aghast at what Mehr's new life was doing to her. She couldn't remember the last time she'd had a delicious scalp massage, fingernails raking into her tresses with fragrant oils and rose water. She missed the gentle way her servants would wash her face in milk to bring out her beauty.

Now it was all gone. She was just an ordinary woman. Her pallor had turned gray. The face staring back at her was nothing but a ghost, a remnant of some other life she could no longer return to. As she looked at her new, hardened features, she spotted movement behind her. She turned around, found the door opening slowly.

"Who is there?" she called out. "Mrs. Shelley?"

Immediately she was embarrassed. The door stood ajar, and within the shadows, she thought she saw movement. She shone the light directly in front of her.

Lucy walked in and gasped, clutching her chest. "There you are!" She laughed.

Mehr couldn't move. She was too stunned by the young woman's sudden appearance.

"I had the manservants turning over every bit of furniture in search of you."

"I was lost," Mehr said.

"Until I found you," Lucy said, staring around at the room. "I have not seen this one before." She shivered. "We should leave before we catch a chill."

Mehr followed Lucy out. They passed the billiards room, and the walls opened up to the large hall. She felt instant relief and scanned the familiar surroundings. The knot of apprehension in her stomach unwound itself. Robert had led her this way when she'd first entered; she understood now where she was going.

In the kitchen, Berger poured stew into a shallow dish and motioned for the two of them to help him. Mehr was surprised to see cuts of meat in it. Perhaps the Lord didn't know about the Shelleys' restrictive diets, even though it had been days now that they'd all been dining together while Mehr was on her own. She gave Lucy a questioning look, but Lucy didn't notice and instead threw a cloth on top of the dish and handed it to Mehr.

"Take this into the dining parlour," Lucy said. "Follow Robert. He will show you the way."

Berger was back to it—roughly slicing bread and placing it on a platter. Robert, holding several glasses in one hand, fingers hugging their heavy bottoms, waited for Mehr at the door. He led her down a different corridor to a set of short steps. She realized there were several ways to enter the kitchen, depending on which room her master and mistress were dining in. The villa was far more elaborate than the small chalet and cottage the Shelleys had been inhabiting since Mehr had entered their world.

Up the short set of stairs, they entered a hallway. The first door that appeared led to the dining parlour. It was a brightly lit, though cramped, room. The gleaming wood table took up most of the space. There were heavy emerald drapes at the window, which were shut against the pounding of the rain outside.

The table had been set with plates and silverware. Two decanters of wine were placed at one end of the table. Mehr positioned the stew in the center. She glanced back at Robert, who was shining the glasses with his apron.

"They do not eat meat," she said.

He stopped polishing and looked up at her. As he set the glass down, he had a distant smile on his face.

She cleared her throat. "The Shelleys. They are Pythagoreans. I thought you would know that."

She heard herself speak and realized just how foolish she sounded. Why she felt the need to protect them, she couldn't understand. Perhaps it was a sensation that arose in ordinary housemaids—the peculiar attachment they'd develop with their masters and mistresses. But she was no ordinary housemaid, and she refused to ever become one. Mehr squared her shoulders, felt the heat of embarrassment creep up her chest as Robert ignored her and carried on setting the glassware on the table.

Mehr retraced her steps and headed back for the platter of bread and rolls from Berger. When she returned to the dining room, Byron, Polidori, and the Shelleys had seated themselves and Robert was pouring wine into their glasses. Polidori noticed nothing around him. He sat resting his head on a fist, staring down at his lap.

It had been a while since she'd last seen him. Before, outside of the hotel where they'd first met, his large, dark eyes had taken hold of her body and she'd been briefly reluctant to move out of his gaze. But his attention rested elsewhere now. She turned away, but Lucy blocked the doorway.

"We are all dining together," she said with a frown. "He demands it."

Byron waved them in. "No more scurrying into your holes in the kitchen to eat out of sight." He placed his hands on the table and leaned forward, eyeing Mehr. "I want to watch you eat."

Mehr hid her scowl as she took her seat with the servants at the other end of the table.

Percy reached for the stew and ladled it into his bowl, then stopped. "What is this?" he asked Berger.

"I will wear you down eventually," Byron said.

"We cannot eat this."

Byron calmly watched him. "You would rather starve?"

"We cannot pimp for the gluttony of death," Percy said. He glanced at Mary, but she was too busy staring at the cube of meat in his bowl.

Byron took a large gulp of claret. "Think about your mind. Your body needs sustenance. Your brain craves it."

"It does not," Percy said. "There is no disease, bodily or mental, which adoption of a vegetable diet and pure water has not mitigated. I have proof."

"Do not you miss it?" Byron asked. His sultry gaze was on Mary.

Mehr held her breath as Mary slowly turned her head to the Lord. She'd been so stoic before, withdrawn as usual, but there was a hint of a smile on her lips. "Why do you tempt us?"

"'A feeble body weakens the mind,'" Byron said, picking at his immaculate fingernails.

"Yes, Rousseau," Percy said, his voice significantly weaker. "My lord, it is the root of all war. On mere principle—"

"If you are starving your spirit, you are impeding your power, your vitality, for the sake of this belief," Byron said, and waved his hand dismissively.

Percy chewed on his lower lip, and then his eyes grew large as Mary dished stew into her own bowl. She produced a lump of meat on her spoon and brought it delicately to her lips. She chewed with her eyes closed, appearing to savor the morsel.

Byron eyed her over the rim of his claret. Mehr found herself also enchanted by the moment. She wondered when it was the woman had last eaten something so decadent, so rich, full of fats and spices and a multitude of flavors. For years, it seemed, they'd been subsisting on the unseasoned slop of root vegetables and cold porridge Mehr had herself refused to eat.

Percy stared at the stew in his own bowl. A series of thoughts seemed to flicker across his face. He exhaled, shut his eyes, and began to eat, though the man didn't appear to enjoy it as much as Mary did.

"Will not you have some, my lord?" Mary asked, chewing a mouthful of bread.

Byron waved it away. "No. I told you, I am a Pythagorean."

Percy dropped his spoon and was just about to speak when the door flew open. Claire barreled in. Her spirits were in disarray. She wouldn't look at her stepsister or brother-in-law, but she gave a meaningful glance to Byron. He looked coolly back at her. She sat down beside Mary, who was so busily eating slice upon slice of heavily buttered bread she hardly saw Claire come in.

With the last of their mistresses in the room, Mehr and the others were finally able to eat. She'd been salivating watching the tendrils of steam rise up from the stew, the light glistening off the cuts of roast beef and slabs of mutton as she made her plate.

Claire was the only one who didn't touch the food. She poured herself a cup of tea and glowered at Byron.

"I had the queerest dream last night," Mary said, finally sitting back from her meal. She glanced down at the table, then met Mehr's eyes. She pointed at Mehr with her chin. "You were there."

Byron smirked. "Our Mohammedan divinity?" His eyes lingered on Mehr a little longer than was comfortable.

Mary laughed to herself, rubbed her forehead. "We were together standing at the staircase and there was such a sound. Unlike anything I have ever heard. Like water rushing in my ears. And I saw someone."

"The Diodati Demon?" Byron asked with a sneer. "I heard a rumor that this villa is haunted."

Polidori jerked his head in Byron's direction. "Haunted, you say?"

Mehr's interest was also piqued. She'd sensed something odd about the house since she'd first stepped in. Though the walls and furniture lay still, she couldn't shake the feeling that everything was in motion. Almost like a presence swirling around, gliding past her when she walked through the halls. But Byron ignored Polidori and didn't say anything more to him.

Mary smiled to herself. "I think it was my mother."

Percy put his arm around Mary's shoulders and squeezed her closer to him. "She has nightmares. Vivid ones. But that is just what they are. Dreams."

"A dream," Mary murmured, staring at a corner of the ceiling. "But she was so real."

Polidori leaned forward. "Tell us more."

Mary closed her eyes and smiled. Her flaxen hair had come undone, and she brushed a lock behind her ear. Mehr noticed a bright patch of scaly, dry skin on the back of Mary's hand. Then Mary opened her eyes and fixed Polidori in her stare. He was taken aback by it. Discreetly, she shook her head and returned to her meal.

Mehr watched it all unfold with a dinner napkin squeezed between her hands. The young woman had dreamt about her. Mehr's confusion gave way to agitation. Her stomach turned, and she realized she was no longer hungry. The room became hot, a flush rose up the back of her neck and into her hair. The smell of meats and sauces and spices was now intolerable. And that humming noise, present with her all afternoon, rose up from the floor and into her ears.

Someone placed a hand on her shoulder. It was Lucy, a shade of concern in her eyes. Mehr quietly excused herself and scurried out of the room. The others were deep in inane conversations—Byron drew Percy into a discourse on Sophocles while Mary and Claire discussed the latest letter they'd received from their sister. Polidori alone stared back at her, one hand cupped around a glass of wine, the other drawing idle circles on the tablecloth.

Mehr stepped out and leaned against a wall, struggling to breathe. She groped her way down to the kitchen, but it was unbearably hot in there too, the fire still crackling in the hearth.

She shoved open the large door that led out to the back garden, breathed in the cooler air. She rested her body against the doorframe, stared out at the darkness. But there was the unmistakable sensation that someone was behind her. She turned and stumbled into Polidori. As she staggered on the spot, he helped her into a chair. The kitchen came into focus then. Polidori poured her a glass of water, and without thanking him, she gulped it down.

He knelt in front of her. "You are unwell," he said.

He hesitated, then reached for her wrist. With one thumb, he rubbed the soft skin of her underarm. She pulled away and stood, holding on to the back of the chair for support.

"The room became intolerably warm. But I am better now." Mehr gestured at the empty glass of water. "You did not have to help me."

"I wished to leave the room as well," he said, returning the glass to the kitchen block. "It was those dull fellows I found intolerable."

So he'd had his fill of them, found them as wearisome as Mehr did. Yet Polidori had returned to their company for the many balls and salons to which he'd recently been invited.

"You were quite taken with them weeks ago."

He leaned back against the sink and eyed her. "I wonder what it is you think of us."

"I am an ordinary housemaid," Mehr said. "It matters not what I think."

"You are not ordinary."

Mehr felt warm again, but it was a different sensation altogether. She held the door open for him. "You must not keep your dull fellows waiting."

It felt like minutes, hours, until he gave up and left her alone. She sat back in the chair and before long was able to breathe again. Perhaps she'd come down with a brief fever and the chill from the rain had made its way inside her. But it was gone, and she felt calmer than she had in a while. She glanced back to the darkness outside before shutting the door. When the meal ended, the masters and mistresses retired to the library, and she and the manservants cleared the table, busied themselves with the washing up, and made preparations for the following morning.

It was well after midnight when she headed out of the kitchen. Through the darkened hallways, she could hear their muffled voices in another room, keeping the night alive. She stopped at the stairs and turned her head to the side. The lingering hum she'd been hearing since entering the villa still rang in her head, blanketing the other noises.

In the attic, she lay in bed staring at the ceiling. The hum had grown louder, drowning the sounds of the rain. She sat up and rubbed her face, ground her palms into her eyes. When she looked up, someone was standing at the foot of her bed. She flinched and crawled back against her pillow.

By their slight build and frail-looking shoulders, Mehr realized it was Mary. It had been months since Mary first sleepwalked into Mehr's room. At that time, her eyes had been closed; now her eyes were wide open. They were enlarged, the blue replaced with an inky black. Void of life.

Mehr reached a hand out, but Mary turned from the bed. The floorboards creaked as she headed for the stairs. Mehr lit her lantern and quickly moved out of bed. As Mehr headed for the stairs, Mary was only a few steps below her.

"Mrs. Shelley?" Mehr whispered.

She waited for the young woman to acknowledge her, but Mary continued down the stairs and disappeared through the door. Mehr held on to the banister and chewed the inside of her cheek. It was one thing for Mary to be sleepwalking in their small cottage in England. The villa was a behemoth. There were ample opportunities for Mary to accidentally hurt herself. And afterward, what would happen to Mehr? To her wages? With a deep sigh, she followed her down the rest of the stairs and into the gallery. Mary had stopped outside one of the bedrooms. She reached a hand out and placed it against the wood.

"Is that Mr. Shelley's room?" Mehr asked her as she neared. "Would you like to go inside?"

Mary withdrew her hand but didn't respond. Mehr moved closer, held the lamp in front of Mary's face. Though she appeared awake, she was still sleepwalking. Mehr reached for Mary's arm to perhaps shake her conscious, but Mary turned away and resumed her slow march down the gallery.

Mehr hesitated and then knocked on Percy's bedroom door. When there was no response, she tried again, then placed her ear to the door. There was no sound, not even a body stirring within. She tried the doorknob and was surprised to find it wasn't locked.

Mehr held the lantern ahead of her, peered in. "Mr. Shelley?" she whispered.

There was no response. From the stillness in the room, she realized he wasn't even there. She turned back to the gallery, but Mary had disappeared. In a panic, Mehr turned in a full circle, shining the light as far as she could, but Mary had vanished. She stopped and listened for light steps, the rustling of a nightgown, but the hum still sounded in her head.

There was something else. A cavalcade of rain. It echoed close by, as if a window had been opened somewhere. She followed the sound down the stairs and to the large hall. The front door was open.

Mehr stepped out into the rain. Mary was outside now, fully drenched. The nightgown clung to her skin, to her thin waist and hips, and appeared to be weighing her down. Her bare feet were caked with mud as she made her slow descent down the lane.

She wasn't alone. A figure walked beside her, a woman holding her hand. Though Mary was drenched, the rain didn't touch the woman. She had the same dark blond hair as Mary but was slightly taller. She also wore a night-gown, and the middle of it bulged outward. A crack of lightning snaked across the sky, and Mehr realized with horror what she was seeing. The figure was in the late stage of pregnancy. Blood dripped down her legs and into the mud below her.

"Mrs. Shelley!" Mehr called out.

The two continued their dogged march to the lake. Mehr took a step forward but found her feet were trapped in mud. She struggled to free herself and, as she fell to the ground, accidentally flung the lantern aside. The light sputtered and died. She dug her nails into the mud, but she couldn't get free.

A hand reached out from the darkness and yanked her up by her hair. A flash of lightning revealed the figure's face. In that brief moment, she saw that its pale blue lips were screwed shut. In the place of its eyes were deep red holes gouged into its flesh. A fat beetle crawled out of one of them.

Before Mehr could scream, she was thrown into complete darkness.

CHAPTER 9

Mehr awoke to the dull chimes of the large clock that lived in the drawing room. She counted each one. It was six in the morning. She sat up, vestiges of the night before coming back to her. She stared at her fingernails. There wasn't a fleck of mud in them. No one stood at the foot of her bed. Her lantern was back on the dresser beside her. She rubbed her face, breathed through her fingers.

It had felt too real to be a dream. She touched the back of her head. It was tender, as if a phantom hand had indeed pulled her by the hair. And was there a touch of dampness to it?

The lightheadedness from the evening returned. She wanted to lie back in bed, shut her eyes for just a few more moments. But it was time to make preparations around the house, and soon Lucy and the manservants would be waiting for her.

She moved slowly as she washed and dressed, then headed downstairs, retracing her steps from the night before. She wondered if she needed to check on Mary but stopped from entering the east wing. She laughed to herself. It had to have been a dream. There was no need to check in on her.

In the kitchen, Byron's manservants and Lucy were already assembled. Together, they divided up the villa, carving out their chores now that Mehr had joined them. She forced herself to focus on her work. She began by cleaning out the grates of the parlours downstairs, though her quality of work hadn't changed.

It was one thing to louse up the work at the Shelleys' cottage, which was a smaller space, already in disarray, but this was a grand villa, and she had little time to be a perfectionist. She was guaranteed employment through September, she was sure of it. And she didn't think Mary had the wherewithal to notice her lackluster work; she seemed consumed by the romance of their new surroundings. But she wondered if the Lord would notice, then was embarrassed by the thought and quickly replaced it with something else.

The nightmare. Her pulse quickened. She should have checked in on Mary, made sure she was in her bed, dry and comfortable, perhaps discreetly examined her feet for signs of mud. But it *was* a dream, she reminded herself, even though her head was throbbing and she still felt phantom fingers in her hair.

Mehr entered the library, which was a large, comfortably furnished room with several tall bookshelves lining the back and plush sofas and armchairs circling a heavily used hearth. It was evident that the writers spent most of their time in this room and had been in there last night when she'd headed to bed. She set to work scraping out the ashes and dumping them into a metal bucket. Once she finished, she entered another sitting room, where an abandoned table full of cards had been preserved from another night.

One by one, she went through the rooms, scraping and cleaning the grates, then took her bucket down to the cellar. After emptying the contents to be used for laundry later, she refilled her bucket with coal and returned to the rooms to light new fires. Then she took a brush to the curtains and rugs to free them of the residual soot from the copious amounts of fires needed to warm the villa.

There was, however, one room she had completely neglected. It was the abandoned room from the night before. It didn't need a fire, as no one had been in there or seemed to want to be in there. She retraced her steps back to the billiards room and through to the darkened hallway. Slowly she crept up to the door and had a strange sensation that there was a presence inside. She hesitated, then placed her ear to the door and shut her eyes. There was an odd noise like the flap of a bird's wing. A gentle sound almost like a sigh.

It felt like her own secret. Something just for her to keep. She opened the door, but found the room empty. As devoid of life as it had been the night before. And just as forlorn. There was a desolate stillness in the air. She placed the bucket on the floor and made her way to the windows. The curtains were plush and soft in her hands. She drew them open and squinted out at the bright light. The sun had made a reappearance, with only hazy wisps of clouds streaked across it. She pulled the other curtains open and a sudden warmth filled the space as the sunlight made its way into the room.

There was a long line of ants on the wainscoting that she'd nearly decimated with the hem of the curtains. They marched along the edge of the wall, then up toward the windowsill and through a crack in the corner of the window. There was a strange formation in the middle of the line. Mehr bent closer and watched as several ants created a circle. They appeared to stand on their back legs, their front legs stretching up to the sky. And then they stopped moving.

Other ants joined the circle, congregating around the first ants, swirling in a confused pattern, no longer in a straight line, losing the path entirely. As they swarmed, Mehr realized the original ants were now dead. Their eyes were milky, and they were completely frozen, unaware the others were now lifting them off the paneling and taking them along. The circle broke, and they resumed their march, carrying their dead with them up the wall. Mehr watched the last of them disappear into the crack.

She stared out the window and found that the room faced down toward the entirety of the vineyard. Among the stalks, the vinedressers moved slowly, reaching up with their pale hands to pull down clusters of grapes. They worked in a circular line, reaching and reaching. And they were singing again, their deep voices mixing in with the rustling of the leaves.

She turned back to the room, to the dusty sheets lying on top of the furniture. One by one, she removed them and took them to the door to dump them in a pile. The mirror that had frightened her leaned against the wall, a sheet barely covering it. She pulled it off and avoided her own reflection.

The furniture had a distinctly feminine look to it, different from the drawing and billiards rooms. The sofas were made of silk, and under one of the sheets was a table with a pot of tea that had been left beside two empty cups. Mehr took the lid off the pot and peeked in, gave it a quick sniff. It was empty, the contents of it having dried long ago.

She glanced back at the ornate marble hearth at the end of the room. There was a large painting on top of it, which she'd missed before in the oppressive darkness. It was hanging at a slight angle and contained the sitting portrait of a woman in a comfortable room, her hands demurely placed in her lap, with a bright window behind her right shoulder. Her face was turned toward the window but her eyes were glancing straight at Mehr as if she had just remembered what she wanted to say to her. Perhaps a secret, because she had a thin smile on her lips. The look was familiar, and it put Mehr immediately at ease, like she was now sharing that secret with the woman. Through the painted window there was a replica of the vineyard. The woman had sat for the painting in that very room.

As Mehr approached the painting, the woman's eyes appeared to be staring at a point above her head. She turned around and looked at the wall behind her, but there was nothing there. She couldn't tell if the woman was beautiful or if the painter had taken certain liberties. Her pale cheeks had an attractive flush to them, and the sides of her face were adorned with small curls. Her long black hair lay straight against her shoulders and was tied back with a gold ribbon. Mehr reached up and straightened the painting.

"This was your room," Mehr said. "Would you like me to look after it?"

Was it the dust moving through the sunlight or had the woman's smile widened? Mehr stepped back, laughed to herself.

Her usual apathy for her duties was replaced with a sense of loyalty to the disused room. It was far too beautiful to be abandoned for long. She tested her ring of keys and found the one that belonged to the room. She separated it from the others and stored it in her dress pocket, feeling as though she'd been given a rare prize and intending to keep it to herself. Satisfied, she got to work brushing dust out of the carpets and the curtains, polishing the furniture so that it shone brightly in the sun, then wiping the windows down so that she could see through to the lush vines.

She realized with a start that the day had approached late morning. The masters and mistresses of the house would be heading down for their breakfasts soon. Mehr gathered up the sheets and bucket, locked the room, then returned to the kitchen. Together, she and Lucy brought out coffee, tea, and platters of cheese, bread rolls, fruit, and cream to the breakfast parlour.

As they set down the platters, Mehr eyed Mary to see if there were any signs of fatigue. But Mary appeared well rested. Her eyes were bright, her hair and clothes dry. Mehr squinted at her feet, but her slippers were pristine, unmarred. Mary had a well of energy; she had already dug into the cheese before she'd poured herself a cup of tea.

Again, at Byron's insistence, Mehr, Lucy, and his manservants sat for a quick repast, but they didn't linger long in the room. Polidori glanced at Mehr several times, but she avoided his gaze, focusing instead on her whispered conversation with Lucy. Mehr and the others ate quickly and slipped out, and with their masters and mistresses thus occupied, resumed their work upstairs. Mehr started in the east wing of the house with Mary's bedroom. The room was much larger than what Mary had in England or in the chalet down the lane. It contained a small sitting room complete with its own hearth and table. Rather than any new writing, the desk was still littered with Greek phrase books. Mehr examined the room for muddy footprints, but of course, there were none.

In the adjoining bedroom, the sheets were dry, clean. Mary had made her own bed, though it didn't matter; Mehr still needed to air it. Her clothes were lying neatly on top of it. Mehr brought the muslin fabric to her face, then stopped herself from smelling them. She didn't need to. Mary's scent was everywhere in the room.

She folded the clothes and laid them on top of the dresser. Then she stripped the sheets off the bed to air it. It was the softest cotton she'd ever felt. The mattress itself was more than just horsehair; it was supple and filled with feathers. It was clear to her why they'd all taken up with the Lord and stopped returning to the chalet. Had Mary known when she'd run off with her atheist poet that she'd enter a nomadic life of periodic poverty? With her own father demanding money from Percy, and talk of numerous other expenses, it was no wonder she was enjoying the finer things in the Lord's company.

Mehr finished her work and headed for Claire's room. Just as she was opening the door, there were quick footsteps coming her way. Robert appeared in the doorway, momentarily blocking her. He was just as startled as she was, and before she could ask what he was doing in the room, he brushed past her and hurried for the stairs.

She stared at him as he disappeared, then turned back to the room. Lucy sat atop Claire's writing table, adjusting her collar, smoothing down her dark hair. Mehr narrowed her eyes at her.

"You saw nothing," Lucy said, a tremor in her voice.

Mehr sighed and entered the room. She set to work tidying the sheets and airing the bed. Lucy stayed back, watching her.

"You will not tell anyone?"

Mehr didn't respond as she struggled with the mattress. She was surprised when Lucy joined her to help turn it over. Silently, the young woman tucked the multitude of sheets and downs into the bedstead.

"I was a housemaid once," Lucy said. "And I do not miss it. Children are better work." She averted her gaze and helped Mehr finish the bed. Then she began tidying Claire's room for Mehr, picking her clothes up off the floor and returning them to the wardrobe.

"You do not have to help me," Mehr said. "I have no one to tell. The villa is large and perhaps you are lonely. There is no harm in it. I have heard of far worse scandals, most of them from you."

Lucy laughed. "I believe this is the longest you have spoken to me of your own free will. Secrets could live and die with you." She hesitated, then added, "As one should keep for a friend."

Mehr headed for the hearth, and as she did her work, Lucy quietly left the room. When the door finally shut, Mehr let out a breath. She was surprised by the sudden sting of tears in her eyes. Quickly, she wiped them with the back of a sooty hand.

As she bent farther into the hearth, something in the grate caught her eye. She shoveled the mix of ash and paper closer to her. It was a half-burnt letter. Quickly, she drew it out and brushed the ash off it. The top half of the letter was burned badly, but she was able to make out of some of it. It cataloged some dire issues with money, or debts. The bottom half, which was nearly untouched by fire, was the most interesting.

> *My dearest Love, God knows I have been guilty of many excesses. I cannot exactly play the stoic with a woman—who had scrambled eight hundred miles to unphilosophise me. You must know, I don't love her and don't pretend to love her. I have never ceased nor can cease to feel for a moment that perfect and boundless attachment which bound and binds me to you—which renders me utterly incapable of real love for any other human being—for what could they be to me after you?*

Mehr read and reread the words, pressing the page so close to her face that her nose almost made an indent in the soot. It wasn't anyone's handwriting she'd seen before. It was purposeful, confident.

Which left two men in her mind. Byron or Polidori. Who was either writing such impassioned lines to? She raked through the still-warm ashes, wrist-deep. From the remaining fragments of paper, she finally came across something that gave her a clue. It appeared to be at the top of the page. *My dear Aug* was all she could make out of the name. The rest had been scorched off.

She sat back on her haunches. It was clear the letter had been destroyed in order not to make it to its destination, and if it was in Claire's possession, it meant she'd stolen it from him for that purpose. Even Shakespeare's finest dramas couldn't rival this. She crumpled up the letter and threw it into the bucket with the rest of the ashes.

With her morning's work done, she decided to take a walk to clear her head. The dream still lingered nearby, no matter how little evidence she'd found to convince her it had truly happened. Still, she dreaded retracing her steps and instead headed out the back of the villa through the kitchen. The sky had a thin haze of clouds covering it, but the sun was able to peek through the curtains and let down a few rays of warmth.

She took the long path around the villa and stopped near the front door. The mud had hardened from the brief dry spell. But there were areas that had raised bumps and small craters. A set of footprints leading from the door?

It was just her imagination. She turned away and headed down the lane.

Mehr took the stone steps to the vineyard. The vinedressers were farther afield, working diligently, their quick hands darting out at the clusters of grapes and placing them in the buckets they wore on their shoulders.

She took her time and walked among the vines. The grapes were an intense shade of blue, mirroring the eye of Leman. She'd never seen grapes with such a shade, and she was tempted to pluck one and taste it. But she moved inward, weaving between the stalks. The air had warmed, and it reminded her of home. She unraveled the cord holding her braid together and raked her fingers through her hair. It fell heavily against her back. She continued combing through her tresses, and from a long-forgotten hollow within her mind, a song emerged.

She hummed a tune, hoping it would bring the lyrics to her. The song started somewhere in her chest and swelled from there. She sang.

"Dikhai diye yun ke bekhud kiya, humain aap se bhi juda kar chale . . ."

She couldn't remember the last time she had sung, and the sound of her own voice was unsettling at first. It belonged to a stranger, she thought, as it echoed around her and dispersed through the vines. But it was her own voice, and freeing it was exhilarating. She shut her eyes and smiled, murmured along to the music in her head, forgetting the next few lyrics. When they came back to her, she let her mind and body go, surrendered herself to the power of her own voice and the beauty of the melody. Her voice rose, high and confident.

"Parastash ki yaan taeen ke ai but tujhe. Nazr mein sabhon ki khuda kar chale—"

"What are you singing?"

Mehr stopped abruptly and turned around, a hand on her beating heart. It was Mary, standing a few feet behind her. Her eyes were wide. She appeared just as frightened.

Was she dreaming again? Mehr stood still, unable to move lest the dream slip away.

"I fear I have startled you," Mary said. "I was headed for the lake. When I heard your singing, it drew me here."

"You don't have to apologize," Mehr said. She moved farther into the vines, but Mary followed.

"Your hair, it—it is beautiful like this," Mary said. "And your voice. You looked enchanted while you were singing."

Mehr stopped and glanced at Mary over her shoulder. She was flushed—blushing, she realized. No, it couldn't be a dream. This felt too real. It made heat creep up her chest to her face. She placed a hand to her cheek and stifled a smile.

"Mir Taqi Mir," Mehr said.

Mary gave her a questioning look.

"It is his poetry," Mehr said. "His ghazal that I was singing."

Mary moved closer, closing the distance between them. It was just the two of them, alone, in the vines. Mehr held her breath, as if a puff of air would make all of it flutter away. The vinedressers had fallen silent; it was as though they were the only ones left in the world.

"Will you translate it for me?" Mary asked, her voice hovering above a whisper.

Mehr shut her eyes, reworked her mind to translate in English. "It is about obsession and love," she said, feeling the blush sting her cheeks. "He says, 'With just a small glimpse, you left me entranced. I lost myself. You estranged me from my own self. I prayed and prayed in my devotion to you. Because in my love, I worshipped you so fervently, that you became a God. A deity.'"

When she opened her eyes, she found Mary had moved closer to her. Among the dry scaly patches that had spread up the sides of Mary's face, Mehr was able to make out light freckles on her nose. The sun had broken through the clouds, lighting her hair like a halo. There were tears in Mary's eyes, and she bit her lower lip to stop it from trembling.

Mehr's eyes were drawn to Mary's front teeth, the soft indentations they made on her lip.

"He must have truly loved," Mary said, her voice small, "to have written something so beautiful." She hesitated, then met Mehr's eyes. "Have you?"

Mehr slowly shook her head.

Mary smiled up at her. "No one worthy enough?"

Mary reached up near Mehr's face. Mehr froze, unsure of what would happen next. But Mary continued reaching until she'd taken hold of a bunch of grapes behind her. With one hand, she pulled them off the vine. She took Mehr's hand with her other, gently dropping the bunch into her palm. Then, she closed both of her hands with her own.

"My gift to you for offering me such beauty," Mary said.

Mehr stepped back as she felt a flurry of emotions, and

hoped none of them showed on her face. Then, with a shy smile, Mary turned away and left. Mehr watched her go, hands still cupped around the grapes.

The silence was shattered when the vinedressers' singing began again. She took her time leaving the vineyard, headed up the stone steps, then back around the villa and inside the kitchen. She filled a small bowl with water and gently laid the grapes in them. It would preserve them for a little while. She wouldn't leave them in the kitchen for the others to paw through; she carried the bowl back up to her room and carefully set it on her bedside table. From within her dresser, she produced a handkerchief and gently covered the bowl.

She realized with an ache in her heart that it was the most precious gift—beyond the gold and silk and perfumes and sweetmeats that had been heaped upon her since her birth—that she had ever received.

CHAPTER 10

After helping Robert and Berger move the platters to the dining parlour, Mehr refused to join the others. She was mortified, but she didn't know why thinking of Mary sitting down the table from her evoked that feeling. She plated her dinner and made herself a cup of tea. She missed the food her cook would make—the meat swimming in masala, the fragrant splashes of kewra water in rice dishes, and a hearty cup of chai after.

She wished she'd learned how to make her own chai. She remembered it needed to be slow cooked over an open fire, the milk and spices added at an earlier stage, but the measurements, or how long it needed to cook, were beyond her comprehension. So for now, it would have to be an English tea—the water poured atop the leaves, then doused in milk. She steeped it with pieces of cracked cinnamon and withered cardamom pods from the more exotic stores in the kitchen.

She took her dinner to the forgotten room. The weakening sun's rays slanted in, lighting the surfaces in golds and oranges. The room was warm and didn't need a fire. She placed her meal on a table and sat on the comfortable sofa. The silence lay heavily around her. As she tucked into her dinner, she spoke to the woman in the painting. She told her about her trip across the seas, how her unpleasant mother had died, how she couldn't wait to reunite with the father she hadn't seen since she was a child.

The portrait watched her with a quiet indifference. Mehr held her cup of tea close to her chest. She glanced down at it, gave it a light swirl, and watched the weak brown liquid rotate in a neat circle. Like the ants she'd seen on the windowsill, the tea continued to move round and round even after she sat still.

She quickly put it down and stared back at the painting. The woman's expression had changed. No, her eyes weren't deceiving her. She stood and moved closer to the portrait and found that the woman's chin now pointed down, was tucked in gracefully. The eyes glanced to the left. Mehr followed her gaze to the window.

Of course she would be looking out at her beloved vineyard. The painting had always been looking out. It couldn't have changed before her eyes. Perhaps she'd only ever given it a passing glance. Still, Mehr brought two fingers to the painting and lightly touched it. It was dry and brittle against her skin.

She moved to the window. The sun was beginning its quick descent over the mountains. Her eyes wandered from the horizon to the vineyard, where the vinedressers were enmeshed. They moved slowly in a circular pattern. Their numbers grew as more women joined the ring. They marched rhythmically, as if in a trance. Their hums grew more plaintive and seemed to find their way into the room. She realized with a start that it was the same noise that had plagued her the night before, in her nightmarish pursuit of Mary throughout the villa.

Mehr backed away from the window and glanced at the painting. The woman was still gazing out the window, but had her frown deepened?

A knock on the door startled her. It was Lucy, holding the infant in the crook of an arm, peeking in with a nervous smile on her face.

"I knew I would find you here," she said, a dimple creasing her cheek.

Mehr pointed at the portrait. "Do you remember her?"

Lucy cocked her head to the side and pursed her lips.

"This painting, I mean," Mehr said. "Do you remember her looking out the window?"

"I do not recall the painting . . ." Lucy said, eyeing the portrait. "It was dark in here the last time I found you." As she spoke, Lucy absentmindedly drew a circle on the door. Her finger was bent at a painful angle, moving roughly against the wood, and when her nail began to scratch against the door, the sharpness of the sound made Mehr flinch.

"Stop that," Mehr said.

Lucy gave her a confused look.

"Stop doing that," Mehr said, now approaching Lucy and pulling her hand free of the door.

"Oh," Lucy said quietly. "What has you so vexed? Hiding in this empty room on your own."

Mehr brushed the hair back from her forehead. "You were looking for me?"

"You were missed at dinner," Lucy said. "We have all moved into the library and you are expected."

"By whom?" Mehr asked, her pulse quickening.

Lucy gave out an exasperated sigh. "His lordship, of course."

"Can he wait?"

Lucy gave her a pointed look, and as she led her out of the room, Mehr glanced back at the painting. The woman's expression hadn't changed again.

Mehr followed Lucy to the library and hesitated at the threshold. Lord Byron was stretched out on a sofa, one arm draped over his face. He appeared to be asleep. Under the window, Claire sat on an armchair, eyes turned longingly in Byron's direction, a book lying open in her lap. Mary and Percy were together on another sofa, tucked away in a corner. Percy chewed on the end of a pencil, then hastily jotted something down, while Mary held a book open in her hands, her eyes darting across the page.

Byron's manservants were nowhere to be found. She peered in the darkest corners, but she and Lucy were the only servants. Even Lucy quickly left after leading Mehr there. Mehr scanned the room and found Polidori kneeling before the hearth, his back to the rest of them, poking at the coals. He turned his face to the side, looked surprised to see her. He gave her a sheepish grin.

Polidori opened his mouth to say something, but before he could, Byron stirred and sat up.

"Now our little menagerie is complete," Byron said to Mehr. "Come in."

Mehr stepped closer, and when he pointed at the end of the sofa, at an empty space beside Mary, she hesitated. Byron raised an eyebrow at her until she obliged. She smoothed the front of her apron flat against her thighs and straightened her cap before sitting, and kept her gaze on the hearth, anywhere but at the young couple.

She met Polidori's dark eyes, like two coals burning into her.

Percy stopped scribbling and sat up. "Listen to this. 'Why aught should fail and fade that once is shown—'"

"Which one is this again?" Byron asked.

"My 'Hymn to Intellectual Beauty,'" Percy said.

Byron grunted, lounging back against the chaise. "And the line before that?"

"I was speaking to the *spirit* of beauty," Percy said. "'Ask why the sunlight not for ever / Weaves rainbows o'er yon mountain-river, / Why aught should fail and fade that once is shown, / Why fear and dream and despair and hope / Cast on the daylight of this earth / Such gloom . . .'"

Percy chewed on his lower lip, staring down at the page resting on his knee.

"It needs something." Byron waved his hand, searching for the right word. "Something . . . more?"

"What more?" Percy threw up his hands. "The . . . the juxtaposition between despair and hope with gloom. It is a metaphor."

"Metaphor?" Byron scoffed.

"If I may?" Mary put her book aside. "'Why fear and dream and *life* and *death* / Cast on the daylight of this earth / Such gloom.'"

Percy shook his head. "Life and death? Feels a little . . . conspicuous."

"I hate it," Byron said, rolling his large eyes toward Mehr. "What do you think, our divinity?"

Mehr was momentarily startled but quickly recovered. "I am not a poet," she said.

"Surely you have read poetry before?" Byron asked.

"Indeed." She would not offer anymore.

"Perhaps in your . . . what is it called? . . . the *zenana* in which you were raised, you would have had plenty of poetry within your reach."

There was a flutter of unease in her chest. She'd shared nothing of her upbringing with anyone. Had she? Unless James had shared her past with Miss Christy, who then had shared it with the Shelleys, who then . . . She wouldn't allow herself to speculate, to be distracted by the man. She stared back at Byron, defiant in spite of the provocative smile on his lips.

Polidori moved away from the hearth. "My lord, must you really—"

Byron put up a hand to silence him. "My dear, your suggestion?"

Mary turned to her with a blank sort of expectation, and Mehr wondered again if their time together in the vineyard had perhaps been a dream. But it emboldened Mehr to have Mary's full attention. She sat up straighter. "Death and birth. 'Why fear and dream and death and birth.' There is your juxtaposition," Mehr said.

Byron gave her a slow smile. "I like it better," he said. "Our divinity has blessed your poem."

Percy contemplated the page, chewed manically on his pencil again.

"'Death and birth,'" he muttered, then took to crossing lines off and rewriting them on the page.

Mary continued to stare at Mehr. "I dreamt about my mother again," she said.

"More dreams," Byron groaned. He lay back down and shut his eyes.

"She felt so real," Mary said. "When I touched her hand, it was soft and warm. Alive."

Mehr met her gaze but couldn't tell if Mary meant to speak only to her.

Byron yawned. "'A lovely Apparition, sent / To be a moment's ornament,'" he said.

"Wordsworth," Polidori barked.

Mary smiled at the Lord and began absentmindedly scratching at her rash. Her fingers scraped under her collar and up to her cheeks. The rasping sound of fingernails against dry skin made Mehr press herself further into the cushion.

Mary went on. "I wonder, perhaps, if it was not a dream? Say we were able to conjure our dead to life. Like Athena springing forth from her father's head. Because he imagined her birth so vividly."

Byron sat up and rubbed his palms together. "And you are Zeus, Mrs. Shelley? The creator of all things?"

Mary looked down at her lap. "I believe I may have something of a story. A vestige of a narrative."

Byron leaned forward. "You have begun a new work?"

A small, inviting smile was all she'd give him. "If I told you what it was about, you would think I had gone mad."

Percy pulled Mary closer.

"I could tell you something about that. 'Mad Shelley' is what they called me at Eton."

Mehr detected a frown on Mary's face while Percy distracted Byron and they began chatting about their university years. She returned to her book, but Mehr could tell she wasn't reading anymore.

"You *can* bring the dead back," Polidori said. He'd long stopped tending to the fire and now stood with his back to the hearth, his features darkened.

"Pray tell," Byron said with a sigh. "We are in need of your wisdom."

Polidori clasped his hands together, a quick, nervous movement, before dropping them to his sides. "Galvanism," he said, looking immensely pleased with himself.

"I know exactly what you mean," Percy said. "Electrostimulation. I studied it at Eton."

"Go on," Byron said with a dismissive wave of his hand to Percy.

With Byron's attention diverted, Polidori slouched, glowered at Percy. In whatever way Polidori had found himself a rival with the other man for Byron's attentions, Mehr knew it would be a losing battle. Percy and the Lord had formed a tight alliance; it was clear for all to see. Mehr realized she was perhaps the only one in the room not clamoring for Byron's approval.

"Galvanism—named for Luigi Galvani." Percy began to stammer. "As I recall, he experimented on deceased frogs."

"What?" Byron laughed.

"It is true," Polidori said.

Mary's keen eyes were on him, unflinching, unblinking. "How do they bring them to life?"

"Animal electricity. A unique way to reanimate the dead. It has been practiced on corpses of criminals. Facial muscles have been known to twitch awake, eyes open, fists unclench."

Mehr shuddered despite the warmth in the room. She looked around at their shining, eager faces and realized she was trapped in a room full of mad people. All of them. Even Mary held on to every one of Polidori's words, her attention rapt. Death and birth and madness and experiments on dead frogs—she was lightheaded, and her dinner churned in her stomach.

"I have had enough," Claire said from her side of the room. She was standing, clutching a book in her hands. She threw it down onto the chair. "I will not sit here and listen to any more of your grotesque stories."

She was glaring at Percy, who appeared surprised.

"I am not the one going on about corpses," Percy said.

Byron chuckled to himself. "I enjoy this grotesque turn of ideas. But I refuse to believe it. I believe death to be an eternal sleep, at least of the body. To our creator we must return. Whether Christian or Mohammedan," he said to Mehr with a smirk.

"You, a God-fearing Christian?" Mehr asked, unable to mask her scowl.

Byron sat forward, elbows on his knees. A lock of hair fell over his eyes, and he appeared so devilishly handsome Mehr could hardly look away from him.

"God knows I have been guilty of many, many excesses," Byron said. "I have a great mind to believe in Christianity for the mere pleasure of fancying I may be damned."

"You want to believe," Mary said, her voice soft, "yet you laugh in the face of piety. Because you are grieved by the same thing that we mere mortals are guided by."

Byron leaned forward. "What is that, Mrs. Shelley?"

Mary fell silent. The only sound in the room was the hissing of coals.

"Love," Mehr finally said. She was glaring at Byron, flushed from her boldness, and something else. Fear, perhaps, was guiding her. She felt more energized by it than by anything else.

"Is it not true, my lord?" Mehr went on. "Is not love what compels us all? A force more powerful than either of our gods? That you think Him your creator, when He was the one created by it."

Byron pursed his lips and reclined back on the couch. "I concede, Mehrunissa of Lucknow."

Oh, it was irresistible the way he said her name. She finally looked away, while Mary, with a triumphant grin on her face, reached over and squeezed Mehr's hand. No sooner had they touched than Percy put his arm around Mary, pulling her closer.

He lifted Mary's hand and brushed it with his lips. "'Love betters what is best.'"

"Wordsworth," Byron said before anyone else could venture a guess. "Is that what you told your actual wife?"

Percy dropped Mary's hand.

"Are not *you* still trapped in holy matrimony with your own wife?" Polidori asked.

Byron chuckled to himself. "Swift says, 'No wise man ever married.' I married on lease. I regret that I will not be renewing it on expiry. Not for all the riches in the world. I am sure our divinity would know something about that."

Byron had a wild look in his eye. She had no idea what he'd meant by this. Percy began to laugh nervously as Mary moved away from him, putting space between them and moving closer to Mehr. Their thighs were so close now they nearly touched. Mehr could comfort her, commiserate with her, but her voice caught and all she could do was sit in silence beside the young woman.

Claire huffed out of the room and slammed the door shut behind her. Polidori also went for the door to follow after Claire.

"It is far too early to turn in," Byron said.

Polidori hugged his wiry frame. "I will not be made to stay up all night and lie in all morning." He gestured at the room around him. "Even if they are all too happy to have taken on your eccentricities."

Percy and Byron began to laugh, which made Polidori grimace and hurry out of the room.

"He is in the sulks. As usual," Byron said, lifting a book from the haphazard pile on the floor beside him. "Maybe I should kill him and be rid of him forever."

"Before we die of boredom," Percy said, "by his hand."

The poets rose from their couches and moved to a darker part of the library, speaking of lines and metrics, melding their minds yet again.

Mehr was alone with Mary now.

"You must write in your letters to your family all about the scandalous Shelleys," Mary said, though there wasn't a hint of sheepishness there. Perhaps more of a desire for it to be true.

She needn't have worried, though, because Mehr had no one she could call family anymore. "I am afraid I must return to my duties," Mehr said.

The faint tremor of raindrops tapped against the windows. Mehr slithered off the end of the sofa, and before she could head for the door, Mary let out a long sigh.

"He is a brute," Mary said.

"Which one?" Mehr asked.

Mary sucked in her breath, bit her lower lip to stifle a laugh.

Mehr found she liked making the young woman smile. It lifted something within her, over the protected, hardened part of herself, leaving the softness exposed and vulnerable. She composed herself quickly.

"I have learned," Mary said, "that you can prove yourself to one man or you can prove yourself to the world."

"I much prefer the latter," Mehr said softly.

Mary raised an eyebrow at her. With Mary's eyes still on her, Mehr took up her lamp and headed for the door.

"Good night," she muttered, then moved quickly out of the library. She turned back once to Mary, who was looking intently into the fire, while Percy and Byron remained within the shelves, arguing about his poem.

Once outside, Mehr realized how stuffy the room had become with Polidori fussing with the fire. The air in the hall was cooler. She had the sensation again that she was standing in moving water. The invisible wave was lifting her, moving her toward the stairs.

She threaded through the darkness. As she passed the gallery, something made her falter in her steps. There was a distinct knocking within the walls. Soft taps that swiftly turned into urgent blows. She touched the wall, felt the echoes of the knocks against her palm. Then the air went silent.

When she stepped back from the wall, the line of paintings had changed. Each was an exact copy of the portrait that adorned the wall of the abandoned room downstairs. She stopped at the last one and held the lamp up to investigate. It was the same background, the same woman, but her eyes had moved. Her gaze was fixed on something behind her. The hair on the back of Mehr's neck stood on end; she realized she wasn't alone anymore. There was a presence behind her. She felt it creeping closer and closer. Then a thud, and a frantic pitter-patter of footsteps.

She whirled around and saw a shrouded, desiccated figure. Mehr had to blink a few times to make it out, and was startled to see that it was a woman. Her eyes were blackened and bruised, her mouth a gaping hole trembling and widening like a deep, dark tunnel. The woman hurtled toward Mehr, hands outstretched, and let out a high-pitched scream. Mehr backed into the wall as the woman reached out to grab her hands, her skeletal body bent over. Mehr could see her vertebrae through the thin, frayed black dress hanging off her frame. She appeared to be crying, pleading, but her face was so horrifying Mehr could only fight her off.

The lantern fell from Mehr's hands, and in the flickering light, the apparition faded into the darkness. She held her hand to her beating heart, gasping for air. She was alone again. When she picked the lantern up and held it to the paintings, they'd all gone back to their usual depictions—men on galloping horses, on battlefields, in their drawing rooms.

She hurried through the rest of the gallery, through the solitary doorway to the attic, and shut the door hard behind her. She held the lamp up the stairs, then slowly took the steps one at a time to her room. The shadows reached and pulled with the swinging of the lantern. But there was nothing else in the attic with her.

She crawled into bed and sat up against the wall, hugging her knees to her chest. Her heart beat against the tops of her knees. First the vivid dreams, and now she was hallucinating. She shut her eyes and, after what felt like years, prayed under her breath. Called out to him to protect her mind, not let her lose herself the way her mother had. She gripped the taweez in her hand, but it was so hot it nearly scorched her palm.

Quickly, she pulled it off and held it up in front of her face. What had Percy called it? A talisman for good luck? Some luck it had brought her. It was a dreadful, evil thing. Ever since she'd started wearing it, she'd been seeing horrific images in her mind. Mehr opened the drawer in her dresser and threw it in. Then her eyes fell on the journal that lay on top. She moved the taweez aside and reached for it, held it in her hands. She unwound it and flipped it open.

Her pulse quickened again as she pored through the pages, searching for meaning beyond the letters she couldn't read. Then she landed on a page that made her gasp out loud and would leave her sleepless the rest of the night.

It was a detailed sketch of the vineyard. The angle and lines looked familiar, and the more Mehr studied it, the more she realized it was the same view she'd seen a few times now from the window of the mysterious woman's abandoned room.

It was unmistakable who used to own the vineyard. It belonged to the woman in the painting.

CHAPTER 11

The following day a terrible gloom fell over the villa. The curtains were pulled away from the windows, yet outside there was a threat of rain from the thick gray clouds blanketing the sky, which made the interior even bleaker. That morning Mehr had to light each and every lamp adorning the villa's many walls, a painstaking task after a sleepless night.

In the late afternoon, Mehr brought a pot of tea and a bottle of claret to the drawing room.

Claire was there, seated at a desk and hunched over a short pile of papers, writing carefully on one paper after studying another. Byron stood at the window, hands locked behind his back, staring out at the heavy clouds over the mountain. Leman appeared to close its great eye as the impending darkness made the vineyard glow a deep, verdant color. Both Percy and Polidori sat on the couch debating something in curt tones.

Yet the one person Mehr was seeking wasn't with them. She withdrew to a corner and poured a few cups of tea.

Percy's voice rose. "My lord, might you please—"

"No good," Byron said. He moved to the writing desk and glanced over Claire's shoulder. "Much better penmanship than your sister's. How is my canto coming along?"

Claire shyly muttered something, catching her breath and writing even slower.

"Did you read it?" Polidori asked him.

Byron grunted. "Indeed I did. From beginning to end."

He placed a hand on the back of Claire's neck. She stiffened and stopped writing. Mehr thought she detected a shudder coming from the young woman.

"You said it is autobiographical?" Percy asked Polidori.

Polidori turned his eager eyes on him. "My life's work."

Byron threw his head back and laughed. "A dull scrawl like *that*." He moved away from Claire and stood over Polidori as he sank in his seat. "You should write something new."

Polidori pursed his lips. "I barely just finished *Cajetan*."

Percy waved his hand about. "Find inspiration in the environment around you."

Mehr brought over two cups of tea and placed them in front of the men. She glanced at Polidori as he fretted over his cuffs again, and noticed a pout on his face. It seemed everyone had literary aspirations of their own, but it was futile seeking his lordship's inconstant approval. Polidori had not yet learned his lesson. His eyes were large and shining as he glared at Byron.

"Writing does not come as easy to . . . some as it does to others," Polidori said.

Even the barest compliment toward the Lord made Mehr's skin crawl.

Unmoved, Byron turned back to the window. "'Full many a flower is born to blush unseen—'"

"'And waste its sweetness on the desert air,'" Polidori spat out.

Percy sipped his tea and smacked his lips. "Thomas Gray. Well done."

Mehr brought the tea around to Claire, who was so focused she hardly looked up when Mehr put the cup beside her. She was copying over lines from one haphazard page to another, neater one. Mehr leaned closer. The handwriting she'd seen before, in the scorched letter in the gate. It belonged to Byron.

She glanced at him as he pointed out the window, and wondered who his beloved "Aug" was.

"We should be off finding the setting of Rousseau's *Julie* before the rains come again," Byron said.

Polidori stood and planted his hands on his narrow hips. "You can go apleasuring without me. I care not for Rousseau or his Julie."

Byron mock-gasped, shared a cruel glance with Percy. Mehr handed the bottle of claret to him. He poured half a glass, and after drinking it in three large gulps, grinned at her.

"Ah, our divinity," Byron said.

The way his eyes held her, Mehr found herself transfixed as usual.

"Would you like to read the doctor's life's work?" he asked.

Given the poor reception of the young man's writing, Mehr hid her grimace. "If the doctor would allow it?"

Byron threw back his head and laughed. "You would need no stronger elixir, more potent than laudanum, to put you to sleep." He leaned in closer. "And how did our divinity sleep last night?" Byron had a mad twinkle in his eye; Mehr stilled as he searched her face for a reaction.

"Leave the poor girl out of this," Polidori said quietly.

Claire looked up. "If it interests your lordship, I have also begun writing something new."

No one bothered to ask her for more. She returned to her lines, sagging now in her chair, blinking away her frustration. Or humiliation, Mehr thought, at her attempt to prove herself yet again to an audience that didn't want her to. A futile task.

Mehr backed away, took up the teapot, and quickly left the room. She brought it into the kitchen, sat down in a chair, and calmed herself. She had been alone in the gallery, she was sure of it. The apparition she'd seen was only a hallucination brought on by too much work, not enough rest. But the Lord was insinuating that he knew more than he let on.

He was a lout, but that was all he was. He enjoyed

pushing people to discomfort for his enjoyment, and he was doing the same to her. She thought of Mary and wondered if that was why the young woman wasn't joining their "menagerie" anymore. Perhaps she was still in bed. A cup of tea might draw her out. She brewed a fresh pot and took it back up the stairs.

When she knocked on Mary's door, there was no response. After a second knock and a few moments of waiting, she opened the door and peeked in. The sitting room was unoccupied, the bed empty and unmade. She stepped in and hesitated, then set the tray down on the messy writing table. She picked up a phrase book from the stack and flipped through it. She'd heard Mary say she was studying Greek, and the language within the journal had looked familiar to her. She pulled it out of her apron pocket and laid it down beside the phrase book. As she compared the lettering, she realized it was a match. Mehr pocketed the journal, then took another look around the room to see if Mary was hidden behind a wardrobe, out of sight.

Something just outside the window caught her eye. She left the table and spotted Mary heading down the stone steps to Leman. Mary turned her head to the side briefly, mid-sentence. Was she speaking to someone beside her? Mehr squinted, but Mary was completely alone.

Mehr didn't see a sign of her the rest of the day. When she didn't come down to dinner, Mehr offered to take it up to her, but Lucy had already been summoned for that task and had to look after the infant as well.

So Mehr retreated to the abandoned room, the only other place she could have found an answer. It was just as she'd left it, spotless and cheery after she'd pulled open the curtains. The woman in the painting stared out the window, down to the very vineyards that were in her own painted window.

Mehr held up the journal, waved it in front of the portrait. "Is this yours?"

Of course the painting offered no reply. She sat down and rubbed her forehead. "I fear I am going mad, trapped in this house with these people. Their absurd and fanciful imaginations are poison to the mind. And I am afraid—"

She stared up at the painting, at the forlorn, faraway gaze of the woman.

"I am afraid I am seeing things that are not real," she whispered. She flipped through the journal, to the page that had a sketch of the vineyard. She stood with her back to the painting and held the drawing up in front of her. It was a near replica of the view.

She turned to the portrait. "Were you trapped here too, like me?"

The wind rattled the windows and made a wailing sound through the chimney. The clouds had come in again. Rain sprinkled down on the vineyards, causing the vines to audibly thrash and flutter. Fat raindrops spattered against the window.

"I wish . . . I wish you would speak to me," Mehr said. "It can be a lonely existence when you're with the living."

There was a series of knocks within the walls. A sudden presence bloomed around her like a warm, tranquil cloak. "Is that you?" Mehr asked, not fully expecting an answer. She let the presence soothe her as she tucked into her solitary dinner.

IN THE MORNING, Mehr hung up the clothesline in the back garden and began the long task of washing the linen. After she retrieved a bundle of sheets from the foul bag, she sat down on a stool to search each one for holes to mend. It was a brief examination. Mary's scolding stayed with her, and since the sheets were thick and durable, of a higher quality than the ones the Shelleys possessed, they needed very little mending.

Mehr carried the bundle to the tub she'd filled with well water earlier that morning, and plunged them all into the cold, holding them down until they were fully drowned. Her sleeves were now soaked to the elbows, and she cursed herself, belatedly rolled them up, and got to work rubbing soap and ash into the linen.

She scoured the fabric quickly, carelessly, then rinsed the sheet in the tub. As she washed, her mind wandered to the abandoned room and how extravagantly it was decorated. Perhaps the woman was a lot like Mehr, a highborn prisoner in a faraway country, and her captors had realized she'd needed a room to befit her nobility. It was only fair that Mehr kept the room to herself. There were such few luxuries for her to claim, and her own captors didn't care to indulge her.

She lifted the linens out one by one, squeezed as much soap as she could from the wet masses. She then laid them on a table under the weak sun to dry momentarily before she hung them on the clothesline. The clouds were tumbling in over the horizon, and she hoped the inevitable deluge would be delayed so that the linen could have a chance to dry and she could move on with her dreary existence.

A movement in the window caught her eye. She glanced up and found Mary staring down at her. It had been days now since she'd last seen her. The young woman had completely stopped engaging with Byron's coterie, instead was sneaking out on solitary walks or staying in her room with the infant and asking for Lucy to bring her meals to her.

Mehr felt Mary's icy eyes on her, two cold pinpricks on the back of her head, as she returned to the foul bag to wash another set of sheets. But there was a commotion near the house that distracted her. Voices echoed, growing louder and louder. She was startled when Percy appeared around the corner, chased by Byron.

The linen fell from her arms onto the soft earth and was then trampled by her boots when she staggered back in surprise. She froze as Byron threw his arms around the younger man and grappled him to the ground. Percy kicked him away and stood up, shoulders square and fists up in a pugilistic stance. Though he was a few inches taller than the Lord, he was slouched over, matching Byron's height, breathing with fury.

Both men's shirts were torn at the collar. Byron swiftly ripped the rest of his shirt off and threw it to the ground before raising his fists as well. Mehr stared hard at the glistening sweat on the man's chest.

Claire came running around the house and pushed her way between the two.

"You will kill him!" she shrieked at Byron.

Percy shoved her out of the way, and neither man glanced over as she fell against the garden wall, one hand covering her face.

"I dare say"—Byron was out of breath, glaring at Percy—"you will not learn how to box if you do not spar better with me."

"He said he did not want to! You forced him!" Claire cried, but again was ignored. Even Mehr didn't approach the young woman, her attention squarely on the two men.

Byron swung a fist at Percy, who neither dodged it nor tried to deflect it. He swayed on his feet, blinking the sweat out of his eyes. Byron inched closer, shadowboxing. Percy moved around him in a semicircle, keeping his eyes on Byron, who was still out of reach.

"You are spoiled by living in your little circles and petty societies," Byron said. He swung again, and this time Percy ducked his head and deflected. "This sort of exercise is the severest of all. Sparring sharpens the mind and wit."

With a sudden uppercut, he cracked Percy under his chin and, as the man wobbled in surprise, jabbed a quick fist into his nose. Mehr flinched as Percy fell to the ground.

Claire immediately threw herself over the prone figure, who let her coddle him to her chest. "I should kill you." She stared up at Byron with teary eyes.

"He said he needed help for a stagnant mind," Byron said with a shrug.

Claire helped Percy sit up and brought a kerchief to his face. He'd cut his lip from one of the blows and pressed his hand to his mouth to stanch the blood. Without a word, he pushed away from Claire and staggered into the kitchen through the backdoor, Claire close on his heels.

Byron watched them go, but he didn't follow. Mehr moved as quietly as she could around the edge of the clothesline, farther away from him. There were a few sprays of blood on the newly cleaned sheet. She stopped and reached for it, wondering how Percy's blood could have made its way several feet to her.

Before she could touch the sheet, the blood spread outward, drenching the linen. She backed away, and a scream caught in her throat. In the window upstairs, she saw another glimpse of Mary staring down at her, her palm flat against the glass. But she wasn't alone. The figure Mehr had seen in her nightmare, the pregnant woman with golden hair and a wrinkled nightgown, stood by her side.

Mehr swooned and felt a pair of strong arms catch her before she fell. Byron held fast to her, his breath tickling the top of her head. She looked up at his handsome jawline, the full, pursed lips, his dilated pupils. The sun shone brightly behind his head, and she shut her eyes. His sweat dampened her hair, which immediately turned cold in the air. She struggled to stand, and together they stared at the bloodstained linen.

"Do you see it?" she whispered. "Do you see it, my lord?"

Byron's nostrils flared as he stared down at her. With one rough movement, he forced her to stand, then let her go. He left her in the garden and strode back into the house. Mehr watched the bloodstain shimmer down the linen and drip clean off, splattering onto the ground and soaking into the earth. Within several minutes, the linen was as clear as when she'd first hung it to dry.

She felt a sudden burning sensation in her chest and realized she was wearing the taweez. It was impossible. Several nights ago, she'd left it in her bedside dresser and swore not to wear it again. She tore it off her neck and threw it into the nearby bushes.

With one last nervous glance, she looked up at the window. There was no one there. She headed for the bushes, found the accursed taweez trapped in the branches. She raked at the dirt, pulled up mounds of earth, then pushed it down into the ground. Her mother could no longer torment her from the grave, send her visions and hallucinations and drive her to the same madness that had made her father run away from them.

She buried that last remnant of her memory, returned it to the worms with whom her mother belonged.

CHAPTER 12

The next morning, a bruised yet sprightly Percy and perfectly unblemished Byron decided to head off to seek *Julie* in Rousseau's land, with Claire and Polidori. Mehr breathed a sigh of relief—the more noxious of the villa's denizens were off on some silly pursuit. She went room by room doing her cleaning and sweeping and slopping, then retired to the abandoned room, curled up on the gorgeous sofa, and flipped through the mysterious woman's journal. But she couldn't sit still for long. Mehr needed a translation, and only Mary could help her.

She left and, for the next hour, searched for Mary in the house. But she'd hidden herself away from all of them. Mary wasn't in her room, and when Mehr looked for her outside, she wasn't on the villa grounds, in the vineyard, or at the lakeside.

Afterward, Mehr slunk into the kitchen to help Berger prepare for dinner, but he shooed her out of the kitchen.

"The Lord has asked you not to serve them anymore."

Mehr was taken aback. Her mind raced with the possibilities. Had it finally happened? Did he not trust the foreigner in their home? That she touched the food they ate? Perhaps he'd grown tired of her speaking out of turn, or maybe her bitterness toward their set was palpable even in his often-inebriated state.

She had to work. She had begrudgingly accepted this part of her fate because she needed the wages to get back home.

"Did he say why?" she asked.

Berger waved her away. "Do not vex me or I will confuse the salt with sugar."

Mehr didn't linger in the kitchen long. She would have to confront the Lord, as much as it both thrilled and repulsed her to do so. She ignored her conflicting emotions and headed straight into the library and, though the others hadn't returned yet, was surprised to find Mary sitting on the sofa alone. Almost like she'd never left the room since the last time they'd spoken.

In the glow of firelight, she looked like she had regained some color. She was ethereal. The scaly rash that had climbed from her neck up to her cheeks and coated the backs of her hands had completely vanished. Impulsively, Mehr sat beside her and reached out and touched her hand. It was as cold as a grave. Mary turned and gave her a distant smile.

"Mrs. Shelley, I have appreciated your allowing me to work for you. And I thank you for your patience."

She could not make herself sound any less convincing. There was a lump in her throat, and she swallowed hard. Mary stared at her blankly, her eyes unfocused.

"I-I must know," Mehr said. "About my wages."

"Your wages?" Mary withdrew her hand and clasped both in her lap. She let out a restless sigh. "What is this about, Mehr?"

"His lordship has asked that I no longer attend to my duties," Mehr said.

Mary laughed out loud. "Oh, Albie. He has a peculiar way of throwing his weight around. Like a child with a bundle of toys."

They were his playthings, Mehr thought with a sinking feeling. She wasn't one of them at all. At least she had hoped she wasn't. "But Berger said—"

"If his lordship has taken a liking to you, why do you resist it?" Mary asked.

Something was wrong. It was Mary's face, but the smile seemed to belong to someone else entirely.

"All of us are at his mercy, and it must remain so," Mary said. "Do you understand?"

Mehr felt a hitch in her chest. "If he relieves me of my duties—"

"He may change his mind in a second," Mary said. "A capricious man."

"What good has it done any of you to oblige him?" Mehr asked.

The question hung in the air between them. Mary

wouldn't look at her, but she appeared agitated and sunk further into the sofa. Mehr felt inside her pocket for the journal, but a sudden apprehension seized her. She couldn't share it with her. Mary seemed to have changed the past few days. She felt distant.

"Mehrunissa," Mary said.

Mehr flinched at the use of her full name.

"I am your mistress and you must oblige my wishes as well," Mary said. "If anyone has the power to relieve you of your duties, it shall be me."

"Indeed, Mrs. Shelley," Mehr said.

She pushed off of the sofa and left the room, the tears coming fast. No, she wouldn't devolve into this, a blubbering, sniveling mess. She was a descendant of the great and esteemed Khwaja Mu'in al-Din Chishti, beloved and worshipped throughout her whole country—a mantra she ran through her mind constantly. How had she, having soared at such heights, fallen so low? Perhaps her mother had cursed Mehr on her deathbed. But she would rise above it. She had such little time left with such odious people.

She quickly dried her tears with her apron as the front door flew open. Claire and Percy bounded into the villa, drenched from the sudden heavy rain shower behind them. They came in laughing, licking rainwater from their lips. Byron ran in after them, holding his coat over his head, letting out a high-pitched manic laugh, the kind she'd never heard from him before. They stood round as Polidori sulked in, soaked and frowning.

"Dinner will be served shortly," she said when they caught sight of her.

Mehr swept out of the hall and down to the dining parlour, but Robert and Berger had already set the table. The wine bottles were uncorked, the steaming pots of tea and coffee in their usual places. Mehr turned back, but she was blocked by Byron in the doorway. He had changed quickly. There were still raindrops in his hair, and his wild curls had been raked back with a severe hand.

"Is everything to your liking, my princess of Lucknow?" Byron asked.

For the first time, she found herself stammering and stuttering in front of the Lord. Even the slightest emotions were perceptible to him, and she was immediately ashamed she'd let him see her discomfiture. She moved out of the way as the others filed in. Though they'd also changed out of their wet clothes, the room smelled heavily of sweat and rainwater.

They took their usual seats. Percy and Mary on one side of the table, and Claire and Polidori on the other. But the Lord remained standing, his eyes digging into the exposed skin of Mehr's neck, the top of her chest. Had she forgotten to button her dress that morning? She placed a hand against her collarbone.

"You will be dining with us now," he said, then lowered his voice. "If it pleases you."

Mehr retreated to the end of the room, where she and the servants had first sat, but Byron came around and pulled the empty seat out next to Polidori. He tilted his head to her, an invitation. Mehr glanced at Mary, who glared back, her eyes shifting to the empty seat.

Mehr gritted her teeth and obliged, sitting into the chair as he pushed it in under her. He poured her a glass of wine and, after placing it in front of her with a flourish, headed to his seat. Beside her, Polidori shifted uncomfortably.

Claire leaned forward and glared at her. "Why is she here?"

"She is my special guest," the Lord said, glancing quickly at Percy and Mary. "*Our* guest."

Claire scowled. "A housemaid is hardly—"

"She has a noble bearing. Would not you agree, my lord?" Percy asked, staring at Mehr. "We noticed it of her as soon as we met her."

It was the first time in a while that Percy had looked directly at her, and his stare lingered as she pretended to take a sip of wine. Byron's manservants brought in platters of food, and Mehr sat stiff in her seat.

"Indeed," Byron said, pursing his full lips. "She has a way with our cutlery, not like the heathen Turks tearing everything apart with their fingers, slurping off their palms."

She bit her lip but wouldn't look at the man. He was, of course, too stupid to know that she had been raised in a home with an English father, who'd expected his children to be be reared with English manners. After her father left, she had relaxed into her maternal family's way of life.

But she had the rare luxury to choose which manners she wanted to display, something he could never possess. And it made her pity him.

"A noble bearing," Byron said thoughtfully. "Would not that be true of your brother? Sikander?"

Mehr flushed, felt blood pinch her ears. Had she told anyone of her brother? She glanced at Mary and faintly remembered telling her that she had a brother. Perhaps Mary had told Byron all about their enigmatic housemaid when they went on their rambles together, made Mehr their object of fascination in between spewing lines of poetry to see who would guess the poet first. Especially as Byron had suddenly expressed an interest in her.

"A peculiar name," Percy said, sharing a quick glance with Byron as he idly swirled his wine.

Her brother had been named after Alexander the Great, her mother inspired by his Persian name of Sikander-i-Azam. Why her father had chosen such a tepid firangi name as James had always perplexed her.

"I dare say, it is pleasing on the ears," Byron said. "A better name than can be boasted by some of our own countrymen."

"The name of a warrior," Mehr said, her voice steady.

Byron's eyes glinted at her. "And where is this brother of yours?"

She felt her pulse quicken. If this was the game Byron wanted to play with her, to briefly lift her up from her drudgery by seating her at their table and pretending she was one of them, expecting her everlasting acquiescence to whatever manner he desired, she wouldn't participate in it. But she would take as much as she could from the rest of them. After all, for as long as he willed it, she wouldn't need to toil after them.

"Home," she said.

"And where is that?"

Byron's sneer deepened, and Mehr found herself unable to look away.

Polidori, likely sensing Mehr's discomfort as she twisted the dinner napkin in her hands under the table, turned his face to her and spoke softly. "You can leave now. If you want."

Mehr shook her head, tightened her lips into a grimace. She was not going to admit defeat or let any of them see or hear her helplessness.

"In hell," Mehr said to Byron. "Where he belongs."

Byron and Percy threw back their heads in laughter, while Claire glared at her through Polidori as if he weren't seated between them. She knew it was a matter of time before his lordship would tire of his subject and move on to torturing Claire or Percy again. But he turned his gaze on Mary instead.

"Mrs. Shelley. You are looking . . ." Byron said, waving his hand in search of a word.

"Thank you, my lord," she replied. She gave him a bright smile. Her cheeks were flushed from the wine, her hair freshly curled and pinned up. She even wore a new dress that Mehr had seen languishing in her drawers untouched. The lace collar sat delicately around the base of her throat. Mehr couldn't stand the look of her and trained her gaze elsewhere.

"You have been healed of your skin condition," Polidori said, leaning forward.

Mary shut her eyes and smiled. "The air here is more curative than the springs in Bath."

"The tincture I made for you," Polidori said, "it worked."

She slowly opened her eyes and fixed him in her stare. "I did not use it. I dare say, not everything must be explained away by medicine. 'More needs she the divine, than the physician.'"

"Shakespeare," Claire said softly, eyeing her stepsister. She pushed food around her plate with a fork, and Mehr noticed the girl still didn't have much of an appetite.

Byron chuckled, an amused smile on his lips. "I thought you did not believe in the divine, Mrs. Shelley."

Mary didn't respond. She glanced at him over the rim of her glass, taking petite sips of wine.

"The divine does not have to be a deity," Percy said to Byron, lolling back against his seat. His black eye and split lip were healing poorly, and new bruises blotched his features. "You can find it in whatever object you want," he said, winding a finger through one of Mary's curls.

Mary delicately carved a piece of roast beef and brought it to her lips, chewed thoughtfully. She was distracted, preoccupied. Unaware of her surroundings and lost in her own thoughts. Mehr wondered what the matter was with the young woman. Then, suddenly, a thought wove into her mind. She behaved like a person newly in love.

"What might our actual divinity think?" Byron asked Mehr.

Mehr stared back at him. "I struggle to believe in the divine when it does not believe in me, my lord."

Byron smirked at her. "Even better," he said softly.

Before he could say more, Polidori cleared his throat. "I have begun a new literary project."

Byron groaned, swatted the air as if an unruly fly had gotten into his eyeline. "You again. I am relieved you gave up on *Cajetan*."

"I did not say I was giving it up," Polidori said.

"What is it about?" Mary asked.

Polidori hesitated before speaking again. "I fear it is in the realm of the macabre."

As thunder rumbled far above the mountains, Byron looked up and poured another glass of claret. "A perfect night for it," he said. "It would be an excellent challenge for all of us to write our own tales of the macabre."

Claire forcefully put down her utensils. "I have already said I quite detest these ghastly stories."

"Quiet," the Lord said.

Claire sat stricken, wide-eyed. She breathed hard, and Mehr wondered if the young woman was going to burst into tears. Claire looked to both Mary and Percy for some sort of support, but neither met her eyes.

"Pray tell us," Mary said to Polidori.

He pulled at his cuffs in that nervous way of his. "It is about a woman. Punished for her curiosity."

Byron snorted and downed his wine. Mary gave him a supportive nod, and Polidori went on.

"She peeped through a keyhole—"

"Why?" Percy asked, hiding a smile behind his hand.

"I have yet to explain," Polidori said. "Her punishment, however, turns her head into a skull."

"Marvelous," Byron said, now refilling Mary's glass of wine. "I will be the first to read it, I hope."

Both he and Percy pretended to busy themselves with their respective dinners, stifling laughter. Polidori glared down at the table, turning his glass round and round. Mehr had the sudden urge to shake him roughly by the shoulders. It was obvious to everyone but him how little Byron and Percy cared to welcome him into their new friendship, yet he reached and reached for their admiration.

She found he looked pleased with himself, perhaps for arresting their attention for even the merest of moments. It made her want to strike Polidori even more, and she hugged her torso to stop herself from doing it.

Afterward, on the Lord's command, they followed him en masse to the library, Mehr using the back of Mary's exposed neck as her guiding light. The fire had weakened, and as before, Polidori took it upon himself to revive it. They assumed their usual places—Byron on a chaise on his own, Mary and Percy together on a sofa, Claire in an armchair under the window.

Reluctantly, Mehr picked a random book from the shelf and joined the couple on the sofa, pressing as far to her side as she could.

"It is your turn to read," Byron said to Mary, pouring himself yet another glass of claret from a new bottle.

She flushed. "I am sorry, Claire," Mary said. "I fear this one is also in the realm of the macabre."

Claire turned a page in her book and didn't look up. "I am reading something far more riveting than that."

"Might you be so kind as to tell us?" Percy asked.

She held up the book, but the title was too small for them to make out in the dim light. Byron strode over, his steps unsteady, and seized it from her. Claire clasped her hands in her lap, glaring up at him.

"'*Pride and Prejudice*, from the author of *Sense and Sensibility*,'" Byron read aloud.

"I have not read it," Mary said.

"I might have," Percy said quickly. "It sounds familiar."

Byron flipped through and stopped on the odd page to read. "Very good," he said under his breath.

Claire sat up straighter in her chair. "A woman writer. Like me." Her eyes darted to her sister. "And Mary, perhaps."

Byron immediately returned the book to Claire and sauntered back to his chaise.

"You seemed to have lost interest in her already, my lord," Claire said with an icy stare.

He threw an arm over his eyes. "I have far too many books to read at the moment."

"And none by women writers?" Claire asked.

Byron didn't reply.

Claire licked her lips. "Might you not like to discover a new writer?"

"Claire, please," Percy said, pinching the bridge of his nose. "You are giving us all a headache."

"You have a headache because the Lord beat you mercilessly yesterday," she hissed.

Mehr laughed out loud, and immediately clapped a hand to her mouth.

"Did you say something, my Lucknow princess?" Byron asked.

"No, your lordship," Mehr said. "Perhaps it was the moan of the wind in the chimney."

Byron stared at her, and Mehr felt the irresistible pull, the longing that wrapped her in a tight embrace when she looked at Diodati from the shore. Byron's eyes acted as the same magnet.

Beside Mehr, Mary put her book down in her lap. "I learned of a new poet. A remarkable one. From her." She pointed a thin finger at Mehr.

"And what is his name?" Byron asked.

Mehr hesitated. "Mir Taqi Mir." Sweat trickled between her shoulder blades. She flushed and looked away from him, calmed her breathing.

"What was that?" Byron asked.

"Mir Taqi Mir," Mary said, with a heavy accent.

"Huh." Byron stared up at the ceiling. "An unusual name."

"He is a celebrated poet, one of the greatest ever known," Mehr said, her voice rising.

Byron waved his hand. "Hindostan is undistinguished by any great bard—"

"Because you have not heard of him does not mean he does not exist," Mehr said. "Might our poets be so undistinguished because they are not English?"

Byron took on a frown so intense even the fire in the grate lessened in awe of it. "If you had let me finish my thought. I meant to say, the Sanskrit is so imperfectly known to Europeans; we know not what poetical relics may exist."

Mehr felt a sting in her cheeks as if she'd been struck.

"My dear," Byron said, softening a bit. "You do not have to apologize if you will do me one task. Mrs. Shelley, let us have our Mohammedan read tonight."

"I do not mind reading," Mary said.

"Show her where you left off." Byron lay back down.

Mary hesitated for the smallest moment. Then she gave Mehr a brief, apologetic look before handing the book over, pointing her finger to the lower half of the page.

Mehr slowly began to read. "'That vain it were her lids to close; / So half-way from the bed she rose, / And on her elbow did recline / To look at the lady Geraldine—'"

"Stop," Byron said, letting out an exasperated sigh. "You are saying it wrong. It rhymes with 'mine.'"

"'Geral*dine*.'" Mehr continued, "'Beneath the lamp the lady bowed, / And slowly rolled her eyes around; / Then drawing in her breath aloud, / Like one that shuddered, she unbound / The cincture from beneath her breast: / Her silken robe, and inner vest—'"

Her breath caught in her chest. She composed herself and read on.

"'Dropt to her feet, and full in view, / Behold! her bosom and half her side—'"

Her heart raced, and she found herself breathless. She struggled to continue.

"'A sight to dream of, not to tell—'"

"Bah!" Byron stood suddenly and yanked the book from her hands. He tossed it into Percy's lap, which startled him. He had been dozing off and was suddenly alert, staring around the room.

Byron pointed a finger in Mehr's face. "*Christabel* deserves better."

He was agitated now, curling and uncurling his fists. He staggered on his feet, and Mehr realized he was heavily intoxicated. She'd seen him drink claret before, but this was something else. She felt the air leave the room; even Mary and Percy sat as still and quiet as possible. He was a wild, hungry beast, and any one of them could be his next prey.

Unfortunately, he drew his caustic attention to Polidori, who was sitting on the floor by the fire, flipping through a book.

"And what are you reading?" Byron asked him.

"That is my concern," Polidori said. When Byron swooped on him, Polidori moved the book away from his groping hand. "You will mock me like you do the others."

Byron planted his fists on his hips. "You are a dull fellow, and all you read are dull things."

Polidori scowled at him and continued reading while Byron stared him down. But he couldn't ignore Byron for much longer. "*The Necromancer*," he said.

Byron swayed on his feet, leaned a hand against the mantle to right himself. "And what is it about?"

"Tales within tales told by two friends Herman and Helfried," Polidori said.

"German?" Byron asked.

Polidori nodded, brightening now under the Lord's attention. He sat up straighter. "About the wizard Volkert who lives in the Black Forest."

"Read it aloud," Byron said.

A sudden burst of rain hit the windowpane, making Claire shriek from her chair. Mehr had also been startled, and both Mary and Percy flinched out of their frozen states. Byron strode over to the window, leaning heavily over Claire to pull the drapes apart. The rain continued to pelt the window, and within the darkness, a streak of lightning illuminated the night sky.

"What a delightful scene," Byron said, then turned around to jab a finger in Polidori's direction. "Read to us about your Volkert."

Polidori stood with his back to the fire. He shuffled

from one foot to the next. "'He strewed sand on the floor, and drew two circles with an ebony wand. Placing me in one and himself in the other.'"

"Why would he do such a thing?" Byron asked.

Polidori let out a sigh. "He is in the process of summoning the narrator's dead mother."

Byron rubbed his chin. "My mother is dead, with no other aim but to vex me. And I do not wish to summon her." He shuddered, then looked directly at Mary. "Anyone here with a dead mother?"

Percy, now fully awake, sat up straighter. "My lord—"

"Her," Mary said, pointing at Mehr, though not quite meeting her eyes.

"Very well," Byron said, turning to Polidori. "He strewed sand? On the floor?"

Polidori nodded at him, perplexed. Byron pushed him out of the way and began poking around in the coal bucket behind him. "This should work," he said. He roughly kicked the rug off the floor and then poured out ash. "What did he do next?"

"This is madness," Claire said, her voice weak across the room. "You are pretending to summon—"

"Let him," Mary said. She turned her head slowly to Mehr, eyes flashing green, red, then suddenly gold—all the colors of madness. "You do not mind?"

Mehr gulped, then took Byron's sooty, outstretched hand. He gently positioned her beside Polidori.

"How many circles did he draw?" Byron asked.

"Two." Polidori's voice came out a croak.

Byron placed his fingers on the scattered ashes and drew two large circles. He stepped into one and gestured for Mehr to do the same. She silently obliged. They were all living in Byron's deranged vision of the world, like it or not.

Percy stood and plucked the book out of Polidori's hands and, before Polidori could protest, shoved him out of the way and continued reading.

"'The stranger was now standing opposite to me in an awful and solemn posture.'"

Byron faced Mehr, a devilish grin on his face. She stared back at him, drew herself up.

Percy continued. "'He folded his hands upon his breast.'"

Byron followed the prompt.

"'His looks being lifted up to heaven,'" Percy read.

Byron was unable to contain his glee as he stared up at the ceiling.

"'Now I heard the clock strike twelve.'"

At that moment the clock began to strike, making them gasp and flinch. Mehr counted the chimes—there were twelve. Her heart was racing, and she felt a sudden wave of dizziness. But she wouldn't let them see her fear.

Another crack of lightning appeared in the window. Claire stood quickly from her seat, hands gripping her face. She made for the door, but Percy ran around and blocked her from leaving.

"You cannot leave the ritual. You have to stay here for it."

"So now you beg for my company," Claire said, tears streaming down her face. "I will not stay here any longer."

Percy took a rough hold of her arm and led her to the sofa. She sank down beside Mary, furiously wiping her tears. If Mehr hadn't been so frightened, she'd have felt pity for the young woman. She was torn between two men who treated her so poorly, yet she could never object to their sudden need for her when it best suited them.

Polidori stood somewhere behind Mehr. "You do not have to do this," he whispered.

"Did I ever have a choice? Do any of us?" she asked him.

Percy continued, a manic smile on his face. "'The clock struck twelve and then,'" he said as he searched for his place on the page. "Ah. 'With the last stroke, the stranger began to turn himself round about within the circle, with an astonishing velocity.'"

Byron turned his hands out and spun wildly. He was immediately out of breath. As he spun, he asked: "What did he do next?"

"'Pronounced the Christian and surname of my deceased mother.'"

"She had no Christian name," Mehr said emphatically, arms crossed over her chest.

Byron stopped and swayed on the spot. He wiped the sweat from the back of his neck.

"What was her name?" he demanded.

Mehr stood even straighter, realized she was nearly Byron's height. "No."

Byron made to reach for her but stopped before he was out of the crudely drawn circle.

"You tell me now or I will throw you out in the rain," Byron said.

"Then throw me out of this godforsaken house!" Mehr screamed back.

There was a sudden boom of thunder that shook the floor beneath them. The windows burst open, bringing rain and hailstones inside. As they cowered from the wind whipping around them, there was a loud groan from inside the house, like a ship struggling against a storm. The walls began to shake, paint cracking off and raining down on them. Byron stumbled and fell to the floor as Claire, with not a glance at either of her paramours, leaped over him and out of the library, her hysterical cries receding down the hall.

The floor trembled again, and Mehr staggered from the circle and into Polidori, who threw his arms around her. She leaned against his chest, both of them gasping for breath. The earth stilled beneath them, and the wind died down, but the rain and hail continued to pepper the room. Mehr and Polidori, careful not to slip in the abundance of rainwater, shut the window and pulled the curtains closed.

But outside the room, there was still the distinct sound of rainfall. Percy pulled Byron up to stand, and together they left the room to investigate the noise. The only one who wasn't panicked was Mary, who had been stoically sitting on the sofa, reading her book throughout the commotion. Polidori and Mehr left her there.

The windows in the nearest drawing room had been thrown open as well. The manservants fought the lashing rain and wind to shut them, while Byron leaned against a wall watching them. But the noise persisted. It wasn't long until they realized every window had been pushed open by the storm. As the manservants went around to secure them and survey damage from the sudden earthquake, Byron, Polidori, and Percy went up to check the windows in their own rooms.

Mehr headed upstairs and realized Mary was following her. When they reached the landing, Mary took hold of her hand.

"You should have told them her name," Mary said.

"I am not amused by their games."

Mary bit her lip. "You might have brought her back?"

"I do not wish for her return," Mehr said, momentarily stunned.

"But that is absurd. She is your mother. I would do anything to have mine back."

Mary held tight to Mehr's hand, taking it in both of her own. Though Mary's palms were soft, Mehr could feel her prominent knuckles under her paper-thin skin.

"Your mother gave you life. Once you have a child, you know what that sacrifice means," Mary said.

Mehr shook her head. "It is my father I wish to see. More than anything."

"Oh, I do love Papa," Mary said. "But he still lives. To see the dead again—"

"Perhaps they should remain where they are," Mehr said, finally pulling her hand away. "It was just a story, after all."

Mary smiled down at her feet. "For a moment, would not that have been wonderful?"

"I should check my room," Mehr said, looking away.

"I am going up to do the same. If you will light my way." Mary headed up the stairs ahead of her.

Mehr followed her to the gallery and watched from afar as Mary entered her room and shut the door softly behind her. Then Mehr leaned against the wall and placed the lantern on the floor. She was still trembling from the tumult that had happened in the library. Her chest ached from alternating between holding her breath and then gasping for air. She was a pawn in Byron's mischief, and she hated how it made her feel. He was a dastardly man. She was sure he was going straight to hell with his antics and impertinent behavior. She was sure the rest of them would be going with him. But she wouldn't allow herself to be dragged there as well.

Mehr took up her lantern and headed across to the west wing for the attic. Upstairs, the windows had been thrown open, but no one had been in to secure them. She grumbled under her breath, hoping Lucy would have been of some help to her. But she was likely locked away in the villa somewhere with her paramour.

After each window had been shut tight, she laid spare

linen on the puddles of water the rain had brought in, then took herself to bed. Since Byron's mischief-making, the room had felt alien to her, the whole of Diodati unwelcome. Shadows danced in the corners of her eyes. But it was all just a game. The sudden earthquake and lashing storm had unnerved her. Nature was intervening in something unnatural happening in the villa. She gathered her blanket and, with the other hand, picked the lantern back up.

She headed down to the abandoned room, where the windows had remained secured. She approached the painting, the downward-gazing woman, and held the lantern up to look at her.

"I hope you do not mind if I sleep here. I feel that if there is anywhere I may find solace, it is here with you."

The woman continued staring toward the window while Mehr found a comfortable spot on the sofa, and finally felt at rest enough to sleep.

CHAPTER 13

Something soft tickled the side of her cheek. Mehr stirred on the sofa and lifted her head. For a moment she was lost, but as she opened her eyes, the heavy red curtains came into view, and she remembered she was in the abandoned room. Though the door was firmly shut, she had a feeling that she wasn't alone. It was an unmistakable sensation—soft breath against her skin.

She sat up and pushed the blanket off, then sighed and stood, stretched her back. As soft as the couches were to sit on, they made for a terrible night's sleep. She couldn't remember if she'd dreamt.

She pulled the curtains aside and looked out. A heavy veil of fog lay around the villa. She could hardly make out the vineyards or the lake. She turned back to the painting and gasped at what she saw. The woman was gone. Mehr moved closer, squinted at the portrait. The painted room was empty of life, its vineyards as well. But there she was, a tiny figure outside the painted window, running toward the lake.

"Where are you going?" Mehr whispered to the portrait. She reached for the canvas, her fingers hovering over the painted chair. Before she made contact, the clock struck and she jumped, stopped to count the hour. It was eleven o'clock. She'd slept far too long. Quickly, she retreated from the room.

Though it was morning, a forbidding gloom had settled inside the house. Mehr lit her lantern in the empty kitchen. She then peeked into the dining parlour, but that, too, was empty. As she walked past the stairs, she found Claire stepping down in her rumpled bedclothes. She let out a big yawn. They shared a glance, and without a word, Claire followed after her. When they passed by the library, Byron stepped out in a daze, leaning against the doorframe.

"What time is it?" he asked.

From the drawing room, Percy emerged, his shirt unbuttoned, bruises dotting his hairless chest.

They congregated in the large hall. Mehr had felt it keenly, an invisible ribbon wrapped around her throat that had guided her out of the abandoned room. From the confused, drowsy looks on the others' faces, she could tell they'd also overslept and been compelled to gather at the front of the house. Mehr's skin was raw, sensitive to the touch, but she had no open wounds that she could see. There were the twin sensations of hunger and thirst, as if she hadn't eaten or drunk in weeks.

They spent the next minute eyeing one another, touching their fingertips to their foreheads, rubbing the backs of their necks. Mehr could not immediately recall what had happened the night before, but she, along with the others, all seemed to be reeling from it.

And then—a timid knock on the front door. They exchanged questioning glances, and even Mehr was unsure she'd heard right. Then a second, more urgent knock. Mehr staggered forward and threw open the door. The fog swirled outside, just out of reach.

"Who goes there?" Mehr called out.

A dim figure moved beyond the veil of mist. As the haze parted, a young woman's face appeared, and she slowly approached the house. Mehr moved aside, perplexed, as a remarkably pretty young woman stepped in. She seemed to be only just out of her teens, with a clear complexion and rosy cheeks. Her long dark hair lay in coils on her narrow shoulders, framing her bright blue eyes.

The young woman stared at Percy, her lower lip trembling.

"Harriet?" Percy's eyes were wide. "What are you doing here?"

Claire moved in front of Percy. "So, you followed them here after all. And for what?" Her voice was strong, but she was visibly trembling. "Is it not enough that he gives you a monthly allowance?"

Percy shrugged Claire off and slowly approached the young woman. "What has happened? The children?"

The woman named Harriet moved aside. Hidden by her skirts were a girl who appeared to be a few years old and a boy who was little more than a toddler.

"I was wrong in keeping them from you," Harriet said. "They are yours, after all. By God and by law."

"Harriet," Percy said softly.

Claire winced when he said her name.

Percy reached out, held the young woman at arm's length. "Are you saying—"

"I am giving up the suit." Harriet smiled at him. "I shall no longer stand in your way."

"You . . . you will allow a divorce?" Claire asked. "You will relieve my sister of her shame and guilt?"

Harriet stared at the tops of her children's heads. A perfect tear dropped down her cheek. Slowly, she nodded. Percy moved to hug her, but she stepped back from him.

"Take good care of them," she said, her voice strained.

"Wait," Percy said, reaching for her again.

Harriet swept outside and disappeared into the fog. Before Percy could follow after her, Claire held firm to his arm, pulling him back. Byron shut the door with force, the clang echoing out around them.

"Who was that?" Mary shuffled into the hall, her hair messily piled atop her head.

Percy threw himself at his children, holding both in one embrace. "We are free, Maie. Harriet gave up the suit."

He wept softly, kissing each furiously on the head, on their round cheeks. But Mary wouldn't come any closer.

She stared down at them, a mix of bewilderment and displeasure playing out on her face. She chewed on her bottom lip.

"Come," Percy said, beckoning Mary over. Reluctantly she drew closer to them, reached out to pat the children on the head, but Mehr could tell she looked deflated, defeated.

Mehr observed the children, their pale glassy eyes. They looked like living dolls. For two small children, they were too tidy, too clean-looking. Something was missing, perhaps had been taken away from them. Mehr shuddered, wrapped her shawl tighter.

"How did she know where we are?" Mary asked. She glared at Percy. "You told her?"

"No, no," Percy said, distracted by the children, who were now giggling madly, their little arms circled around his neck.

"Then how did she know to come here?" Claire asked.

"I do not know, and I do not care," Percy said, a petulant look in his eyes.

Claire bristled, turning on Mary. "I told her—"

"You do not speak to her," Mary said, her eyes flashing. "And you do not speak for me."

Claire glared at her sister, mouth agape. Mehr thought Claire would have more to say, but she turned away and swept out of the hall. Percy was on the floor, wrestling with his children, poking their little stomachs.

"Eat, eat," the little boy said, gesturing to his mouth, his teeth.

"You must be hungry," Percy said. "Let's see what Berger can make for you."

He led them out of the hall, followed by a somber Mary. She stopped in front of Byron. "Was it you?" she asked.

"I would never go behind your back, Mrs. Shelley," he said with a bow.

He managed to look even more unconvincing than usual. Mary frowned at him and followed after Percy, the children babbling and baby talking down the hall.

Mehr glanced back at the front door. Did she hear a carriage leave?

She moved past Byron, into the library, where there was a broken bottle of claret and a glass shattered beside it, the piles of ash still on the floor, undisturbed. She glanced out the window, nearly stepping on a large piece of broken glass. But the fog was so dense she couldn't tell if a carriage was making its way down the lane. She sighed and began to collect the shards in her apron.

A movement in the doorway caught her eye. She glanced up, thinking of something quick to say to Byron if he were to annoy her. But it wasn't him. With a sharp intake of breath, Mehr realized it was the figure that had been shadowing Mary in Mehr's nightmare. She had blackened eyes and a twisted mouth. The figure smiled at her, and Mehr shuddered, unable to look away as its gums dripped blood down the front of her nightgown. It stepped farther into the room, its distended stomach swelling forward.

Mehr was unable to move as the figure's gaunt fingers

reached for her. She felt a sharp pain in her hand. She stared down and found she'd been gripping a piece of broken glass. She dropped it immediately and watched as blood trickled to the floor. Slowly, it melted into the wood and disappeared. More droplets fell and also were sucked into the floor. She looked up and found that the figure had disappeared but Byron stood in its place.

He blinked hard, his gaze uneven. She wondered if he had seen the figure as well, but he appeared intoxicated, as he often was, no matter the hour of the day.

Mehr wrapped her apron around her hand to stanch the bleeding. As Byron wavered in the doorway, she pushed past him and to the stairs. She took them two at a time and headed for the west wing. She hesitated, then knocked on Polidori's door. When he appeared, his shirt was loose around his neck and his cuffs were rolled up. He looked like he had just awoken.

Immediately, his eyes landed on the crimson bloom in her apron. He took hold of her hand and gently unwrapped it. She shivered when the cold air suddenly hit her wound.

"How did this happen?" Polidori asked.

"An accident," she said, swallowing hard.

He stepped back and opened his door wider. "We will have to wrap it quickly."

Mehr stared back down the hallway, wondered what other figures waited for her in the shadows, then slowly entered his room. It was as cavernous as the other rooms were, had the same layout as Mary's and Claire's.

She followed him to the sitting room. He inspected her hand by the light of the window, rainwater dribbling down the pane. "It might feel worse than it is," he said. "The amount of blood must have startled you."

Mehr nodded but said nothing.

He brought over a washbasin and poured water into it. With a wet handkerchief, he gently cleaned away the dried blood around the cut. His hands were firm, determined, as he dabbed at her palm. Then he was gone again, retrieving his medical bag. He'd left the bloodied handkerchief on the table. Slowly, the blood seeped out and was absorbed by the wood.

When Polidori returned, Mehr suddenly stood.

"Did you see that?" She pointed at the table.

He gave her a questioning look.

"My blood," she said.

Polidori bent over the handkerchief. "It is gone." He glanced up at her, a nervous smile on his lips.

"It was not my doing," Mehr said, closing her wounded hand into a fist. She winced at the pain. "The table took it."

"The table?"

"I don't know," Mehr said, sinking back into her chair. She shut her eyes as Polidori laid a bandage over her hand and wrapped it in gauze.

"I think it most unkind of you to see me as untrustworthy," Polidori said.

Mehr opened her eyes, stared at him in the glinting lamplight. There was so much more she could tell him—the dreams, the hallucinations, the ever-changing portrait in the abandoned room. And the memories from the night before were coming back to her. A failed ritual, the earthquake. Was it all real? Or was she turning into her mother, letting her inherited hysteria take hold of her mind? No, she'd made enough excuses for the strange happenings. She wasn't her mother. She'd never be her.

"Do you recall the fight between his lordship and Mr. Shelley?" Mehr asked.

He pulled over another layer of gauze and shook his head. "They were sparring."

"Call it whatever you like," Mehr said. "His blood splattered on the sheet. Then it turned everything red. All of the linen was dripping with his blood."

He stared at her a moment, then continued bandaging her hand.

"The Lord saw it. You can ask him."

Polidori grimaced. "He finds me irritating at best. He will not speak to me of his own free will."

"You are not listening to me." Mehr pulled her hand away from him, tearing off the gauze and squeezing her fist over the table. As her nails dug in and reopened the wound, a small puddle dripped down.

"What are you—"

"Look," Mehr said.

The blood slowly disappeared into the wood.

Polidori shot out of his seat and backed away, nearly falling over the second chair. "Good God!"

Mehr tried her best to rewrap the bandage. "Doctor, I need your help."

"A parlour trick," he said.

"It is not!"

Polidori ran his palm along the top of the table. He hunkered down and inspected the other end of it. Mehr resisted the urge to slam her fists down. She winced at the new pain in her hand.

"Have you seen strange things?" she asked. "Unexplainable things?"

It was a while until he stood, eyeing her warily. He gripped the back of a chair and nodded.

"What have you been seeing?" Mehr asked.

"Nothing."

"Tell me the truth," Mehr said. She laid her good hand on his arm and felt him flinch under her fingers.

"It is not something I am seeing," Polidori said. "It is something I am feeling. Eyes on me even when I am alone."

He walked to the other side of the room, placed a hand on the wallpaper. "From here."

She joined him, and together they put their ears to the wall. There was that hum again, nearly lulling her to sleep. Mehr looked up into Polidori's eyes and realized how close he was to her. One of his curls had freed itself and lay on top of his forehead. She wanted to reach out and touch it, feel the softness between her fingers before moving it off his face. He stared down at her, his breath warm on her skin.

"It sounds like a song," he said, running his hands against the wall.

For a brief moment, she wondered how his hands would feel running down her bare back. She stepped away from him.

"Perhaps that is the way it speaks," Polidori said.

"It?" Mehr asked.

He gave her a meaningful look. "The Diodati Demon."

"That was his lordship's joke," Mehr said.

"But there is something here." Polidori trailed his gaze from the wall to the ceiling. "Something alive." He knelt on the floor, inspected the skirting board. "It resembles speech. There is a cadence to the sound. Sometimes I hear it knocking."

"I do too," Mehr said. "Something trapped within the walls, begging to be released."

"No, no." Polidori shook his head, deep in thought. "Something dark wanting to pull us in."

Mehr felt herself straying further and further from reason. "I do not think we have a demon plaguing us. It is someone else entirely."

He glanced up at her. "More malevolent than a demon? Pray, explain yourself."

Mehr nearly shouted at the young man, but contained herself. "She . . . she is trying to tell me. The lady of the villa. She is no longer here, but she remains. I think. In the walls, as you say. It is she who is trying to tell us something."

He shook his head. "There is no one else here but us."

"All the answers lie in her room. I am the only one to whom she grants entry."

He raised an eyebrow, then took hold of the gauze and began to rewrap her hand.

"And her painting speaks to me," Mehr said. "It is no demon. Perhaps an embittered ghost. Yearning to free herself from this terrible place."

"A ghost?" Polidori stared at her from the corner of his eye.

She held her breath, realizing just how deranged she sounded. But she recalled that the young man was already receptive to the strange, the unordinary.

Reluctantly, he gave her a nod. "Where is this room?"

Mehr didn't respond. She moved quickly to the door, throwing it open to the gallery and bounding with purpose through the house. Her hands barely touched the banister as she flew down the stairs, so fast that she nearly lost her footing on the last few steps. When she stopped to wait for Polidori, something grabbed at her leg.

She started. It was Percy's son, holding on to her with a fierce grip, his coarse little teeth gleaming up at her. When she yelped and tried to move away, he dug his tiny fingernails deeper into her skin through her skirts.

Polidori came down the stairs and stopped when he saw the child at Mehr's feet. "What *is* that?"

"Not what, who," Percy said, striding up to them and picking his son up in his arms.

Polidori eyed Percy as he took the child down the hall to the cellar, the little boy glaring back at them as he rested his head on his father's shoulder.

"Is that his child?" Polidori asked.

"One of them," Mehr said. "His wife left them here."

"Harriet Shelley?" Polidori took the last few steps down and placed a hand to his chin.

Mehr moved in the opposite direction. "The room. This way."

"I would have heard her carriage pull up," Polidori said. "There was a bitter suit between them. Why would she relinquish the children so easily?"

Rather than follow her, Polidori turned toward the kitchen.

"I have to show you her room," Mehr insisted, but Polidori seemed not to have heard her. She followed him down to the cellar and into the kitchen, where the two children sat atop stools and were being hand-fed little slices of cake by Lucy. Percy was up on the kitchen block beside them like a large child, while Mary watched mournfully from the corner.

Polidori cleared his throat. "I hear your children are visiting."

"Visiting?" Percy narrowed his eyes on him. "They are here to stay."

"Do you mind if I inspect them?" Polidori asked.

"I do mind." Percy shoved off the block and squared off against Polidori, who, to Mehr's relief, did not back down.

"They have had a long journey," Mary said, her frown deepening. "And you heard about the pox going around."

Lucy stopped to examine them. "They seem healthy to me," she said.

"Lucy," Mary said loudly. "When did you last look in on Willmouse?"

After Lucy averted her gaze and wordlessly left the room, Mary turned to Polidori. "Go on," she said, with a dismissive wave of her hand. "See what they have brought with them."

"They need no examination, Maie," Percy said.

"Think of *our* child. Or have you already forgotten him?"

Her eyes flashed, and for the first time since Mehr had been in their employ, Percy was first to relent. He grumbled and moved away from the children. As Polidori approached, they glared at him, their pupils suddenly dilated, like predators encountering their prey. Their sharp little teeth gnashed on bits of cake.

Polidori hesitated, then reached for the little boy. He cupped his face in his hands, peered into his eyes by candlelight. He turned his head side to side. Then he was on to the next child.

Percy took on a stern tone. "As you can see, they are healthy and free of pox."

"I need to examine one last thing," Polidori said impatiently.

He bent and placed his ear to the little boy's chest. The boy giggled and slapped the top of Polidori's face. When

Polidori rose, he glanced at Mehr in the doorway, and she could tell he was stricken by something. His face had grown pale, and his eyes widened. He did the same with the little girl, who whined and pushed him away, her lower lip jutting out.

"Fit as can be," Polidori said with a nervous laugh. He walked past Mehr, but not before catching her arm. He motioned for her to follow him and guided her into the salon, glanced outside the room before shutting the door.

"There is something wrong with the children," Mehr said. It wasn't a question; she'd noticed it the moment she'd first seen them.

"I am perplexed," Polidori said. "Something happened to them. Perhaps on their journey over."

"You said they were fit as can be," Mehr said, her confusion rising.

Polidori pinched the bridge of his nose and took a few deep breaths. She watched him struggle for a while.

"Doctor . . . ?"

"They should not be living," Polidori said, shaking his head.

"Beg your pardon?" Mehr asked.

"Do you believe in . . . the dead rising?" he asked softly.

She stifled an anxious laugh. "I thought I was the one losing my mind."

"Listen to me," Polidori said, a sudden wild look in his eyes. "There are stories about people going to their graves only to reemerge alive."

"I have heard of no such thing," Mehr said, crossing her arms. "Am I supposed to be amused?"

Polidori glared hard at her. "I listened to you about your lady of the villa. Quite patiently, I must say."

"What does any of this have to do with her?"

"Do you know what a vampire is?" Polidori asked.

Mehr shook her head.

"Vampires. Creatures who were once human. After death, they reawaken and seek out humans to feed on," the doctor said. "Most times they target their family members."

"That cannot be true," Mehr said.

"But it has been documented. Coffins have been reopened to bloated bodies with blood pouring from their mouths, while their family members become ill and slowly wither away. I have researched it. I have seen these bodies."

The rain picked up, droplets lashing against the window. Mehr shuddered and hugged herself. Of course she'd placed her trust in someone who would believe in forces outside of the realm of the ordinary. But even this was too much for her. She needed his help. There was so much more she needed to explain to him, all the unsettling feelings, the incessant humming. The dreams. The woman in the white nightgown. The taweez lying buried in the bushes behind the kitchen . . . Its power still had a stranglehold on her. But she realized placing these details out bit by bit would make her seem madder than Polidori's tales of vampires and bloodthirsty undead children.

Mehr headed for the salon door. "I was a fool to trust you."

Before she could step out, Polidori caught up to her and blocked her path. "I have a theory. But it needs work." He gripped her arms and drew her closer. Mehr held her breath, looked up into his young face. "Even if you think my ideas are deranged."

Mehr pushed away from him, though he still held his grip on her.

"I know those children are peculiar-looking, perhaps having the inhumane qualities, but . . ." She didn't know how else to describe them. They unnerved her, but weren't all children strange, otherworldly creatures anyway?

Polidori lowered his voice. "They do not have heartbeats."

Mehr felt her own pulse in her ears. "Impossible," she said.

He shook her hard. "I examined them both. How can a child—how can anything—live without a heartbeat?"

Fear prickled against the back of Mehr's neck. The noise in the walls hummed louder, and in the midst of it, there were urgent raps within the wall. Both she and Polidori looked around the room.

"There it is," he said softly.

They were interrupted when Mary walked into the salon. Mehr immediately pushed away from him, stepped back several feet to put distance between them.

"Oh," Mary said, her hand touching her throat. She glanced between the two, until finally settling on Polidori.

"The children?" Mary asked.

He struggled to smile. "I have never seen a healthier pair."

Mary began wringing her hands. "If they are ill, we must send them back to their mother."

"No need," he said with a falsely cheerful voice. "They seem to have taken their journey well."

Mary rubbed her temples. "My head has been splitting since last night. Will you bring me a cordial?"

"We shall have one sent straight up to you, Mary," Polidori said.

Mehr glared at him, at the familiar tone he'd taken with her. She detected a blush creeping up his neck. There was manic child laughter in the hall behind them, and Mary quickly left before she could be found.

As Mehr attempted to leave the room again, he touched her forearm. "No one can hear of this. We must keep it a secret, the two of us."

He left her leaning against the wall. As the house carried on its soft song, the wallpaper rustled against her back, hands reaching out to caress her. She moved away, and the wallpaper lay still. She hesitated, then rested her cheek against it.

"Will you help me?" she whispered.

The paper bulged under her face, another soft caress against her cheek, then the walls fell still and silent.

CHAPTER 14

Mehr threw open the front door and stepped outside the villa. There was a damp wind, but the rain had briefly stopped. Her boots squelched in the mud, furrowing up around her feet to her ankles. She pulled each foot out and carefully circled the house, peering under its foundations. She was unsure of what she was searching for. Perhaps a tunnel leading straight to the pits of hell.

She shoved the gate open and struggled around to the back garden. She squatted in front of the bushes and searched for the taweez, found the little mound of dirt where she'd laid it to rest. She clawed at the mud, winced as small pebbles pierced the tender skin under her fingernails, the wound on her palm straining. But it was gone. Instinctively she touched her chest. She stood and went back around to the front of the villa but slipped and fell in the frigid mud, landing roughly on her hip.

As she hauled herself up, wiping as much mud off her hands with her apron as possible, there was a noise above her. She was under Byron's large balcony. As she stared up, three women came into view, all leaning against the edge. Two were speaking to each other, and one accepted a glass of wine from Byron. He glanced down and made eye contact with Mehr, raising a glass to her.

She backed away and hid underneath the balcony. There was a foreboding feeling, like the fog lying over the lake, that pressed in on all sides of her. Usually there were scores of people out on their boats—those on holiday, intent on enjoying themselves no matter the weather. They often swam close to the shore to gape and point at Byron on his balcony. Yet what little she could see of the lake's surface was empty.

She carefully went back around the house and into the hall, dripping mud in with her. But cleaning wasn't her concern anymore.

There was a commotion coming from upstairs. She crossed the hall and followed the noise up to the men's gallery. Byron, Claire, and Lucy argued in the hall. She crept closer but remained in the shadows, unnoticed by the three of them.

"How will the children sleep with all this bedlam?" Lucy asked.

"His menagerie may stay in our chalet down the shore, but they are not to stay here," Claire said to him, her voice shaking.

Byron stared down at her. "Jealousy looks hideous on you."

"For the children's sake," Claire said, clasping her hands together as if she were prepared to beg.

Byron rolled his eyes. "I shall have whatever company I want. I do not belong to you," he said, and pointed in Claire's face. "Or to those brats."

Claire glanced over Byron's shoulder into the half-opened door behind him, but he moved in her way. He glared at Lucy. "Make sure there is enough food and drink for all of us."

Lucy planted her hands on her hips. "I don't work for you."

"Know your manners," Byron said sternly. His eyes flashed hot, and even Mehr shrank from them.

Lucy was also taken aback. She looked like she was on the verge of apologizing. Though her lips trembled, she kept silent.

"Do not forget yourself," Byron said. "Or I fear I will need to remind you of your place."

Lucy stalked down the gallery, then stopped abruptly when she saw Mehr, taking in her muddied clothes.

"When did they arrive?" Mehr asked.

Lucy scoffed. "Perhaps in the middle of the night, like the heathens they are." She had a deep frown on her face. "All this carousing and no one is thinking of the children. That man will ruin us all." She stomped down the stairs.

Claire began arguing anew with Byron, holding on to his hands, but he shoved her off. Before turning back to his room, he glared back at her.

"I thought you already knew how to share." He slammed the door in her face.

Claire's shoulders sagged as she hurried past Mehr, and with her tear-streaked eyes, she seemed not to notice her. Mehr wondered if she should stop to console the woman. But there were more pressing matters. The mud was drying into itchy scabs on her arms and legs, and she needed to get into warm, clean clothes before she caught a chill.

She wandered into the gallery and laid her ear against Byron's door. There were the distinct sounds of glassware tinkling and voices chattering coming from inside his room. One guttural laugh, then nothing more. She headed to the attic and changed out of her dirty clothes. As she rifled in her drawers, searching for a new cap, her hands found the mysterious woman's journal. She sighed and sat on her bed, flipped through the pages and landed on the drawing she'd seen before, the one of the vineyard from the point of view of the abandoned room. But something about it had changed. She pulled the page closer to her eyes.

In the drawing, the figure of the woman seemed to be fleeing past the vineyard and to the lake. It was just like in the painting. She flipped another few pages and found one that had been shaded with a rough pencil until it was all black—except for a scarred face emerging from within the darkness. She flipped again and landed on one more. It was the gallery in the women's wing. Each bedroom door was open. And from each, a pale face glared out at her.

Mehr gripped the journal tight in her hands and quickly headed downstairs. The dining parlour was empty, though piles of dirty dishes had been left behind. But there was a gathering elsewhere within the villa. She followed the sounds of conversation to the salon. Besides the villa's usual denizens, there were extra bodies in the room. Two women stood on either side of Byron, cheerily talking to each other.

She looked at their faces, their gleaming eyes, the skin on their hands. Their dresses shone with an ethereal, otherworldly light. She had never seen designs like these before—the cloth looked like it would have been laid out for a queen. Their smiles were empty, and like dolls, their eyes were lifeless. The salon had gotten hot, and the multitude of voices overwhelmed her. On top of that, the house continued its low, growling song. She found Polidori going from woman to woman, trying to stand close enough to assess something, pretending to fiddle with his trousers or shoe but bending low and close enough to gauge a heartbeat, Mehr realized. His behavior was earning Byron's distaste, and he shooed him away.

But Polidori wasn't the one she was looking for. The Shelleys sat together on a sofa, where Mary was engaged in conversation with a beautiful woman with thick chestnut hair. Percy nodded along but wasn't paying much attention to them. He discreetly smiled across the room to Byron, some unspoken secret dangling between them.

As Mehr approached the sofa, Byron swept forward, putting his arm around her waist and pulling her into his circle. His fingers dug into her side. Mehr flinched and instinctively placed her hand on top of his. He moved her in front of him to present her to the women he was talking to.

"Look at this!" Byron said. "A Hindostani bird flown all the way over the seas to be with us."

Everyone in the room stared at her like she was an exotic peacock chained to a post.

"Such an *interesting* complexion!" one of them declared, and reached out to touch her face. Mehr shuddered when the woman's icy fingertips grazed her ear. They were joined by the alluring woman who had been speaking to the Shelleys.

"How do you manage to surround yourself with such beauties?" the woman asked.

With Byron distracted, Mehr pulled herself free from his grasp.

"Ah, Lady Caroline," he said, kissing the woman's hand softly, lips touching her skin longer than was decent. "None more so than you." He pulled her close, nuzzled her ear.

"When did you arrive?" Mehr asked her.

Lady Caroline smiled at her, but it was all wrong. Too perfect. "Just this afternoon."

"I was out this afternoon and did not hear you arrive. Or the rest of you," Mehr said, staring at the other women.

Polidori was beside her in an instant. "The storms did not delay you?"

The strange women were giggling, patting their hair, beaming at him, a hint of malice in the glint of their teeth, which were brighter than Mehr had ever seen on an ordinary human. Hair so well coiffed that not one strand was out of place.

"These are my friends," Byron said.

"You mean former lovers," Polidori cut in.

"Former?" One of the women shrieked with laughter.

Polidori wrapped his fingers around Mehr's upper arm and led her to a corner of the room. She yanked herself away, tired now of being led like a show horse. When they were out of earshot, he leaned in.

"Automatons," he whispered furiously.

In spite of her confusion and the growing sense of unease caused by the strangers, Mehr stifled a laugh. "Automatons?"

"Look at them, they are perfect. Polished like fine silver. The knocking within the walls. The humming sound. It is a machine!"

Polidori's outburst caught Mary's attention from across the room. She looked up from her conversation with Byron and one of his women, and gave the two an odd look.

Mehr lowered her voice. "I have cleaned every room of this villa. I would know if there were an automaton factory here."

Polidori grimaced at her. Behind them, she heard a

small squabble. Percy was holding Mary's hand, pleading with her to stay.

"We are turning in," Byron said, yawning loudly. He put his arms around the two women and grinned at Lady Caroline. "You lead the way."

The strange woman gave him a coquettish grin and sashayed on ahead. As Byron headed out of the salon, he turned back to Percy. "Will you be joining?"

Percy dropped Mary's hand. He gave her a look like a child begging to be allowed to play with a new toy. Mary waved him away with an exasperated, loud sigh.

As he passed by, Byron glanced at Polidori. "You are not invited. You will bore them to sleep before we've even finished with them."

Percy and Byron laughed and left the parlour with their women. Mary wavered on the spot, rubbing her temples, then headed for the door. Polidori reached out to stop her.

"Your headache still persists?" he asked.

Mary nodded. "Have you anything stronger?"

"Indeed, though I fear it may be too strong for you."

"Do not condescend to me," Mary whispered to Polidori.

"Mrs. Shelley?" Mehr ventured forward, the journal in her quaking hands. "I must ask you something."

"Not now, Mehr," she said, then left the room.

There was a crack of thunder, and Mehr and Polidori both jumped. Through the parted curtain, the moon became obliterated by clouds. Lightning streaked over the lake. Another clap of thunder and the rain came hurtling down.

"Listen." Mehr pointed at the ceiling. The rain battered away. Within that noise, the hum of the villa vibrated, like a pair of vocal cords.

"She is trying to tell us something," Mehr said. "We need to listen to her."

Polidori rolled his eyes. "Your lady of the villa." But still, he looked up to where Mehr pointed.

"She wrote it all down. Look!" She rifled through the pages for the illustrations, but when she noticed Polidori had averted his attention, she gave up at once. Desperate, she felt time slipping away from her, pushing her further and further from home. If not the deranged doctor, then someone else had to help her—Mary, perhaps, who'd grown more remote since joining Byron's circle, but who still seemed trustworthy enough to Mehr.

She stalked out of the room and into the hallway. As she made her way to the stairs, she stopped in her tracks. The pregnant woman was slowly making her way up, one step at a time. She appeared to glow of her own spectral light. Mehr held her breath and watched her turn the corner to the gallery. Mehr inched her way up, held back as far as she could.

When she made it to the top of the stairs, she saw Mary's door was ajar. She crept closer and peeked in. Mary sat in front of the hearth, a book in her lap, her eyes closed. There was a faraway smile on her face. The pregnant woman stood above her, combing her hair. She ran her pallid fingers through it, then trailed them down to Mary's chin and tilted her face up. The woman leaned in and gave her a soft kiss on the forehead.

"What has you so vexed?" the figure asked Mary. Her voice was warped and low, nearly inaudible.

"I began a new novel, but I feel no inspiration as of late."

"Perhaps I can help," the woman said. "What is it about?"

Mary sat up, smiled eagerly at the woman. "A man of science who uses it to be God. In pursuit of creation, though it is most injurious to the ones he loves."

"A modern Prometheus," the woman murmured.

Mary touched the woman's hand. "Will this be a passing moment? Or will you be here forever?"

The woman stroked her head. "I am wherever you want me to be, Mary."

Her voice was like a whisper from where Mehr stood. Mehr sucked in her breath when the door creaked from her moving closer to it. But they appeared not to hear.

"The man wishes to bring the dead to life," Mary said. "What if I could? Would you want to come back to me?"

The woman laughed to herself and began humming a song. Mehr realized she was humming along with the house, rising with it, falling with it, all while raking her cadaverous fingers through Mary's hair.

Slowly, the two turned in unison to stare at Mehr. Mary's eyes were bright, awash in tears. But there was something else too. Something missing from her gaze. Something lost. The pregnant woman tucked her chin in and smiled at Mehr, the fire creating two bright pinpricks of light in her eyes. She placed a thin, pale finger to her lips, pressed down gently.

Mehr backed away, and as the woman's smile faded, the door softly shut on its own. She moved quickly back through the gallery, down the stairs, and to the abandoned room. She threw open the door and was alarmed to see a large fire roaring in the hearth. She stalked up to the painting and held up the journal.

"Do you know what is happening to us? Why we are being plagued by these strange visitors?" Mehr asked.

The woman in the painting was frozen in mid-flight, still trying to make her way to the lake.

"Why do you not tell me?"

She slammed her fist down on the painting. The frame wobbled and slipped to the floor. She stepped back as it fell face up. The fire crackled in the hearth, casting long shadows onto the painting, making it seem like the figure was moving, getting closer to the lake.

"You escaped," she whispered. "That was the only way you could save yourself."

She ran to the front entrance of the villa. She hesitated at the door, thought of the others trapped with the unnatural strangers in the house. But she waited only a brief moment. She pulled the door open to the roiling mist and heavy rain. Bolts of lightning illuminated the path outside. Without another glance back, she hurried out into the rain. It was colder than she'd thought it would be. Water dribbled down her collarbone and snaked its way into her ears. She struggled down the lane without a lantern, using only the weak lights from the villa's windows and the lightning to guide her way.

Mehr stopped to wipe the rain from her eyes and hurried on, but the mist blanketed her and she suddenly found herself standing in several feet of water. She took a few steps back, just as a sudden wave crashed into her. As she flailed in the water trying to find her footing, she was deeply submerged and there was no way for her to see where she was drowning. Her lungs squeezed under the pressure as she reached and reached. For something, anything. She couldn't hold her breath anymore and screamed, felt the ice-cold water enter her lungs.

But there was something pushing against her. Her hands ran over a hard wooden surface. She banged her fists against it, frantic to find a way out. She felt a round object like a doorknob and pulled it hard, her mind spinning and giving way to the darkness.

The sound of rain brought her back. She was crouched in the doorway of the villa, coughing up water. Her lungs burned as she took in deep breaths. Someone had a hold of her shoulders. She screamed and wrestled them off.

It was Polidori, attempting to throw his coat over her. She shoved him away and ran back outside. But moments later, she was drowning in the dark. The door appeared within her reach, and she pushed it open to return to the villa, spewing even more water from her lungs. Polidori was there again, shaking her hard by her shoulders. He dragged her inside and shut the door.

She collapsed on the floor, shivering uncontrollably. This time she allowed him to cover her. He threw his arms around her, rubbing her back, smacking at her cheeks, attempting to revive her. But the cold had reached her bones; it had a firm grip on her now.

He laid his chin on top of her head. "What in the devil were you doing?"

"Escaping," she managed.

Polidori let out a laugh. "A poor attempt. You ran out in the rain only to return drenched every time."

The trail of water running down her face was no longer the rain. She realized why the figure in the painting was stuck, neither making it to Leman nor back in her chair inside the room.

Polidori brushed the wetness from her face.

"I worried you might never return," he said.

"It did not let me leave."

"It?" Polidori asked.

Mehr sat up, Polidori's coat sliding down her shoulders. "You must listen to me. It will not let any of us go."

"The automatons?" he asked.

Mehr gripped his face in her hands. "Diodati."

THOUGH POLIDORI HAD given her several drops of laudanum, Mehr didn't sleep. The coldness still hadn't left her. She lay awake in her bed as the rain battered against the window. Below her in the house, there were too many new bodies occupying the space. The children, Byron's women, and Mary's mother. She could feel them moving around their rooms like ants crawling on her skin.

She had thought she was going mad like her mother, but it seemed the madness had reached all of them. Even Polidori. His theory of automatons was still less sensible than what was running through her mind. They were all damned, and now so was she.

Mehr had trouble remembering what day it was, what month. It felt like they'd been in the villa for years. She rolled over in her bed, squeezed her fists to her eyes. She was meant to return home, to the safety and warmth of the zenana. She was trapped now, stuck forever, a pretty bird in a gilded tomb.

Her chest heaved as she fought back tears, but it was too late. She was sobbing now, thinking of Amma lying alone in her bed, her eyes staring into nothing. She needed a mother's warm and protective embrace. For the first time, she wished she was with her. Perhaps lying beside her, being held by her. But Mehr was alone. And she'd die alone too. She spent the rest of the night trapped in the odd state between sleep and consciousness.

In the morning, she crept down from the attic to conduct her own search of the villa. In the gallery, she stopped and listened at each of the doors. But all was silent within the rooms. She took the stairs one at a time, waiting for the reason for their madness to appear. Yet she was mostly alone. As she approached the front hall, she noticed the door was open a few inches. It creaked in the wind but wouldn't open further. Mehr peeked out and found Claire standing on the other side, staring out at the rain. She flinched when she realized someone was behind her.

"I went for a walk," Claire said. "But I cannot seem to get very far."

"You cannot leave." Mehr reached for her. "Come inside."

"Not with all his women surrounding him," Claire said.

Mehr didn't know which man she was talking about.

"You envy the wrong things," Mehr said.

Claire scoffed. "How would you know? Look at you."

Mehr looked down at her maid's uniform and back at Claire's pretty, ruffled dress. Yet she still felt richer than Claire, far more privileged, because she was going to find a way out of the villa and leave the others behind to be lured into Byron's damned machinations. No one was worthy of being saved, she realized, and she would be the one to save herself.

"I am merely a housemaid," Mehr said. "I know nothing of loneliness or despair."

Claire sighed and finally looked at her. "It can be lonely being in love with the wrong man."

"But you have Mrs. Shelley," Mehr said.

"It can be even lonelier having a sister who hates the sight of you," Claire said. "I brought them all here, I brought them together. Was I recognized for it?" She absentmindedly touched her stomach. "I have fulfilled my duties to all of them yet have been cast out. And here I am, staring out at the rain, with you."

Mehr had the sudden urge to push her into the fog, to see if she would return drenched and choking on lake water as well. Instead, Claire headed back inside, just as Polidori was making his way to the front door. He pushed past, hardly noticing them, and held the door wide open.

"I hope you will oblige me in removing yourselves immediately," he said.

Mehr followed his gaze to two strange men. One had a crutch and was missing half his shin below the knee. The other walked beside him, his head tilted at an unusual angle, a large scar scribbled underneath his jaw and running the length of his neck. The sight of it shocked Mehr. She'd never seen an injured man in such a state. She'd never had the opportunity, sheltered and lovingly cloistered as she'd lived before. In spite of the manners she'd been raised with, she could not stop staring.

Claire backed away, her handkerchief against her mouth, and let out a muffled cry. The two men shuffled to the door but wouldn't step in. They stared at Polidori.

"I thought you might be happy to see us," the man with the scar said.

"I would be perfectly glad never to see you again," Polidori responded, his voice shaking. He pointed at the door. "Leave."

The wounded men stood outside, side by side, staring out at the rain the way Mehr and Claire had moments ago.

Polidori shut the door and stomped back down the hall.

"Who were they?" Claire asked, following after him. "Wh-why did they look like that?"

"Former patients of mine," Polidori said.

Claire persisted. "Why were you rude to them?"

"Rude?" Polidori asked, his voice high-pitched. He brusquely moved the hair out of his eyes. "They cannot care for manners if they are already dead."

Claire stopped in her tracks, unsure of what he'd just said. Polidori turned to Mehr.

"They appeared to me in my room moments ago and expected me to be relieved to see them reanimated."

Mehr gave him a puzzled look. Percy's children and Byron's women all looked pristine and unsullied. Far too perfect to be human. Even Mary's mother's skin shone like white ceramic. None of them had seen any trouble or sorrow. But if these men were also strange creations that Diodati was spewing out, why hadn't it made them as immaculate and faultless?

Polidori stalked away, and both Mehr and Claire followed him as he headed for the dining parlour. Byron and Percy had congregated with their guests over a breakfast spread.

"I have let this go on far too long," Polidori said, then turned to Byron and the three women huddled behind him as he ate. "They are not real people!" He pointed at both of Percy's children sitting in his lap. "Neither are those children of yours."

Percy hugged them close. "Beg your pardon? Have you gone mad?"

Mehr stared at the children, at the women. She realized they all, including the pregnant woman who was doting on Mary, shared the same peculiar trait.

"Look," she said, pointing over Polidori's shoulder. "Look at their clothes."

Though Byron's women stood still, there was movement on their bodies. The cloth of their dresses moved in ripples against them like they were underwater. It was subtle and noticeable only if one took the time and care to look for it, but it was there on the children as well.

Percy looked to what she was pointing at and quickly set the children down.

"It is Diodati," Polidori said. "Churning them out like a machine. Automatons. Bringing the dead back to us whether we want them or not."

"Good God," Percy shrieked. "My children are not dead!" He pulled his children into a tight embrace.

"They have no heartbeats!" Polidori yelled back. It was the first time Mehr had ever heard him truly raise his voice.

Percy hesitated, then laid his head on his son's chest. His face turned pale, his lips swollen like he was on the verge of tears. He glanced from child to child as they innocently stared back up. One of them reached for his hand, and he reluctantly took it.

Polidori stepped closer, eyes on Byron. "And your women do not have heartbeats either."

"You stupid man." Byron laughed aloud, then his eyes darkened. "Of course they don't."

CHAPTER 15

The stillness in the room made the walls' hum even louder. Byron pulled Lady Caroline into his lap.

"And no, they are not dead," he said. "Her ladyship is perfectly well and alive. But this one here is something else. As perfect as a memory." He bent his face in Lady Caroline's undone hair and took in a deep breath. "Like the first time I gathered her intoxicating scent. It is how she speaks to me, how she loves me. So different from the real Lady Caroline Lamb. The difference I always wanted."

He glared at Polidori. "I know they are artificial, and I want them here all the same."

Percy wept as he held the children to his chest. The little boy began to cry as well. Mehr realized Mary was the only person not in the dining room. She turned back to the hall and found her standing in the darkness, her mother one step behind her, holding her hand.

"It is Diodati," Mary said, echoing Polidori's words. "It

is giving us what we want. Whom we want." She peered in at the others, then at Claire.

Polidori stared back at her. "That is exactly what I said."

"Not automatons, you fool," Byron said. "Something else entirely."

Claire drifted into the doorway, gaze fixed on Mary.

"Would you like to meet my mother?" Mary asked, her voice tender.

Claire let out a soft cry. She threw her arms around Mary, weeping against her shoulder. Mary held Claire's face in her hands, softly kissed her cheek. "It is a gift. For all of us."

Percy stroked the tops of his children's heads. "I have wanted so badly to hold them again."

Byron chuckled and shrugged, gave Lady Caroline a long kiss. "I might never leave this house again," he said.

"And you," Mary said to Polidori. "A chance to ask for forgiveness."

Polidori bristled. Mehr touched his arm, and he visibly relaxed.

"I did not *ask* for forgiveness, nor do I want it," he said. "I never wanted to see them again."

"Are you certain?" Mary asked, her voice sounding far away.

"You suggest this house knows better than I?" Polidori asked.

"It knows everything," Mehr said quietly to him. "Whether we want it to or not."

Mary held a hand out to her mother, then took Claire's in her other and began to lead them away.

"Find Berger," Mary said to Mehr over her shoulder. "Our guests are hungry. Make sure we give them a good feed."

FOR THREE DAYS, no one attempted to leave the villa. Not one of them missed their long rambles among the vineyards, their trips to the lake, the carriage rides over the mountains, the traipses through the village.

Byron was entertained endlessly by his women. While Percy partook in his carousing, Mary paid no mind to him, nor to her son, who had fully become Lucy's ward along with Percy's children, causing a minor tiff with Robert. Instead, Mary happily distracted herself with her mother, spent hours walking around the rooms with her and Claire, who herself was a changed creature. She'd come back out of her shell, transforming into the vivacious young woman Mehr had first met. She'd found her voice again. Some color had returned to her cheeks, and the gauntness in her face seemed to be filling back in. Perhaps her body was settling around her, around the child growing inside her, like the villa was settling around them all.

Mehr realized why no apparitions had appeared for Claire—the people she desired already existed under the same roof, but the one whose affections she sought the most was finally granting them.

Polidori kept to his room. His two former patients

lingered in the house, stood in the shadows, unable to leave but not able to pursue Polidori either.

Mehr completely removed herself to the abandoned room. She'd taken a strong devotion to it, cleaning it every morning, lighting the fire, wiping dust off the portrait frame. She knew the lady of the villa would look kindly upon her for doing so. And when the time was right, she'd keep Mehr safe, explain away everything, and help her find her way out. The thought made her breath catch. She'd be able to leave Diodati. She'd return home. But she had to placate the woman first to be set free. Then she would decide whom she would save along with herself.

One evening, when she brought dinner up to Polidori and placed the tray outside his room as she usually did, he opened the door and peered out. There was sparse, dark stubble on his young face. He wore a wrinkled shirt that Mehr realized he had not changed out of for days.

"Are you alone?" he asked.

She nodded.

Polidori looked both ways down the gallery, but didn't reach for his dinner. "They are still here?"

"All of them," Mehr said.

He ran a hand through his disheveled hair. "I cannot continue to live like this."

She glanced past him into his room. Candles covered nearly every surface.

"The darkness. It frightens me," he said, following her

gaze. She was reminded of how young he was. Only one and twenty, several years younger than Mehr.

"I will not go out there and be surrounded by those . . . things," he said.

"Then you will remain in this room for God knows how long?"

He sucked in his breath. "We must find a way to leave."

"I have tried and failed," Mehr said. "I have searched every room for a tunnel, every wardrobe for a secret passage. There is no escape. Nowhere to go."

"Fool, fool," he muttered to himself, resting his forehead against the door. "Just my fate, to be wretched forever."

There was a creak in the hallway. Polidori flinched and glanced out into the darkness. Then he picked up his dinner and beckoned her into his room. She obliged and entered, found his room stuffy with the overwhelming smell of candle wax. Behind her, Polidori gave one last peek in the gallery before shutting the door.

He pushed pages of his manic scrawls off the table and sat down to eat. "I have been thinking about Diodati. It is replaying our memories for us. Conjuring people from our minds."

Mehr banished the thought of her mother. "I confess I do not know how it is happening. But you must stop hiding—"

"I am not hiding." Polidori frowned at her, his mouth full. "I do not want to conjure up any of my memories. You do not know what I have seen."

He stopped eating and swallowed hard. "Perhaps we shall be stuck here forever," he said with a dark laugh, which was interrupted by a sudden thump from above them.

They stared up at the ceiling in silence, waited for something more. Then a scream in the hall distracted them. Mehr was the first to run to the door. She pried it open and ran out into the gallery, leaving Polidori at his table, his mouth hanging open in shock. Lucy was on the floor at the bottom of the attic stairs, cowering against the wall. She was pointing up into the attic and crying while Robert stood over her, perplexed. Her wails were long and searing. The noise brought Byron and Shelley out of their rooms and down the gallery. They converged on Robert, roughly yanking him away from her.

Lucy crawled to Mehr and hugged her around her waist, trembling. The young woman's tears and snot were ruining Mehr's apron, and she looked to Robert for help.

"Did you do something to her?" Percy asked, suddenly a gallant. He puffed out his chest and shook Robert by his collar.

"No," Robert said. "We were only—"

"What are you crying about?" Byron glared down at Lucy, a look of distaste evident on his face.

"I saw him, I saw him," she said, her voice muffled by Mehr's clothes. She began to cry anew.

Mehr pulled the woman off and held her by the shoulders.

"Who did you see?" Mehr asked.

"I saw him!" She pointed again at the attic stairs, a look of terror on her face. "He was in the room. And his arms . . ." She shivered. "He had no arms!"

"There was blood gushing from his body," Robert said, seeming to choke back vomit. "Blood everywhere."

Percy looked about the hallway. "Where are my children?"

Lucy cried uncontrollably while Percy bore down on her. "Where are they?"

"With your wife," Robert hissed, pushing him away from her.

"Blood, blood," Lucy said, hugging herself tightly. "He was bleeding all over his clothes, all over me!" She looked down and shrieked, started to rub her clean clothes.

Byron and Shelly shared a glance, then valiantly made their way up the stairs. Their footsteps scuffled above as they walked the length of the attic. Lucy whimpered at their feet, and Mehr and Robert stood tense in the gallery. She stared at him, at the way he opened and closed his fists.

"It was her father," Robert said, his voice coming out hoarse.

"He said . . . it was my fault," Lucy said.

Robert knelt and wrapped his arms around Lucy as she lay against his chest. Mehr recalled the time he had come to fetch her from the lakeside chalet. He had seemed so stern to her, so unmoved. Perhaps the way Byron had wanted him to be. But Lucy had softened him. He'd started to bring levity to their gatherings, whistling as he polished the silverware or set the table, poking at Berger with silly jokes to make the taciturn cook laugh.

Mehr's thoughts were interrupted by a shout from above. A heavy object crashed onto the floor. Lucy screamed, pulling at Robert's clothes. Something, whether it was the commotion upstairs or Lucy's piercing cries, summoned Polidori from his room at last. He came running down the gallery to the group assembled there, but before he could say anything, Percy and Byron bounded down the stairs, laughing pitiably.

"Oh, look at your faces!" Percy said.

Byron gave a mean smirk. "And you, Polidori. Was that your womanish scream I heard?"

"Did you see him?" Robert asked, his face flushed.

Percy laughed again, but it was twisted and cruel, not unlike Byron's. "There was nothing there," he said.

Lucy viciously shook her head and pointed at the stairs. "No, no. He is up there! My father!"

Byron rolled his eyes, then glared at Robert. "Take her to her room. The noise is hurting my head."

Robert picked Lucy up off the floor and led her down the gallery. He kissed the top of her head, murmured something to soothe her. Percy and Byron retreated to the latter's room, loudly shutting the door behind them.

When Mehr and Polidori were alone again, she cleared her throat and her voice came out raw. "He had an accident on their farm when she was young. The horses tore his arms off."

"She told you?"

Mehr nodded. "It never left her. The grief."

Polidori rubbed at his bristled chin. "'As perfect as a memory.'"

"And this was a bad one," Mehr said. "Perhaps she always thought it was her fault."

Polidori nodded. "The house is bringing him back to her but in such a horrific state." He turned his head to the side, listening for something. "Who is cooking our meals?"

"Berger." When he didn't immediately respond, she shook her head. "He is not poisoning us. We might all be dead by now."

"I am not saying poison," Polidori said. Then he lowered his voice and added, "Perhaps we are being influenced."

"Influenced?" Mehr asked.

"When I first met you, I told you I was here to document his lordship's travels. I am, but I am also his personal physician. I procure and administer all of his . . . tonics."

"And what of your literary plans?" Mehr asked. "Might not that be the reason for his company?"

Polidori sighed and looked away. "I am his physician first and foremost. He happily reminds me on a daily basis. His lordship enjoys laudanum and opium on a steady schedule. I fear he may be using it to influence us."

Mehr admitted to herself that it wasn't the first time she'd sensed the diabolical in Byron. The way he seemed to peer right through to her thoughts, the inner workings of all their minds. The Lord had insisted they all stay at the villa, then immediately shut them up in it. He'd hardly blinked at the sight of blood the times he'd seen it and had been fully aware of what the apparitions were before anyone else figured them out.

"Might one man be responsible for all these apparitions?" Mehr asked.

"To fight his incessant boredom, he would do anything." Polidori unclenched his jaw. "We are his playthings, after all."

He staggered toward the stairs. Mehr followed him down to the kitchen, where he banged the dirtied pots around, glanced in jars, opened cupboards, and sniffed inside the hearth. She stood back and watched him in his mania, unable to help him. If the Lord was behind all of it, she didn't think it was through temporal means. She already had an idea of what a brute he was to those he called his friends. She wondered what else he could be capable of.

She left Polidori to his search. Outside the kitchen, her path was blocked by Lady Caroline Lamb, who was cradling a glass of wine in one hand. The woman glared at her, then gave her a waxen smile. It was as if her lips were doing it for the first time. There was a strain on her face and a tic in one eye.

"If you'll allow, I must be on my way," Mehr said.

Lady Caroline eyed her back, and Mehr realized she hadn't blinked since the moment they'd walked into each other. Mehr took her time circling the woman, taking in her perfectly coiffed hair, impossibly smooth skin, the dullness to her eyes. Her clothes rustled, moved on their own as if she were standing in a room full of water.

"How is he doing it?" Mehr asked.

Lady Caroline giggled and took a long gulp of wine. "The way you all have been doing it," she said, then tsked. "Your beauty is being wasted here." She reached for Mehr's face. Her fingers were like ice on her chin. "A pity you were born the way you were."

"I pity *you*," Mehr said.

The woman continued to grin at her, but there was a confused look in her eyes.

"You are not the real Lady Caroline Lamb. You are a memory of her. You will never live. Never feel what it is to be a woman. To be alive."

At this Lady Caroline turned her lips downward and stared at her wineglass. "I am serving my purpose," she said as she slowly tipped the glass forward. The wine sloshed out and splattered onto the floor. "Now you can serve yours."

The woman drew nearer to her. There was a small cut in her bottom lip. As if reading Mehr's mind, Lady Caroline stuck out the tip of her tongue to touch it. "We will draw them out," she said. "Your demons. I can feel them swimming around inside of you."

Mehr glanced away from her lifeless stare. Caroline thrust the empty wineglass into Mehr's hand and headed down the hall to the library. Mehr looked to the spilled wine. It pooled like blood. She could not do the phantom woman's bidding, but the lady of the villa would be disappointed in her. For her sake, she retrieved a rag and bucket and mopped up the wine, as Polidori stormed out of the kitchen and down the hall to some other useless pursuit.

After, she threw the rag into the bucket and sat on the floor, placed her back against the wall. The deadness in Caroline's eyes. The way she was inebriating Byron, leaving him even more senseless than he usually was of his substances and intoxicants. The same could be said for Mary's mother. She'd removed Mary from the others, lulled her into a sense of childlike obeisance.

It was taking too long to wait on the lady of the villa. She had to know what was in the journals. She shored up her courage and headed upstairs to Mary's room. Before she could knock on the door, though, she found it was already open.

She stepped into the sitting room and glanced at the writing table. A new manuscript sat on top of it. It was a healthy number of pages, more than she'd seen since Mary had written, then discarded, *Hate*. Mehr realized this was the most prolific Mary had been with her writing since they had departed from England.

As she passed the table, the light from the fireplace flickered onto the stack of papers, and Mehr could just make out the words scrawled across the top page: "I have love in me the likes of which you can scarcely imagine and rage the likes of which you would not believe."

Though she could not fully comprehend them, Mehr

shuddered at the words. She turned away and headed to the bedroom, where she found Mary sitting on the edge of her bed, facing the window.

"Mrs. Shelley?"

Mary turned to her, sat up a little and brightened.

"I feel I have not seen you in years," she said in her faraway voice.

Gingerly, Mehr pulled the journal from her pocket and approached Mary. "I need your help, Mrs. Shelley." She held it out to her. Mary gave a small glance at it, then turned back to the window.

"Please," Mehr said, her hands trembling. "It is the only thing to explain what is happening to us all."

"Beg your pardon?" Mary turned to her, and Mehr was surprised to see her glaring. "Explain what?"

"The apparitions. Your mother. The children. All of it."

"I do not wish for any explanations," Mary said.

Mehr sank to her knees in front of her. She thrust the journal at her. "It has happened before. To the lady of the villa. She was trapped here like us."

Mary stood and placed her hands on the windowsill. Her breath fogged the glass. "I do not feel trapped."

"But you are. We all are! We must make it stop, and this"—Mehr said, pointing to the journal now in Mary's hands—"will help us find a way out."

Mary turned and glanced at something over her own shoulder. Mehr followed the direction of Mary's gaze to a dark corner of the room.

"I have everything I need," Mary said.

Mehr thought she saw a figure move within the shadows. The darkness swirled around a dark object. But when she blinked, there was nothing there. Mary absentmindedly scratched her neck, her finger moving in a circle, round and round and round. The humming grew from a lull. It was all around her now.

Mehr picked herself up off the floor and hurried out of the room, leaving Mary and the journal behind. As she ran down the gallery to the attic stairs, a hand reached out from the darkness and grabbed her. She yelped and fought against it, thinking it was an apparition. But it was Byron who had a firm grip on her.

"You ignored me all day," he said, the wine heavy on his breath.

She was taken aback by the fervent desire in his eyes and immediately stopped struggling.

"You are pretending like you don't know me," he said.

"My lord, I do not know you." She held her breath as the man moved closer to her. In the half darkness, the devilish glint in his eyes was far too alluring.

"You came to me last night. Slunk into my room. The things you did to me."

"I did no such thing!" Mehr said forcefully. "I have never been in your room."

He looked at her, his eyes downcast. "Now, I do not easily get my heart broken."

In an instant he had his hands on her waist and was

drawing her in. He pressed his lips to hers. Mehr was overwhelmed and didn't exactly resist him. She'd be a liar if she were to claim she hadn't imagined variations of this moment. All too easily she yielded to his embrace.

He suddenly pulled away with a confused look on his face. He let go of her and brushed his fingers against his lips. "But it was you?"

Mehr couldn't speak as she caught her breath. She wanted him to kiss her again, to be touched so fiercely, but he was staring at the wall opposite them, lost in thought. She reached for him, but he swept past and headed down the stairs, muttering to himself.

What had she done? A stupid, stupid thing. Momentarily lost herself in the one man the whole of the villa was in thrall to. Whom they thought more brilliant than perhaps he deserved. Though his mind *was* dazzling, his spirit was rotten. And she'd succumbed to it just as easily as the others. Even she couldn't break free from the spell he had on them all.

She fled to Polidori's bedroom door and beat against it with her fists. He opened it in alarm, holding a candlestick up to ward off an attack. He was shirtless, and a single layer of sweat lay over his young chest. She placed a hand against his glistening skin. After a few breaths, he placed his hand on top of hers, then drew it to his face, brushed it against his lips. Before she could change her mind, she wrapped her arms around him and kissed him ferociously. The candlestick clattered to the floor.

Just as she'd yielded so easily to Byron, so Polidori gave in to her.

When she pulled away, it was no longer the young doctor who stood before her but Mary. Mehr looked at her mistress with surprise and confusion, but her reticence was short-lived as the door swung open to her deepest desires. Holding Mary like this felt familiar to her, in a way Mehr recalled from a distant dream.

Mary's hair grew brighter in the candlelight. She had a deep, irresistible blush to her cheeks, and she let Mehr go, turned her around. Mehr was powerless to her touch as Mary kissed the back of her neck, then untied Mehr's apron from around her waist. Mehr's intense heartbeats choked her breaths. Mary pulled her dress off and encircled Mehr in her milky arms. She turned back to Mary, pressed her lips against her, felt the softness give way to a sudden, sharp bite on her lower lip.

Together they toppled over onto the bed. When Mehr opened her eyes, it was Byron who lay on top of her. Gently, he moved a stray hair away from her temple. "You are beautiful," he whispered as he pulled the rest of Mehr's layers off, one tantalizing bit after the other. She felt exposed suddenly as he ran his hands from her rib cage to her breasts, then circled his hand around her neck.

Mehr tilted her head back, let him grip her throat however he wanted, but his touch became light. He was Mary again, her tresses rolling down over her shoulder and softly tickling Mehr's collarbones. Mehr reached up and cupped Mary's cheek in her hand. A tear rolled down the side of Mehr's face, and Mary moved closer to brush it away with her lips, her breath heavy in Mehr's ears. Gently, Mary took each of Mehr's hands and pinned them up over her head. Mehr instinctively wrapped her thighs around her.

Mary kissed her again, but Mehr could tell she'd changed to Polidori. His kisses were gentler, artful. When his caresses changed to Byron's, she nearly lost her breath. He rolled her over, took her from behind, dug his nails into her hips until she screamed. His grip relaxed, and she rolled over, climbed onto Polidori's lap. As she moved against him, he wrapped his arms around her and held on to her for dear life. And then it was Mary. She was romantic, full of raw passion. She laid Mehr back down, trailed her lips down her navel to the most tender part of her, where her heart beat strongest.

And so it went. Byron was rough with her, greedy with her body. Polidori was hungry for her touch. And Mary would slow the two men down, take her time with Mehr. The evening's minutes stretched into hours as one by one the three of them brought Mehr to ecstasy.

Afterward, Mehr lay on her side staring at Mary, at the illusory way her hair glowed in the candlelight. Mary reached over and placed a hand on one of Mehr's breasts. Slowly Polidori's form returned. Mehr sighed and moved away from him, lay on her back and stared up at the ceiling.

"Was it your first time?" he asked after a while.

She wondered at the question. It was a first for many things, sure. But the first time sharing her bed? She shook her head. There had been many an errand boy losing himself in the zenana. While the other women kept themselves hidden in purdah, she'd sneak into the darkness and pull them into her room, have her way with them. She didn't need to ask him to know that for him, it was.

"Who did you see? The most?" Polidori asked.

She tightened her lips into a hard line, but he moved closer to her and gently turned her face.

"I think you know," she said softly. "They were the same for both of us."

He sighed and touched his sweaty forehead to hers. Then he let out a sheepish laugh. "Are you real?" he asked. "Am I?"

"Would it matter?" Mehr asked.

She moved away and sat up, began to dress herself as Polidori watched.

"We will die here," he said.

She stopped to stare at him. "I hope when I truly die, it will be after a night like this."

Polidori crawled back to her just as she was pulling her dress on. He laid his head on her chest, placed an arm around her waist. Like a child, Mehr thought.

He looked up at her, chin digging into her ribs. "You are alive. I can hear your heart."

She pulled herself from his embrace and went to leave, but Polidori had quickly thrown on his breeches and reached out to hold her hand. He looked like he wanted to kiss her, say something more. She gave him an impassive look, and an understanding was forged between them. He nervously threw open his door, moved aside for her to leave.

"Good night, Doctor," she whispered, and left him standing in the candlelight.

In the attic, Mehr undressed for bed. Her body was a mingling of scents and odors, and she hated herself for enjoying it. She reached out and touched the wall, felt the light pulses of the villa grow stronger. The humming rose up. It sounded like the house was acquiring language, playing with vowels and consonants. It wanted to speak to her.

She stood on her knees and pressed the front of her body to the wall. The house vibrated through her, rattling her teeth. Mehr spread out her arms, realized quite sheepishly that she was hugging the wall. She listened as hard as she could, but the house didn't make its intentions clear.

A wave of tiredness overtook her. Mehr reluctantly moved back to her bed and slipped under the covers. The humming arose from the walls, and Mehr was lulled in its arms to a gentle, restful sleep.

MEHR SHOOK AWAKE to the chiming of the clock. It was three in the afternoon. She'd been sleeping through the mornings, waking later and later. And now she'd slept even longer. There was a queer sensation that she wasn't alone in the attic either. When she rolled out of bed and peered around the corner, Robert stood over one of the empty beds, where Lucy lay asleep.

He was muttering something insensible when he looked up and flinched at the sight of Mehr.

Mehr took a closer look at the sleeping form, at Lucy's young, pale face. She waited for her to blink, to sit up demurely and cover her bare breasts. But she lay still, her lifeless pallor taking on a yellow tinge

Mehr took a step back from Robert, from the crazed way he rubbed at his face.

"What have you done?" she said.

Robert turned away from the sight, sagging against the wall for support, hastily wiping away his tears. "Nothing at all. When I should have done more."

"Is she—"

"I don't know, I don't know," Robert said as a tear trailed out of an eye.

"How long has she been like this?" Mehr asked.

Robert wouldn't meet her eyes. "Hours, perhaps?"

"You must get the doctor," Mehr said. Though she spoke calmly, her body quaked, and she waited until Robert had headed down the stairs to approach the bed. She touched Lucy's hand. It was colder than the lake water, colder than empty corners of the villa. A cold like she'd never felt before and that she knew she'd never forget.

Polidori stomped up the steps, his shirt creased, hair in complete disarray. He'd brought a medical bag and was so intent on finding Lucy that he nearly didn't see Mehr watching him from the corner of the room.

He bent over the body and inspected her. Touched her wrists, cradled her head in his hands. He produced a small mirror from his bag and held it up to her nose. Then he stared up at Robert. "Were you the one who found her?"

"It was Berger. He found her at the front door, and we both brought her in together."

Polidori stood. "Show me your hands," he said.

"What?" His voice trembled.

"I said show me your hands."

"Are you accusing me of something, Doctor?" Robert's voice shook.

Mehr approached Robert, placed a comforting hand on his upper back. Polidori flushed at the sight of her but quickly composed himself.

"Show him your hands," Mehr said, attempting to soothe the man, though her body trembled as Lucy's corpse lay just in the corner of her eye. "You have nothing to hide."

Robert did as he was told. Polidori took his time examining Robert's fingernails and palms. Once he was finished, Polidori bent down and covered Lucy's body with a sheet.

"I should have kept a better watch on her," Robert said. "She was troubled and I abandoned her."

"A natural death." Polidori stared hard at the floor. "There is nothing you could have done."

"But what do I do now?" He began to cry in earnest, covering his face with his hands.

"Go down to the kitchen and have something strong to drink," Polidori said.

"How can I leave her like this?" Robert asked.

"We will take care of her," Mehr said.

Robert nodded slowly, then took one laborious step after another to the stairs. Mehr watched him go, then turned to Polidori, who had a dark look on his face.

"She has been murdered," Polidori said softly.

"Murder?" Mehr stared at Lucy's twisted body under the sheets. "But you insisted it was a natural death."

"I said that to *him* because I have not ruled him out as the one behind it," Polidori said.

"It was not Robert. He is kind, gentle. He could never." She thought hard, resisted the urge to chew on her nails. "It was the apparitions behind this."

Polidori shook his head. "They have been preoccupied serving their new masters."

"It is them. Your vampires that feed from the living," Mehr said. "No human could have done this."

"There are marks of strangulation around her neck."

"Because his lordship is the one controlling them," Mehr said.

Polidori frowned. "Lord Byron?"

Mehr wrung her hands. It was logical in her mind, but Polidori was making her seem like she had lost all sense. "He hears and sees everything. At times I think he can read my mind. He knew about his lifeless women all along. And last night . . ." She laid her hand on her chest, became breathless for a moment. "I believe that was a part of his game too."

Polidori turned from the window, leaned against the pane and looked at Mehr. "I know he is a corrupt man. But I do not think he is capable of murder. Why would he risk his title, his peerage?"

"He cares little for propriety."

"He says these things. He does not believe it. He cares very much what society thinks of him. It is why he is here and no longer in England. The scandal with his sister Augusta, their rumored child, has forced him to escape to the Continent."

So that was the "Aug" he had written such an impassioned letter to, Mehr thought. The one the hotel guests were gossiping about. The subject of his frenzied, obsessive scrawls. He was clearly in love with her. She felt too disgusted to speak, but she went on.

"He is a brute. He tortures all of you, *especially* you. He mocks and ridicules. You believe he drugs our food."

"He has not been drugging our food," Polidori said.

"You are defending him."

Polidori met her eyes. "I am saying I found no evidence of it."

"But he has proven to be far more fiendish than that," Mehr said. "Since he dragged us into this house, we have all been taking part in some devilish experiment of his."

He began placing his medical equipment back into the bag. "If you think he is the one responsible for all of this, how is he doing it?" Polidori asked.

"I suppose I will have to ask him myself."

Polidori froze. "You cannot confront him. Cannot accuse him of murder."

Mehr took a deep breath, held on to the bed frame and steadied herself. "He said he would show her her place. Threatened her. Now he is keeping us here against our will. He will not let us leave the villa. You saw my feeble attempts. I know you have tried as well."

"What do you suggest we do?" He sighed, then frowned. "Not your lady of the villa."

"She is the only one with answers. It is her house, after all. If there is anyone who can free us, it is she."

Polidori finished packing his bag and held firm to it. "I am afraid of this house. I do not know my days, my hours. Everything blends into one long nightmare. Even this theory of his lordship trapping us here for the sheer opportunity of torture." He rubbed his forehead. "I find your lady of the villa difficult to believe."

Mehr bristled. She gritted her teeth, stopping herself from screaming in frustration. "Then you are just like the rest, content to be controlled and manipulated, run your days in complaisant captivity. Your fascination with that man will be your ruin. He will see to that."

She pushed past the doctor and stormed down the attic stairs. In the bowels of the house, she found Percy and Byron in the salon, Lady Caroline too, with her arms wrapped around Byron's waist. Mary was nowhere in sight.

"Our princess of Lucknow, there you are," Byron said, placing an object on the table that was draped in a kerchief. "It was very unkind of you to hide these from us." He lifted the kerchief to reveal the grapes Mary had picked for her, which she'd kept so carefully in a bowl of water. They seemed to have ripened further on their own.

She was unable to move, her memories of him from the night before clouding her thoughts.

"Why would these be so special to you?" Byron asked.

She narrowed her eyes at him. "You had no right taking my belongings."

"I rented this villa. I have a right to all the rooms. I hope you will allow us a small taste."

The last word made Mehr wince. She shook her head, but her mind was fuzzy; the endless fog outside seemed to have taken up room inside her. Byron plucked a few of the grapes off the bunch and threw them at Percy. He caught all but one, which rolled and stopped to rest at the wall. Byron lifted the bunch from the bowl and held it over his head. Water trickled off it and onto his face in slow, silent drips as he opened his mouth.

As he bared his teeth and took one of the nearest grapes into his mouth, Mehr found herself instinctively chewing, as if she were doing the eating for him. Percy suddenly gagged and spit the grapes into his palm. Blood dribbled out of his mouth as he spat again.

"What is this?" Percy asked, retching violently.

He stared in astonishment as Byron struggled to chew the bloodied grapes, then impetuously ate another. Blood splatter lined the outside of his mouth.

Lady Caroline shrieked with laughter, mouth wide open, the darkness inside reaching out.

"Stop it!" Polidori cried, wrenching the grapes out of Byron's hands and throwing them against the wall. Blood splashed out of them on impact, then dripped down the wall to join the errant grape below. Polidori, mad with rage, began to stomp on them, the blood splashing on the table, on the chairs, on Mehr. Percy and Byron joined in Lady Caroline's laughter; they doubled over, their teeth and gums stained with rust.

"He is making wine," Byron managed, flecks of blood on his cheeks as if he'd been shaved by a clumsy barber.

Polidori slipped and fell to the ground amidst the muck, earning more choked laughter from the pair. He crawled to Mehr, and she helped him to stand.

"I told you this place is cursed," she said. "And so are you."

As she attempted to pull him out of the room, a movement distracted her at the window. A familiar figure stood outside. It was the fakir who would take his post outside her mother's bedroom every day at sunset. She saw him as clearly as she had the day her mother died. His eyes were sunken and heavy but had that lively twinkle they always did despite his haggard appearance. His cloak was terribly soiled, threadbare where it hardly covered his gaunt chest.

She watched the bones of his rib cage puff in and out as he breathed and saw his heart beat against his paper-thin skin.

The fakir lifted a frail hand and placed it against the window. Mehr reached for him, wanted to touch her hand to his. But he turned it into a knobby fist and smashed it down, leaving a long crack in the glass. The walls undulated, drew in and out as if they were screaming. She swayed on the spot, and her legs gave way beneath her. She felt nothing as her body met the floor.

She awoke on wet earth. As she attempted to sit up, her fingers squelched in muck. She realized she was on the lakeshore. The mist blanketed the air around her, swirled against her breath. Then a hand darted out of the mist to pull her to stand.

It was the woman from the painting. She was shorter than Mehr had imagined her to be, with a slight yet strong build. And the painting didn't do her justice; she was far more beautiful.

"You!"

The woman tucked her chin in, an invitation.

"Did you ever escape Diodati?" Mehr asked.

The woman solemnly shook her head.

Mehr tried to reach her, but her hand passed through the figure.

"Is this death?" Mehr whispered.

Again, the woman shook her head. She turned and walked away from the lakeshore, back toward the villa. Mehr hesitated. She looked to where she remembered the

Shelleys' rented cottage to be. She set out in that direction until the fog became intolerable and she could see neither in front of her nor below to her feet. A figure emerged from the mist, and she jogged up to it.

It was the same woman, the lady of the villa.

"No! Please," Mehr said.

But the figure waved a beckoning finger and led her to the vineyard. Mehr followed at a distance, breathing in the mist, keeping her eye on the figure. They moved among the vines, and for a moment, Mehr lost sight of her. She reached out for her and was yanked suddenly forward, face-to-face with her mother. Amma.

Amma's face was waxen, her eyes tinged with yellow. Her lips were scarred and cracked. Sallow skin hung off the bones of her face. A line of ants marched across her forehead, entering the corner of an eye. Mehr stepped back and nearly toppled over a mound of earth. Beyond it lay an open grave. Mehr peered in and found a skeleton lying curled on its side, a train of long hair blanketing its shoulders.

She looked up, but Amma was gone.

A whisper arose within the vines. She found a line of vinedressers standing just beyond the mist. Their whispers grew louder until they filled her head. She clamped her fists over her ears, but it was inside her now, laying a nest made of earth and blood.

CHAPTER 16

When Mehr awoke, Polidori was kneeling on the floor beside her, cradling her face with one hand. She glanced around; she was on a sofa in the salon. The window's glass was intact; there was no one outside. It was only the ever-present roils of mist moving against the current of wind.

"They think it is their intoxication making them hallucinate," Polidori said, his eyes wide, searching her own. "You see the blood as well?"

He glanced behind her with a worried look on his face. Percy, Byron, and Lady Caroline were drenched with bloodied grape juice and pulp. Lady Caroline held on to Byron's arm, but he grimaced and shook her loose. For the first time, Mehr noticed deep, dark circles under his eyes. There was dried blood on his chin. She attempted to sit up and leave the couch, but Polidori wouldn't let her. She shoved him away.

"You arrived at the villa first," she said to Byron. "What did you do to her?"

Byron turned his gaze on her, but rather than anger, it was softer this time. "What are you accusing me of?"

Mehr gripped Polidori's hand. "The lady. I must show you her room. Then you will believe me."

Byron scoffed. "Our Lucknow princess has gone mad. Yes, yes. Do show us 'her' room."

"Stay back, murderer," Mehr said.

Byron leaned over Mehr. "I said show us your damned room," he said, his voice hovering above a growl.

Mehr hesitated before moving off the couch, her head swimming. Polidori attempted to help her, but she moved as quick as she was able, leading them all out of the room. She didn't need a light; she knew exactly where she was headed. If he could see the room, the painting, Polidori would finally believe her, and perhaps the lady herself would confront her murderer and explain what was happening to them. How Byron had taken her life and also murdered Lucy. How they could all be free of his spell.

Mehr led them to the abandoned room.

"There, see for yourself," she said as the door slammed against the wall.

It was empty. The furniture was gone. There was no painting. Only the heavy red curtains remained. Mehr rubbed her eyes—but no, they hadn't deceived her. Nothing was there. She moved frantically to the hearth and touched the wall above it. There was a fine layer of dust, and no portrait had ever disturbed it. The grate looked pristine and untouched, not a fleck of ash inside.

Polidori was first in behind her, then Byron and Percy; Lady Caroline lingered in the doorway.

"But she was here," Mehr said. She turned on Byron. "It was you. You removed her things. You murdered her."

"Mehrunissa," Percy said, a warning in his tone, blood cracked against his lips.

"He is guilty." Mehr was bordering on mania now, like the doctor. With a trembling finger, she pointed through the window. "Her body lies in the vineyard."

Byron narrowed his eyes on her. "You do not know what you are saying."

Her heart hammered in her chest as she tried to read his expressions, what he was hiding inside.

Percy threw up his arms. "She is accusing his lordship of murder. Talking of buried women, and . . . paintings? Lock her up in this room. I do not want this hysteria near my children," he said.

"They are not *real*," Polidori snarled.

"They are still my children!" Percy shouted.

Byron glared at Percy, who clamped his mouth shut and backed away to the corner of the room. Then he turned to Polidori and impatiently snapped his fingers. Polidori hesitated, swallowed hard, then strode up to Mehr, pulling something out of his inner coat. He held up a book, and Mehr realized with a start that it was the lady of the villa's journal.

"Looking for this?" Byron asked.

Mehr snatched the journal back from Polidori, squeezed it in a hug. Her heart beat against the cover, and she pressed it even harder to her chest.

Byron took out a handkerchief and began wiping his fingers of grape pulp, then the sides of his face. "There is nothing in there. No drawings of the paranormal. No trapped madams or mysterious ladies."

"She is here," Mehr said. "I saw her."

"Pray, calm yourself," Polidori said softly. "It is a harmless travel guide."

Mehr peeled the journal off her and flipped manically through the pages. "No, no. These are her words."

There were lines and lines of writing, but the erratic sentences and grisly drawings had disappeared. Mehr glared up at Byron. "You tore out the pages."

He began to laugh. "I have nothing to hide. You, however"—he glared deeply into her eyes—"have plenty of secrets."

Mehr began to tremble and wondered just how much he knew about her. Without another word, he swept out of the room, waving at Percy to follow him.

Polidori reached for her, but she flung the journal at him. He didn't try to defend himself, and it bounced off his chest and fell on the floor between them. She was a fool, and she'd been duped by the others, seduced by the house, by the madness of the Lord. She squeezed her fists together, felt her blood pumping inside.

He took hold of her arms and, no matter how much she fought him, managed to draw her into a hug, cupping his hand against the back of her neck.

Mehr gave up and lay against him. She let out a sob. "What happened to her?"

"She does not exist, Mehr," Polidori said. "You imagined her. Just as we are seeing the blood-filled grapes. The apparitions. We are sharing this delusion. All of us." His voice vibrated through his chest.

She shut her eyes, circling her arms around his waist. The Lord had them all in thrall. She knew the delirium was coming for each of them. She didn't want to think of what could come next at Byron's hands, in whatever mood he happened to be in at the time.

"Do you believe me?" Mehr asked.

It was a while until Polidori responded. "Lord Byron is the Diodati Demon. I see it now. But we mustn't vex him. We must be patient. He cannot trap us here forever."

"He can and he will," Mehr said, wiping away her tears.

"Then I would take forever if it were here with you."

Polidori held her chin in his hand and drew her in for a kiss. She knew from the fervency of his lips what he wanted, but she broke away and stepped back from him. There was sudden disappointment in his eyes. Diodati had had its way with her, orchestrated by Byron himself. She was ashamed now of yielding so easily to him, to all of them.

She left Polidori in the abandoned room and went back

upstairs. In the gallery, she hid in the shadows as Robert struggled with the sheet around Lucy's body, carrying her down the stairs while Byron watched from his bedroom door. She heard Robert mutter something as he passed, perhaps a prayer to console poor dead Lucy's soul.

When Byron had retreated to his room and shut the door, she moved quietly up to the attic and locked the door behind her. It was still daytime, though time was an endless circle now. She headed to bed and lay awake for minutes, or perhaps hours, until the light outside the curtains dimmed and, sometime later, brightened again.

Sleep was futile. Her mind raced with what she'd seen and felt. Every creak on the stairs made her flinch. She pushed herself out of bed and, at her washstand, splashed water onto her face. Just as she was drying the droplets from her forehead, there was a presence behind her.

Mehr froze, her hands shaking on either side of the washbowl. The figure stepped forward. It was the woman in the painting, a sad smile on her face.

"You!" Mehr whispered.

Her features rippled, stretched against her skull. Then she changed. She was her mother again, but she was beautiful, young, the way she had been before her father left.

"Are you happy, Amma? That I threw myself at the first firangi I could find? Just like you did."

Her mother remained stoic and held something up in her hand. The taweez glinted in the candlelight. Her mother's dying wish came back to Mehr—to give the taweez to her father. It had to be Mehr who delivered it by her own hand.

Mehr fell to her knees and began to sob. Long ago, she'd thought she'd see her father again and have her beloved little brother back. The conversation with her uncle, the long voyage to London, the stay in the home—it was all meant to be temporary. But her brother had abandoned her. She was trapped in the villa, moving along its whirlpool current, like the dead ants caught on the windowsill, like the Shelleys and Claire and even Polidori gravitating around the Lord. Swirling and swirling, arms open to him. She knew that eventually she would also surrender to his pull on her.

She was stuck, her wings painfully clipped. The only way she'd ever be leaving Diodati was in death, like Lucy. As if reading her mind, her mother frowned at her. Wordlessly, she held the taweez over her head, and Mehr wept but obediently bowed her head. The cord was soft against her neck as the taweez nestled onto her chest.

Her mother pointed to the window.

"It will not let me leave," Mehr whispered.

Her mother shook her head and pointed again.

"I told you," Mehr said, "I cannot leave!"

The window flew open on its own.

Mehr gasped, cowered against the sudden wind. Then she crawled to the window, held her hand out. The rain slapped against her palm. She squinted out at the early-morning fog. It twirled in a circle, round and round and round.

She tore the sheets off all the beds, then tied them into a long rope. After tying one end to the foot of the nearest bed, she hesitated, then threw the end over the sill. It fell down like a soft sigh against the window below her. She climbed over, held tight to the cloth, and swung her body out. She hit the side of the house hard, and the wind was knocked out of her. She caught her breath and took her time, her arms straining, the sweat blinding her as she slowly lowered herself toward the end of the linen. When she hovered a few feet off the ground, she let go.

She landed on the attic floor. The window was shut, the bundle of linen in a heap at her feet.

"No!" she screamed. She ran to the window, unlocked the latch, and pushed against the pane, but the window wouldn't open. The humming grew louder around her. She screamed, threw her weight against the window, but it didn't budge. She picked the pitcher up off her nightstand, hurled it against the window; it shattered into pieces. Not a mark was left on the glass.

Mehr moved quickly to the stairs, took them down two at a time, tripping on her skirts. In the gallery, she plucked the paintings off the wall, threw them against the floor, stomped on the frames. If anyone were to wake from the furious clamor she was making, she didn't care. Then she was down the stairs, to the kitchen, searching for the largest knife she could find. She found one and took it with her into the drawing room, then the salon, and slashed the furniture to pieces. She stabbed at the walls, felt the pulse on the other side grow stronger, angrier.

"Let me go!" she cried.

She ran to the library, grabbed an armful of books, threw them into the weakened coals. The fire built up quickly, roared back at her. But to burn the whole library would take too much time. She picked up the chair in the corner of the room, smashed it down heavily. Then she pried a leg loose and lit the end of it in the fire. She held the torch aloft and walked back down the hall.

The rain whipped against the villa, pattered on the roof, howled furiously through the chimneys. She headed for the abandoned room, the start of all her trouble. With an angry cry, she held the torch against the door. In an instant, the fire snuffed out. Gray smoke trailed up from the leg of the chair. She tossed the useless torch to the floor, threw herself against the wall to cry out her disappointments.

There was movement inside the room. She felt it through the wood, under her skin, but she knew better than to throw the door open. She bent down and peeped through the keyhole. The apparitions stood in a line with their backs to the window. She spotted Mary's mother at the front, her belly having swelled even larger since the last time she'd seen her. Like the grapes that had been taken from her room, engorged with phantom blood. Then Byron's women, clasping their hands in front of them as if waiting for a sermon, Lady Caroline glaring straight ahead, a faint smile on her lips. And Percy's two small children, side by side, holding hands. Behind them, Polidori's two mangled patients.

All of them were as still as death. Then, slowly, they tilted their heads back and moved into a circle, emitting a strange hum, the same tune as the vinedressers' song. She realized where she'd heard it before. It was a lullaby. The one that never failed to ease her to sleep as her mother cradled her to her breast and hummed it into her ear. It was the one that had soothed her loneliness after her father and James had left. Slowly, the other apparitions joined Lady Caroline and looked directly at the keyhole. Mehr's spine stiffened and her blood turned cold; she gasped and fell back against the opposite wall.

A noise down the hall startled her. She looked up and found Byron stalking toward her, Mary gripping his arm, Claire following closely behind them. Mehr moved into a darker part of the hall to hide, holding her breath.

"You cannot do this!" Mary cried.

"I am the master of the house," Byron said, pushing her off him. Mehr flinched as she watched Mary fall to the floor.

"Think about what you are doing," Mary said. "What about Percy? You will break his heart."

"We have thought about it," Claire said, chin jutting out in defiance. "His lordship has grown tired of them, and so have I."

So, she'd reclaimed her position with him and moved her ever-shifting loyalties. Mehr scoffed, but no one heard her.

"The incessant chatter of those women," Byron said, rubbing his temples as one of the apparitions let out a high-pitched laugh through the door. "The constant distractions. I cannot think. Or sleep. And worse—I have not written a word in weeks."

Mary hauled herself up and held on to Claire's knees, crying pitifully into her dress, but Claire stared down at her with contempt and something close to triumph. She shoved Mary off and leaned down to stare into her eyes.

"I have spent far too many years being in your way," Claire hissed, "so I am taking my own path. You would do well to remember that."

She and Byron left Mary in the hall. She sank to her knees, sobbing uncontrollably, and crawled to the door, placed the side of her face against it.

Mehr felt around in her apron pocket for the key she'd faithfully kept there since she'd first found the room. She waited until Mary's cries subsided to emerge from the darkness. Mary turned to her as if she knew she had been hidden there all along.

"No," Mary cried weakly, her eyes on the key. She shook her head, seemed to beg for something with her tear-streaked eyes. But Mehr wondered how Byron and Polidori had gotten their hands on the journal she'd given to Mary. Had she turned the pages, found them mundane and devoid of mysteries, then laughed about them to the Lord? Mehr knew a vast distance had grown between them.

Mary was, and always would be, a stranger to her. Her mistress, her employer, and nothing more.

She slipped the key into the lock, heard it catch, and let out a loud click. It echoed in the hall around them.

"Mama," Mary whimpered, and Mehr backed up, felt the twin feelings of disgust and pity rise as she walked away.

CHAPTER 17

Mehr floated through the halls like a ghost. The humming within the walls hypnotized her. It could have been minutes since she'd first entered the villa. Or hours, or weeks, or years. Time was a vortex, sucking everything into its darkened eye. She realized there was a sudden quiet that came with Byron banishing the apparitions. There was room to breathe. But no one was breathing anymore.

She passed by the dining parlour, stared at the others gnawing on bread, slurping their stews, stuffing large blocks of meat into their mouths. She touched her stomach and couldn't remember the last time she'd felt hunger or thirst. Perhaps it was the same with them. They were going through their routines, eating because it was the only thing they had left to cling on to—their mundane human habits.

In the kitchen, she found Berger laughing over a pile of dirty dishes with a strange, withered old woman. When he caught sight of Mehr, he moved to block the woman from her view. In his eyes was a plea. Mehr shrugged. She left the cook with his apparition. It would be a matter of time before Byron found her, and it wasn't Mehr's concern anymore.

She moved out of the cellar and walked through the familiar rooms. Dust coated the furniture, crawled into the carpets, floated in the air. The furniture had resewn itself; the walls healed the wounds she'd carved into them. In another life, she was a poor housemaid neglecting her duties in favor of the drama going on around her. But now she was a phantom, trapped in a large villa, like the mysterious woman her mind had created.

In the drawing room, she found Robert alone, sitting on the sofa, slouched and gripping tightly at his knees.

"Can you see her?" he whispered.

Mehr shook her head.

"She is there," Robert said. "Behind you."

Mehr wouldn't look, didn't want to. "Who do you see?" she asked.

"Lucy," Robert said. "She stands far enough away, but close enough to see. Just in the corner of my eye."

"She is not real," Mehr said.

"I used to be married. She left me, took everything with her. I never thought I would be capable of love again. Until I met Lucy. Now she'll never leave my side."

Mehr sighed. "She died, Robert. You carried her body away. Where did you put her?"

"I left her in the cellar," he said. Robert suddenly

laughed. "I saw a man there. Young. Battered and bound. But I did not recognize him."

"Perhaps another figure from your past," Mehr said.

"Why does she persist in tormenting me?" Robert asked. "Because I should have saved her?" He looked up at her. "Perhaps I ought to follow her? Let her lead me away to where she's gone."

He winced, stared hard at the corner behind her. Mehr left him to his mania and decided to hide herself away in the attic. She didn't need food, didn't need any earthly sustenance. The silence would be her only companion. Mehr returned to her bed. She would wait for death to approach, to take her in its arms and carry her like a bride to hell.

Within the silence, a small voice slithered through the darkness to her.

"Mehrunissa."

It was only a whisper. She sat up and trained her ears to listen again.

"Mehrunissa."

It was gravelly, as if buried underneath sand. She lit her lantern, glanced around at the shadows. There was a creak in the floor, and Mehr braced herself. But nothing happened. She moved out of bed and looked around for some sort of weapon to wield. Something glinted in the corner of the room. It was a discarded, heavily tarnished candelabra. She picked it up and held it out in front of her in her wavering hands.

She turned the lantern around, shined it on the line of

empty beds. Mehr's breath caught in her chest. There was something occupying one of them.

The whisper again. "Mehrunissa, come here."

It was Lucy's voice. Mehr gripped the candelabra and took a small step, then another, as the lantern illuminated the bed.

Lucy lay as she had in death, her body twisted, arms splayed beside her. Her head was tilted at an odd angle, just as Mehr had seen her last. She inched closer, rounded the bed to face her.

"There you are," Lucy whispered, her blue-tinged lips barely moving. She did not turn her head, only blinked her cloudy eyes.

Mehr sank to her knees, touched the edge of the bed. "I am so sorry. For all of it."

Lucy continued to stare at the ceiling.

Mehr held back a sob. "I abandoned you."

"I don't have much time," Lucy said, her tongue twitching beneath her exposed teeth.

"You will haunt me until I lose my mind like Robert," Mehr said. "Won't you?"

Lucy was silent for a while. She blinked again.

"You are going to survive, Mehr," Lucy said. "You are going to leave Diodati. You will be the one to make it end. For yourself. For all of them."

Mehr stared at the odd and lumpy way her neck bulged, the skin twisting around itself. "Am I next?" Mehr whispered. "Is the Lord going to kill me too?"

"You are not listening."

"Just tell me!" Mehr cried. She held her breath in the silence that followed, crawled even closer to the corpse.

Lucy's eyebrows twitched into a slight frown. She blinked once, twice. "Only you can make it end. First you must save them. Mrs. Shelley's life is in peril."

"She does not care for me," Mehr said. "I was a fool to think that. Even if my father had chosen me, I still could not be one of her people."

"You must save them before you can save yourself," Lucy said, her voice fading away.

"But I do not wish to save them!"

"What of James?" Lucy whispered.

"Wh-what do you mean?"

Mehr waited for more, but Lucy had fallen silent. She picked up the lantern, shined it on the bed, but it was empty again.

"What *of* James?" Mehr asked. "Tell me!"

Lucy's voice echoed in the air, swirled around the room with the flecks of dust. "Go . . . go to them . . ."

Mehr hugged the candelabra to her chest. She moved off the floor and stood at the top of the stairs, her heart pounding in her ears. She took each step slowly, her body trembling, imagining Byron hiding in the darkness, his fingers reaching, reaching for her.

She entered the gallery and froze, her ears twitching. But the villa was as silent as a tomb. She crept toward the staircase, took each step one at a time. As she stood at the bottom, the lantern heavy in her hand, a bloodcurdling scream rent the air. Mehr cried out, dropped the candelabra from her hands. As it clattered onto the floor, there was another scream. It was unmistakable where it had come from. She ran through the villa to the abandoned room and tried to look through the keyhole, but something was blocking it. She threw herself at the door, pushing with all her strength.

Mehr backed away, retrieved the candelabra from the bottom of the stairs, and began hammering the doorknob. By the fifth swing, the wood cracked and the doorknob flew to the floor. She heard Mary's palms frantically slap against the floor as Mehr moved away. The door burst open. Mary crawled out, crying hysterically.

Mehr shined her light in. All the apparitions had disappeared except for Mary's mother. She lay on the floor, stabbing herself in her stomach, slowly opening up her insides. Out of the blood and bits and entrails, a golden-headed child emerged. It was streaked in blood and birth matter and looked exactly like William, Mary and Percy's infant child.

Mehr hauled Mary up by the shoulders and dragged her away. They ran to the library, the only place that felt safe. The air was icy, and Mehr, with little else to do, stoked the fire in the grate. Mary sat on the floor beside her, shivering hard. She sat in a stupor, then finally spoke.

"Where have you been?"

"Mrs. Shelley, I have always been here."

Mary touched the side of her head. "I feel . . . I feel I have lost a great amount of time."

"Did she—did it hurt you?" Mehr asked, only now

catching her breath as the fire came to life. As Mary slowly turned to her, Mehr found a streak of blood along her jawline, another slash on her wrist. She wanted to reach out, help her in some way. But the wounds were shallow enough that they were already beginning to form a scab.

Mehr glared at her. "We must not let him get away with it."

Mary's eyes were bleary, and she blinked several times before answering. "Who?"

"Lord Byron. He has been bewitching us," Mehr said. "The whole of Diodati."

"His lordship? Oh dear." Mary slowly shook her head.

As the fire blazed higher, there was movement in the doorway. Mehr found Byron peering in at the two of them. His skin was sallow and sagged from his jowls. His teeth were the color of dishwater. He'd been so beautiful before, an ageless Adonis. Since summoning the apparitions in the past few days, he'd aged terribly. She supposed that's what a rotten spirit would do to a person. She supposed it was as Polidori suggested, that they were vampires drawing out his lifeblood. She held the candelabra in front of her.

"Stay back!"

Percy pushed past Byron into the room and huddled before of Mary. He inspected her wounds. Then, with a pitiful cry, he held her to his chest. Mehr tore her gaze away from them and back to Byron.

"This is all your fault," she said, feeling the curl in her lip as he had the nerve to look around him in confusion.

"You are accusing me of that?" Byron pointed with his whole hand to Mary.

"My mother," Mary said, her voice far away. "She said I let our daughter die, that I was the reason for it. She wanted to take Willmouse away to save him from me."

"You did not let our daughter die," Percy said, crouched in front of her, rubbing her arms to warm them. "There was nothing we could do. Maie, you must remember that."

"My little girl," she whispered. "Mama is right. If only I had warmed her by the fire a little longer."

In the hearth, a piece of coal broke free and was briefly alight. Byron flinched at the sudden spark. "The apparitions. They were too perfect. Lulling us like babes at their breasts."

Mehr let out an exasperated laugh. "I thought your playthings were as 'perfect as a memory'?"

Byron grimaced, looking even more haggard. "Perhaps we change a detail here or there. But you cannot alter a memory. Even memories have flaws."

Polidori hurried into the room, then halted when he saw the blood streaked on Mary's face. Mehr held the candelabra out in his direction.

"She is hurt," Mehr said. "Because of him. He has been manipulating us all this time. Just like you said."

Before Polidori could flee further into the room, Byron growled and yanked Polidori up by the collar. He shook him hard, and Mehr could hear Polidori's teeth rattling.

"What ghastly things are you saying about me?" Byron asked.

"You . . . *you* are the Diodati Demon!" Polidori spluttered, clawing at Byron's hands to free himself.

Byron laughed hard in his face. "You are trapping yourself in your own delusions again."

"Lucy is dead," Polidori managed. "Because of you."

"Was it not *you* who gave her the laudanum?" Byron asked, a manic glint in his eye.

"That is not what murdered her," Polidori said, his voice rising.

"A murder?" Mary asked softly. The rest had fallen silent. Mehr realized the young woman was coming out of the spell the villa had cast on her.

Percy spoke to her quietly, and as he did, Mary's eyes widened. She placed her thin fingers to her lips. "Poor Lucy," she said, and began to weep. She stared up at Percy, a look of confusion in her eyes. "Where is my son?"

Behind Byron, the hall was suddenly illuminated. An unmistakable smell of burning cloth and flesh filled the air, and Mehr's eyes watered as she covered her face with one hand. A beautiful pale woman appeared in the doorway. She had dark ringlets piled atop her head and wore a sumptuous lilac dress. She would have been otherwise striking if Mehr weren't so intent on the fire consuming her skirts. When Byron spotted her, he fell back against the wall. The phantom's eyes grew large as the fire climbed up her dress.

"Augusta." He reached for her, then drew back his hand as if singed.

"Will not you try and save me?" the apparition asked, as her dress turned to ash and the skin and fat on her legs dribbled down her charred bones into a sizzling puddle at her feet.

"Forgive me," he said, holding back a sob. "How many times must a man humble himself?"

The apparition's eyes flicked to the others. "You told them?"

Byron had a panicked look on his face as he squirmed against the doorframe. "I did no such thing."

She sneered at him as the fire burned at her breasts, began to climb up her face. "That our child, the 'ape,' is not yours. She has your face!" She reached a hand out to him, grabbed hold of his arm as the fire spread rapidly across her sleeve to Byron. He screamed as flames quickly engulfed her upper body, coating her face and hair like an unholy halo.

"The world will know what we did," the apparition said, her voice rising into a cackle.

Claire bounded into the room and threw herself at Byron, wrenched him free of the apparition's grasp. Augusta fell away, burst into a cloud of ash. Byron collapsed to the floor, his arm on fire. Claire beat it with her skirts until it was extinguished, but the hiss of charred muscle and bone remained—and Mehr resisted the urge to cough, forced the nausea to retreat.

They cowered in the library, staring anxiously at one another. Mehr was the first to move. She slammed the doors shut, placed her back to it, and held the candelabra out in front of her.

Byron groaned on the floor as Claire lay protectively over him. "You called him a murderer," Claire said. "He could have been burned alive."

Mehr ignored her and instead turned to Polidori. "He orchestrated it to make himself look innocent."

Polidori backed farther into the room, pulling at his cuffs again. Behind him, two figures emerged from the darkness and shambled forward. They were Polidori's patients, but more grotesque than before. The men were nude, their genitals distorted and shriveled. Their putrid, gangrenous limbs were an odd assortment of mismatched parts, stitched together with thick, ugly sutures. Mehr lost the ability to speak, to warn him, as the figures lunged. Their eyes were crazed and glowing from some demonic light.

Mary finally noticed them, turning her head swiftly, then letting out a long scream. Before he could escape, one of them took hold of Polidori, wrestling him down to the ground. He fell in a heap, then rolled over and kicked at them. Byron found a way to sit up and, with his good hand, immediately pulled out a pistol. He aimed at the apparitions.

As Polidori again attempted to crawl away, the figures grabbed hold of his legs and dragged him back. Byron shot once—the noise sharp, sudden. Mehr clapped her hands to her ears, a tinny ringing sound filling her head. The bullet had struck one in the neck, but it was undaunted by the blackened blood streaming from its wound. Byron fired again, and the other was struck in the arm. It shuddered but didn't let go, and with one quick twist, it snapped Polidori's ankle.

Polidori let out an anguished cry. Byron shot the apparition in the head, and both of them melted into the darkness. Well before the bullets had found their mark, Mary had pushed Mehr aside and flung open the library doors; Polidori scrambled up and limped out of the library as well, and the rest followed suit. They all congregated in the hall, catching their breath. There was a sudden pounding, a banging within the walls. Voices whispered in the air, whisking past like fallen leaves. Byron pointed the pistol wildly around him. His hands were shaking.

"Byron . . . do not you miss us . . . ?"

"Leave us, demons!" Byron shouted.

"Come out, Mary," a woman's raspy voice called.

Two mingling voices spoke at the same time: "Papa, we are hungry. Feed us."

Mary shrank into Percy as he furiously wiped a tear from his cheek. Then, a long, loud wail of an infant within the other voices.

"William!" Mary cried.

She plunged straight into the darkness. Percy made to follow her, but Claire held him back. He shoved her off, then sprinted after Mary.

"Percy!" Claire shouted, and hurried after him.

Mehr, Polidori, and Byron ran in the opposite direction,

to the entrance of the villa. Polidori tripped and fell to the floor, crawled to the door, but Byron kicked him away from it.

"There is no way out!" said Byron.

Mehr shrank from the timbre of his voice as Polidori cried openly in his hands.

"What *were* those men?" Byron asked, dangling his burnt arm away from his body.

Polidori's eyes were shut. "I am a monster."

"Are not we all?" Byron grimaced.

Mehr was not one of them. She was no monster. She tightened her grip on the candelabra as Byron pulled Polidori up by the collarand slapped the doctor across the face, sending him sprawling back to the floor. Then he turned to Mehr, grabbed the candelabra easily from her hand, and threw it hard against the wall. Before she could flee, he grabbed her by the back of her hair, pulled her tight against him.

"I may be damned, but I am no diabolic conjurer." He held up his burnt arm, the smoking, hot flesh against her cheek. She gagged, struggled to free herself.

"Look at me," Byron said.

Mehr held her breath, stared up into his eyes.

"We, all of us, are condemned. Even you," Byron said. "There is a disease coming for our minds. One by one. I will not let it take me."

Mehr couldn't look away from his wrath. But there was something else there, on his face, she hadn't ever seen before. Abject fear. There were tears in his eyes. He roughly nudged them away with a shoulder.

There was something malevolent going on—far more powerful than the Lord. Than all of them. Diodati had targeted each one all equally, to get inside them, push the hurt down to the bone. But there was something else she hadn't wanted to admit. The noise, the reverberations: Diodati was reaching out to her, pulling her in. It was asking a question of her, not demanding an answer. She realized she was clutching the taweez around her neck.

Byron glared at her chest. He snatched the taweez in his good hand and yanked it to pull her closer. "What is this thing?"

Mehr bit his hand and he let her go, withdrew in shock.

A noise in the darkness distracted them. A soft sound, the shuffling of feet, grew nearer. Mehr stood still, even as she trembled. Polidori had stopped weeping to squint into the darkness ahead of them. Slowly, he got to his feet, bearing his weight awkwardly on his good ankle.

From the darkness, a pale face began to emerge. In one second, Byron had his pistol back out and shot directly at it. There was a small cry, then the sound of something hitting the floor. They waited in silence, until Byron took the first step.

"Light my way," he said.

She followed with her lantern as he limped down the hall. A body came into view, and Mehr froze. It was Berger, a surprised expression frozen on his face. Byron had somehow aimed perfectly at his heart—a puddle of blood pooled beneath him.

In the darkness beyond them, Mehr found the old woman's visage. Her face was twisted, her nails long and curved like claws. She cackled once and evaporated into the shadows.

A voice whispered in the darkness. "Lord Byron . . ." It was Lady Caroline. As her voice grew nearer, Mehr and Polidori exchanged a glance, but Byron seemed not to hear anything. He continued to examine Berger, the pistol limp in his hands.

"You do not hear it?" Polidori whispered. "Her voice."

"What?" Byron barked, looking around him. "I hear nothing." Then his face settled, became serene. "I cannot hear them anymore." He began to laugh.

Horrified, Mehr watched as Berger's corpse rose, blood spurting out of his mouth. Polidori had been transfixed by Byron and didn't notice Berger grab hold of him. Mehr didn't wait to see the rest—she took her lantern and ran ahead of them, a single gunshot ringing out behind her.

As her lantern swung wildly in her hand, out of the darkness Percy's demonic children staggered out, their faces stretched into hideous leers. From the dining room, Mehr saw two of Byron's women standing side by side, holding hands, their mouths open and drooling blood, their tongues cut out, wriggling in their free hands.

She kept going, threw open the cellar door and headed down into the depths of the villa. Rather than entering the kitchen, she veered left, threw her weight against the storage room and fell inside. She shut the door and sank to the floor, caught her breath. Inexplicably, her lantern sputtered and burned out. Mehr plunged her hand into her apron pocket and found a lone candle she'd stowed away long ago with a box of matches. She quickly lit the candle and held it out in front of her. Her hand trembled as she walked the length of the room, turning the candle to her left and right and behind her, to make sure she was alone.

There was a light rustle in the room. She whirled around. The candle was inches away from her mother's face just as the wax melted down to Mehr's fingertips. The sudden burning sensation made her drop her candle. She crawled on the floor in search of it and lit it again.

Her mother was crouched on the floor.

"Tell them," she whispered.

Mehr began to weep. She reached for Amma, but her hands went through the form. She felt nothing when she touched her; even when her hand was grazing her shoulder, she had no sensation of cloth or flesh under her fingertips. The house's hum became louder. Her mother was humming along with the noise, the lullaby. The flame blew out.

"Mehrunissa," a voice whispered behind her.

When she turned, something took hold of her. She screamed and fought back. She heard the rattle of her matchbox, the strike of a match. A light flared in the darkness, a familiar face shone out. It was unmistakable who it was.

It was her brother, James.

CHAPTER 18

Mehr threw her arms around him. It caused the match to fall out of his hands, and they were back in darkness.

"Baji," he said, his Urdu heavily accented. "Aap kaise ho?" He laughed sheepishly. "As you can hear, I have lost practice."

She pulled away from him. "Are you one of them?"

"One of who?"

She held his face in her hands, felt the warmth under her fingertips. She placed her palm against his chest, and a strong heartbeat answered back.

"What are you doing here?" she asked.

A soft laugh in the darkness. "I should ask you the same thing."

"I am a prisoner here," she said softly.

James sighed. "I fear I am the same."

"Who did this to you?"

"Lord Byron. He had written me a letter weeks ago.

Said he had important business with me. I-I was honored. Struck by his celebrity. His lordship, writing me a letter?" He scoffed. "He was with another man."

"Percy Shelley," Mehr said, nearly spitting with disgust as she said his name. "What business did he have with you?"

"I was too flattered by the man's attention, I never had a chance to ask. They met me at a coffeehouse in Geneva. Dazzled me with their wit. I suddenly became ill, drowsy. They offered to help and dragged me into this house. Then threw me in here. Left me crumbs to eat."

Mehr retrieved her lantern, righted the candle inside, and had James help her light it. The storage room contained a pile of discarded candle bits, ones that were meant to be melted down to create new ones. They lit what they could of the remains until Mehr was able to see her brother better than she had in the brief spurt of light.

"How long ago was that?" Mehr asked.

James shook his head. "I have no way of measuring time here. If they serve my meal once a day, I would wager two weeks. Perhaps three?"

In the decade since she'd last seen him, her baby brother had grown into a handsome young man. He was nearly one and twenty now, and would have indeed looked every bit the pukka sahib if his collar weren't torn, his shirt and breeches soiled, his hair in complete disarray, his cheeks gaunt from hunger. There were the yellowing, faded remains of a bruise under one eye and a scabbed cut in his lower lip. She could tell he had been wearing very smart-looking clothes until something calamitous had befallen him. A dirty piece of rope bound his hands. Mehr helped untangle the knots and found twin burn marks on his wrists.

She glanced at his bruised knuckles. “It was you, knocking on the walls. Trying to alert us.”

“You heard me?” James said. “I fear my desperation faded once . . . she arrived.” He held his candle up and pointed at the wall behind him. A slight shrouded form appeared. Mehr realized with a jolt it was Lucy.

Their mother materialized in the darkness beyond the candle’s reach.

“Amma,” James whispered, a boyish smile on his lips.

“You can see her?” She pushed back from him. “She is dead, James. For nearly a year.”

“But she is always here in this room.”

“She is not real; she is an apparition.”

Mehr thought of her own supposed hallucinations. She had been sure it was something cruel that had been passed down only to her from her mother. A penchant for the dramatic, a unique inclination to delusion and derangement. But Diodati had been toying with her, and it had done the same with James.

“She is the only comfort I have had.” He quickly wiped a tear from his eye. “To see Amma again after so many years—”

There was a noise in the hallway, a banging in the

kitchen. Mehr pressed her fingers to her lips, then moved to the door and placed her ear against it. There was shouting between two men, loud thumps that echoed through the walls. Then a long scream that was cut short.

Slowly, she backed away, held her breath and clamped a hand over her mouth. James beckoned her closer to him, and together they stared at the door. But after a while, it was apparent no one had seen her escape that way.

"You shouldn't be here," Mehr said. "Trapped like this."

"I had to find you, Baji," James said.

Mehr recalled all the months she'd spent wondering when James would show up at the door and take her home. She'd had so many curses ready for him, so many horrible things she would have said. But it was futile. Because even then she'd known if she were ever to see him again, her heart would not be able to bear it.

"You never tried to find me," she said softly. "I waited months to hear from you."

"Believe me, I tried," James said. He rubbed at his freed wrists. "I would have found you sooner, but he would not let me bring you home."

"Who?" Mehr asked.

James hesitated. "Our father."

The door flew open behind them. Footsteps scuffled in, and before she could turn around, she heard James shout a warning. Something struck her hard on the head, and she was plunged into an ice-cold darkness.

CHAPTER 19

Within the darkness, the adhan punctured through, bringing Mehr to consciousness. The crisp, cool air caressed the side of her face. With the morning call to prayer still in her ears, she sat up, surveyed her surroundings. She was back home in the zenana. The curtains billowed softly as, little by little, the darkness outside turned to light and the sun rose.

Had it all been a terrible dream? Mehr moved out of bed, plunged her toes into the plush rug below her. The window brought in a warm, perfumed breeze. She parted the curtains to look out. She stepped onto the windowsill as she usually did, but the room changed around her.

She was in the zenana courtyard, lurking in the garden. The cook had her back turned to Mehr. She squatted on the floor, stirring a mash of lentils and rice in a pot hovering over a fire. Then the cook let out a soft sob. From her sleeve she produced a vial, carefully glanced around to make sure she was alone. She didn't see Mehr far down the courtyard, peeking at her from around the garden wall. The cook sprinkled the substance into the food. It wasn't an ordinary spice, Mehr realized, because, hastily, the cook hid it back in her sleeve and glanced around again.

Mehr moved out of the garden, approached the cook, who wouldn't meet her eyes as she continued to mash the khichdi with a large wooden spoon.

"How is your mother?"

"Better today."

The cook slowed her mashing, appearing to take a few breaths. She spooned the kichdi into an earthen plate, held it out to Mehr without looking.

"Make sure she eats all of it," she said, her voice breaking. "It will help her regain her strength."

Mehr stepped out of the courtyard, and as she did, the grass gave way to a rug underneath her feet. She was back with Amma, who was sitting up in bed, glaring at her.

Mehr held a tray in her hands, and she placed it down beside her mother. As she turned to leave, her mother took hold of her hand.

"Did you bless it?" she asked.

"We do not need to bless everything every waking moment," Mehr said.

"Bless it," her mother said. "Then feed it to me."

Mehr sat beside her mother. She pretended to pray a blessing on the meal. She then blew air at the mashed lentils and rice, the onion salad, the achar adorning the side of the plate. Mehr used her fingers to create a small ball, the oil from the pickles helping the mound keep its shape, then held up her fingers to her mother's mouth. Amma delicately took the food in, shut her eyes as she chewed. Mehr also closed hers.

When she opened them, she was lying on a sofa in a strange room. She sat up slowly, her head swimming, her vision blurred at the edges. In the dim light, she made out four figures nearby. It didn't take her long to know who they were.

"Is it true?" Mary whispered, clasping her infant to her chest.

Mehr turned her head, saw Byron's unmade bed. There was a hazy apparition of Mehr and her mother sitting on it; Mehr hand-fed her mother. Then the scene slowly dissipated. They had all been watching it play out without her knowing.

James was nowhere in sight. "What have you done with my brother?" Mehr asked.

"A murderess," Byron said.

"No," Mary said quickly. "She was not the one who poisoned her."

Claire scowled at Mehr. "She knew what she was doing."

"My mother said that the only way she could be with my father again was in death." She stared at Byron. His sleeve was torn clear off, the burnt arm wrapped in a bandage. "And I am not the only murderer in this room."

"It was an accident," Byron said. "I thought Berger was one of those . . . things."

"He was fleeing his mother's apparition. He was scared. And so was Lucy," Mehr said. "Did you think she was one too?"

Byron let out a grim, pointed laugh. "I was not the cause of poor Lucy's demise." He waved in Claire's direction. Claire flushed crimson red, began patting her neck with the handkerchief clenched in her hand.

"I didn't mean to do it," Claire said. "I was scared. It was dark and she surprised me."

"You would have known who she was once you had her by the throat," Mehr said. "Or did she deserve to die because she was allowed to have her lover all to herself?"

"Be quiet!" Claire yelled. "Nothing happened in this house until you arrived." She produced Byron's gun from the pocket of her skirts and aimed it at Mehr. The others gasped and backed away; Mehr didn't flinch.

"Claire," Byron said in a strong voice. "Give me back my pistol."

Claire's eyes filled with tears. "She has been bewitching us, bringing her wild demons in here to haunt us."

Mary held a hand out toward her sister. "This place is not haunted. We are."

Claire shook her head, her hands trembling.

Mary took a few steps closer to her. "It knows who we are. What we are. What we have done," she said. "We are the ones bringing them out."

"I am innocent," Claire said, the tears streaming down her face. "I have suffered, more than you know. But I am free now. And if you want to be, then you know what you must do."

"What are you saying?" Mary asked.

"A small sacrifice. That was what your mother—what *it* told me, Mary. Whispered it in my ears. And now I cannot see or hear them anymore."

Mehr stood from the sofa, her legs shaking. At the other end, she found a figure lying on the floor. It was Robert, his throat slashed, eyes open to nothing and everything. After the shock subsided, she felt a twinge of regret. She wanted to mutter some apology to him. But he'd never be able to hear her. His and Lucy's romance had mattered so much to them before; now it didn't matter at all.

Percy stood over Robert, blocking her path, a bloodied knife in his hand. With Claire distracted by Mehr, Byron fought to free the gun from her. Claire resisted but, at the fierce look on his face, let it go and backed away from him.

"You already had your turn," Byron said. "And Percy. It is Mary's now."

He held the gun out to Mary, but she averted her gaze, nuzzled her son's head instead. Slowly, Percy approached her. "Maie, I am so unburdened. My thoughts, my mind, have cleared. I can think again. Feel again. The noise in the walls? I hear nothing." He frantically touched his neck. "I feel a great shackle has been wrenched free from my neck."

"I will not be a murderess," Mary said.

He touched the side of her face. She shut her eyes.

"Do you not want to be free?" Percy asked.

"Not like this," Mary said into the infant's sparse hair.

Percy grunted and pried the child away from her. Mary's shoulders sagged. She took the gun from Byron's outstretched hand.

Mehr shook her head, willing Mary to read her thoughts, but Mary's mind was elsewhere now. A tear streamed down Mary's cheek as she raised her arm, pointed the pistol at Mehr's heart. But then her eyes flashed to something over Mehr's shoulder.

Polidori stood in the shadows, his arms up in surrender, trembling. "Mary, please," he said softly. "Do not believe their lies."

"You disgust me," she said. "What you did to those men, their bodies."

He let out a deep, rattling breath. "I was young. A fool. A student of science—"

Mary pulled back the hammer, fixed her aim at him.

"This will not fix us. You must know that." He watched her a moment, then his bloodshot eyes widened. "Whose approval do you really seek?"

Mary took a few breaths. She appeared to be wrestling with a response. Instead, she fired. Mehr flinched and cried out. But it was too late. Polidori fell face-first to the floor.

Percy sighed and hugged Mary, buried his face in her neck. "You sweet, pure spirit. Now we can be free."

Byron snickered, snatched his gun back from her. "We shall see once we have conducted our business. You—"

He snapped his fingers at Mehr. "Help her take his body downstairs. Then I will sort you and your brother out."

Mehr drew herself up, though her legs trembled and she resisted the urge to throw herself at the man, to beat him merciless with her fists. "What have you done with him?"

Percy sneered at her. "Nothing yet."

Mary took hold of Mehr's arm and guided her over to Polidori's body. Blood pooled underneath him, and Mehr fell to the floor beside him. Mary took one arm, and Mehr the other. They struggled as they dragged him out of the room and into the gallery. As they made their way to the stairs, Mary immediately stopped, craned her neck toward Byron's room. But no one was following them.

Polidori stirred from the floor, and Mehr rolled him over, placed her head on his chest. His heart beat slowly, but he was alive. When she helped him sit up, he clamped a hand on his wounded, bloodied shoulder.

"Stay away from us," Mehr cried, glaring at Mary.

Mary pulled Mehr off Polidori. "Keep quiet," she whispered. "He would be dead if it were not for me."

"You tried to kill him," Mehr said.

But Polidori was staring up at Mary, no longer frightened. "I had no idea you had such good aim," he said, then groaned, squeezing his shoulder tighter. The bullet hadn't entered his body; it had grazed the meat of his upper arm. The blood soaked his sleeve, but he was otherwise unhurt.

"My girlhood years in Scotland were not wasted." Mary

gave them both a rare smile. "We will need to bandage it quickly."

She beckoned Mehr to help Polidori to his feet. The three of them made it down the stairs, Polidori wincing with pain, limping on his newly wrapped ankle. Now, a safe distance away from the others, Mary tore the hem off her dress and wrapped it tightly around Polidori's shoulder.

Mehr watched it all unfold in disbelief. "Do you believe them that if we make a sacrifice, we will be freed of this torment?"

"I do not know," Mary said. "Perhaps it is something they say to comfort themselves." Mary bit her lip, stared at Mehr through the fringe of her lashes. "I know what you think of us. That we are monsters, cut off from all the world."

"I do not care for monsters or men," Mehr said. "All I want is to escape this cursed place."

Mary finished tying a knot on Polidori's tourniquet. "There is only one way. Through your brother."

Polidori gave Mehr a questioning look. "Your brother? He is here?"

"They kidnapped him." Mehr said, the sorrow nearly choking her words. "Lord Byron and your husband."

Mary pressed her lips together, though they still trembled. She squeezed Mehr's hands in her own. "There is nothing I can do to change the past," she said. "But I can fix the present. I know where he is." Mary pulled her along, down the hall toward the library.

As Mehr's thoughts muddled together, Mary gestured to Polidori to hide in the library, then led Mehr to the drawing room. Mehr didn't have time to wonder what alliance had been created between the two, because as soon as she stepped in, she found James tied to a chair, his head hanging at an odd angle.

Mehr threw herself at her brother, slapping his cheeks to wake him. As he coughed himself awake, she smoothed the hair back from his forehead. He stared up at her in confusion. A mottled new bruise arose on his forehead. She hugged him tightly, but when she turned to Mary to ask for her help, she noticed the others had congregated in the room.

"Is it done?" Byron asked Mary, a pistol in his hand and a bottle of claret tucked under his bandaged arm.

"Yes, my lord," Mary said. She sat on the sofa with Percy, took his hand and held it in her lap. Claire slouched in the doorway, watching Byron, as they all were, as he approached Mehr. James stirred in his seat, but when Byron pointed the gun at him, he immediately stilled. Then Byron turned his steely gaze on Mehr.

"I knew there was something special about you," he said. "When I first met you. The way you looked down on us all."

He handed the claret to Percy, then produced an envelope from his pocket. Mehr squinted at the writing. It was her uncle's expert penmanship. Her heart leaped into her throat. The inheritance letter she was meant to give James.

Byron held the letter up for everyone to see. "You are the daughter of Franklin Hammersmith. An Englishman. A soldier. He had business with your grandfather, the grand nawab of Lucknow," he said with a sweep of his hand. "He seems to have found his way into your mother's bed when she was . . ." He pulled the pages closer to him, found his place. "A budding flower of fifteen? Took advantage of her innocence, swiftly put his seed in her. Built himself a fortune from your grandfather's dowry. Even had his own harem!"

He slapped the page, laughed out loud. "And he squandered it all, did he not? Your greedy father? Despoiling your mother's, then your grandfather's, fortune."

Mehr shut her eyes, took her memories back to the day her father left. He'd appeared so handsome to her, his benevolent face stricken with sadness as he turned back to Mehr one last time before carrying James out of the playroom forever. But her true memories nudged their way in. He had a rough voice; there was never any softness she could remember. The way he'd bellowed at Amma, struck her when he thought the children couldn't see. She and James would cower in the shadows, watching his abuse take place week after week. He'd been a tyrant with them as well. They'd had to be silent, respectful, move softly through their rooms, through their little lives. And when they disturbed him, he'd take away their meals, their toys, even the privilege of spending time with their own mother.

On that fateful day, he'd abused Amma for the last time. There was nothing left for him to take from her anymore. Mehr and her mother were destitute, and her family's remaining wealth was cut off from him. He'd picked James up in his arms. When Mehr had clung to his leg, cried to be held as well, he'd kicked her away. They'd lost everything because of him and were made to move to her uncle's zenana. Two new burdens for him to look after.

These memories, the real ones, took over, and Mehr wondered why she'd ever turned her resentment toward her mother. Hating her for her weakness, for crying and prostrating herself to God for a man who'd destroyed her life.

Byron continued paraphrasing the letter. "Your grandfather left only his lands to your eldest uncle. And the rest of his wealth to your mother—remorse for letting the man ruin his daughter."

Her grandfather, so heartbroken with guilt, gave up all his earthly possessions and became a fakir in the shrine of their ancestor Shaikh Mu'in al-Din Chishti. Every day at sunset, he'd post outside the wall where he knew his daughter's bedroom to be.

"And of that fortune, she left only a quarter to her son. Everything else," Byron said, pocketing the letter and turning to Mehr, "she left to you."

At first, she thought she hadn't heard right. Her brother was meant to inherit nearly everything, not just from her mother but from her grandfather as well. But the nawab, perhaps through his shame, had paid penance to the women he thought he had wronged. And Mehr's mother had gone one step further.

Mehr wiped the tears from her eyes, a surge of affection for the fakir and guilt for her mother. Amma had been difficult to live with, but only because Mehr could not manage being around her constant bouts of sorrow and despondency. Mehr blamed her for their misfortunes, for not having a father or brother anymore. She'd been so cruelly oblivious. But now she was seeing everything clearer than she ever had before.

It all fell into place. Byron's sudden interest in her, his attempts to both impress and seduce her. She had a swift, bitter taste in her mouth. He'd known for quite some time that she was an heiress and had begun to woo her before she had even known. Byron approached her, held tight to her hand, and brought it up to his generous lips to kiss.

"There is only one way out of here," Byron continued. "You, Mr. Hammersmith, are going to sign over the rest of your inheritance to your sister. And, once my divorce has been agreed to, I will marry your sister and come into possession of her fortune."

Byron headed to the table, lifted the quill and ink and a few pages, and placed them in James's lap. He took his time untying James, then stood back, gun held out in front of him.

"I will not," Mehr said, her voice rising. "Do not listen to him."

"Your precious Sikander's life must mean so little to you," Byron said.

"Then shoot me and be done with it," James said.

"No!" Mehr cried out, and reached for James, but Byron took hold of her and held firm. With his eyes still on James, he turned the gun on Mehr instead. James attempted to move from his seat, but Byron pushed the muzzle into Mehr's cheek. She flinched as the metal stung her skin.

"Pray, write to your solicitor, Mr. Hammersmith," Byron said.

James hesitated, distracted by movement behind them. Percy had stood from the sofa and crept up to Byron. He suddenly lunged, threw his arms around Byron's neck. He dragged the Lord backward, freeing Mehr, who immediately ran to James and shielded him from the others.

Byron howled in pain as Percy twisted his bandaged arm and then punched him hard in the face. He staggered on the spot, unable to stop Percy when he took the pistol from his grasp. Byron pressed a hand to his nose to stanch the bleeding. "You fool. Think about what you are doing."

Percy laughed. "I have grown tired of being pushed and pulled by you."

"You came to *me* for help," Byron said. "I will help you if you give me back the weapon."

As Byron stumbled toward him, Percy ducked away, circling him like a feral animal. "I don't need you. I never did."

Mary didn't move to intervene in the tussle. Her eyes flicked between the two men, yet she showed no inclination to stop them.

Mehr stared at her. "Mrs. Shelley?"

"I hope you understand, Mehrunissa." Mary joined Percy's side, held his free hand in her own.

"How can you do this to us?" Mehr asked. For a brief moment, like in the vineyard, it was just the two of them in the room. But Mehr was afraid she already knew the answer. She was just their housemaid after all. And, like Claire, a pawn to bring the Lord closer to the Shelleys.

Mary stood firm. "For weeks Percy flees across the country, dodging our creditors. And I have to answer my door and explain his whereabouts when at times they are perfectly unknown to me."

"*His* creditors," Byron said.

Claire attempted to clean the blood from his face, but he evaded her attempts. She threw her handkerchief down in frustration.

"I must live alone, alone. Like a widow," Mary said. "And we must think about our child."

"And what of my child?" Claire hissed, cradling her stomach.

Mary flinched. "Claire?" She shook her head. "You cannot possibly—"

"How?" Percy asked, his lips quivering.

"*His* child," she said, glaring at Byron. "I no longer need to rely on you or on Mary's meek coffers."

Mary moved away from Percy's side. She hesitated before gently touching Claire's hand. "If you are with child," Mary said, "we will always look after you."

"I am only a burden to you," Claire said. "You say you feel alone when Percy leaves you. How must I feel to have no one? Nothing?" She angrily wiped her tears away. "Let it be signed over to Lord Byron," Claire said. "And I will be the one to look after you."

James sat still, his hands trembling in his lap as he looked between them all, confusion knitting his brow. He held a quill in one hand and a page in the other, glancing at Mehr for guidance.

"Sign it to me," Percy said, waving the gun at him.

But before James could comply, wholly unknown to them, Polidori had slunk into the room, Mehr's candelabra in his hand. He swung wildly, and with a loud crack, caught Percy against the side of his face. As he tumbled to the floor, Mary gasped and rushed to him.

"You dear, stupid man," she said as he lay unconscious. She pulled him up and cradled him in her arms, kissed his forehead. It was surprising to Mehr that Mary would continue to attach herself to such an unworthy man.

It had happened to her mother, and it would continue to happen again and again and again to Mary, despite everything she had endured with Percy. A tide of rage rose within Mehr, higher and higher. The apparitions melted out from the walls, their faces further distorted, their flesh pouring out a putrid odor. Claire screamed as she joined Byron in the center of the room. Mary's pregnant mother appeared with her stomach cut open, entrails dragging at her feet, Percy's demonic children, the burnt corpse of

Augusta, and so many others that they'd seen in their terrifying private moments. Byron tripped over Percy's legs and fell in a heap, Claire cowering beside him. Polidori's former patients hulked close to him, swiped at him. He, too, limped to the center of the room.

"Good God!" James said, standing. Mehr held fast to his arm.

"It cannot be," Byron spluttered. "We were freed from Diodati."

"It is not Diodati," Mehr said, facing the apparitions, glaring back at them. She pulled the taweez off her neck and held the locket in her palm.

"My mother gave this to me. She often prayed I would be the one to deliver vengeance to him, but I never knew what it meant before. Just a curse from a bitter, despondent woman. Now I know she wanted me to bring this to my father so she could avenge her broken heart. To bring out all his demons and force him to confront them. Instead, it coaxed them out of all of you."

Byron had a curious smile on his face. "The love of women. A lovely and fearful thing."

They congregated in a knot, Claire furiously crying into her handkerchief. Polidori shielded Mary from the sight as Percy awoke, staring in horrified shock around him. Byron pulled himself away from the outstretched arm of his burnt half sister.

Mehr shut her eyes and pried open the taweez. This time it gave way easily. Nestled underneath a gray-streaked lock of her mother's hair was a whispered prayer. It floated into the air above her. The humming switched its tone. It was the prayer, now, all around her—her mother's whisper enveloping everything. The earth shifted beneath her.

"I will take you home," Mehr whispered. "I promised you I would."

She kissed the contents of the taweez and then held up her palm. The walls began to tremble as the apparitions stood frozen, awaiting her command. She glanced over at James as he stared in wonder at it all. One by one, the apparitions burst into clouds of white mist. James held his arms over his face in fear, but Mehr stood her ground, watched as the mist sped straight into the opened locket. As the room emptied, the fog outside the villa dispersed. Suddenly, in the quiet, there was the sound of birds, then sunlight streamed in, illuminating every surface into brilliant silvers and golds.

The villa's front door flew open, and without a glance back, the others ran out, shielding their eyes from the bright sun. They scattered in all directions, running or limping as far as their lungs would take them. Mehr gently shut the taweez and placed it back over her head. She led James outside, stared out at the brilliant blue eye of the lake.

Mehr spotted Mary in the vineyard; she had stopped to look at the house. The sunshine illuminated her form as she appeared to let out a laugh. Her intense gaze, fixed on Mehr, conveyed something like a promise. Perhaps she would always remember her, remember this summer, remember that since the day they met, their lives were irrevocably changed. But within that moment, a warning—Mehr would also have to confront this all again, much as she wanted to leave it all behind. It was only a glimpse of a thought, though. Gone as soon as it came. Then Mary turned back and was lost among the vines.

Mehr wouldn't realize until much later that glimpse of Mary Shelley partially hidden within the vineyard, her hair a shining halo, would be the last time she'd ever see her again. And even that would be too soon. Their paths had briefly cobbled together over the better part of a year and just as quickly veered back to where they belonged. Mary with her husband and their coterie of poets and writers, who, despite how Mehr truly felt about them, were geniuses and who would continue scattering into the four winds, leaving their individual marks upon the world.

Mehr, now a sudden heiress, turned to her brother. There would be no yearning for greatness or glory, for a legacy. No, she knew she had everything she'd ever wanted.

James was in shock, wavering on his legs, leaning into her. She held his arm to steady him.

"What do we do now?" he asked.

She cupped the taweez in her hand and smiled.

"Sikander, now we go home," Mehr said. "It is time for our parents to be reunited."

ACKNOWLEDGMENTS

Without the constant support and encouragement of my husband, Paul, and my twin sister, Ruby, this book could not have been possible. They are my first readers and critics, and I strive to be the best writer I can be for you.

To my agent, Lane Clarke. I had almost given up my writing career. This novel was going to be the last I was willing to write for an unforeseeable amount of time. The week I decided to quit writing altogether was the week Lane reached out to me. She's been an incredible champion for my career.

My editor at Soho Press/Hell's Hundred Nick Whitney for helping me push the envelope and really take this book to the deepest darkest depths I couldn't have imagined. The immense passion and intuitiveness you've shared while we toiled away on edits, and the abundance of patience are all things for which I'm deeply grateful.

And to the Soho Press/Hell's Hundred marketing and publicity team—Rudy, Steven, Johnny, Emma, Erica, and Paul for your enthusiasm and hard work on this book, and letting this little horror author feel really appreciated.

I also couldn't have done it without my friends and writer's group members—Stephanie Kelly, Christine Hung, Oriana Clapper, Sarah Reck, and Jaimee Garbacik. Your early critiques were so valuable in shaping the novel as it is today. And my friends Liz Agyemang and Roxanne Jones—I cherished your expert industry advice and constant support as I navigated this book on its prepublication journey.

A novel of this scope required quite a bit of hands-on research. I'm indebted to the New York Public Library's Carl H. Pforzheimer Collection of Shelley and His Circle housed in the Stephen A. Schwarzman Building (the one with the lions, if you're curious) inside a very cute though very inaccessible room. Still, I had the ability to check out and read journal entries and diaries on-site, which was incredibly invaluable.

Diving into John Polidori's diaries, the letters of Lord Byron and Claire Clairmont, and the travel journal that Percy and Mary cowrote gave me deep context into their inner lives and helped shape the narrative around these dynamic yet very flawed people.

I also leaned on the work of multi-award-winning historian William Dalrymple, who has dedicated his life to research on India and written extensively on the history of British colonization of the Indian subcontinent. His book *White Mughals* inspired parts of Mehrunissa's story along with my own personal history that I was able to cobble together from what little remains of it.

Young Romantics: The Shelleys, Byron, and Other Tangled Lives by Daisy Hay, *In Search of Mary Shelley: The Girl Who Wrote Frankenstein* by Fiona Sampson, *If Walls Could Talk: An Intimate History of the Home* by Lucy Worsley, and the 1770 edition of *The Complete Servant Maid: Or Young Woman's Best Companion by Mrs. Anne Barker* helped while I researched the era.

And last but not least—to you, dear reader. I hope you got exactly what you came for.